THE WAY OF]

By

H A Culley

Book four of the Saga of Wessex

Published by

oHp

Orchard House Publishing

PLACE NAMES

Note: *In my last series of novels I used the modern names for places in Anglo-Saxon England as some readers had said that my earlier novels were confusing because of the use of place names current in the time about which I was writing. However, I had even more adverse comments that modern names detract from the authentic feel of the novels, so in this series I have reverted to the use of Anglo-Saxons names.*

Ægelesthrep	Aylesford, Kent
Alba	Scotland
Apuldre	Appledore, Kent
Basingestoches	Basingstoke, Hampshire
Baðum	Bath, Somerset
Beamfleote	South Benfleet, Essex
Beamfleote Hýþ	Benfleet Creek
Bebbanburg	Bamburgh, Northumberland
Bedaforde	Bedford, Bedfordshire
Berncestre	Bicester, Oxfordshire
Berrocscīr	Berkshire
Biceilwæd	Biggleswade, Bedfordshire
Blæcmere	River Blackwater
Brigge	Brignorth, Shropshire
Britannia	The island of Britain (Roman name)
Brunanburh	Bromborough, Merseyside (disputed)
Buccascīr	Buckinghamshire
Cæstir	Chester, Cheshire
Cæstirscīr	Cheshire
Cantwareburh	Canterbury, Kent
Casingc Stræt	Watling Street (Roman road)
Cent	Kent
Cicæstre	Chichester, West Sussex

Cilleham	Chilham, Kent
Danmǫrk	Denmark
Dēvā	River Dee
Dingesmere	Heswall, Cheshire
Dofras	Dover, Kent
Dornsæte	Dorset
Dyflin (Viking name)	Dublin, Ireland
Dyfneintscīr	Devon
Earninga Stræt	Ermine Street (Roman road)
Ēast Seaxna Rīce	Essex
Eforwic	York, North Yorkshire
Englaland	England
Escanceaster	Exeter, Devon
Eveshomme	Evesham, Worcestershire
Favresham	Faversham, Kent
Fearndune	Farndon, Cheshire
Fearnhamme	Farnham, Surrey
Frankia	Parts of France, Belgium and Germany
Frisia	Most of the Netherlands
Fŏsweg	The Fosse Way (Roman road)
Glowecestre	Gloucester, Gloucestershire
Grárhöfn	Near Birkenhead (fictional)
Guilforde	Guildford, Surrey
Hamtunscīr	Hampshire
Hamtun	Northampton, Northamptonshire
Hamwic	Southampton, Hampshire
Herewic	Harwich, Essex
Hreopandune	Repton, Derbyshire
Hrofescæstir	Rochester, Kent
Hwicce	Part of Mercia,
(most of Gloucestershire and Worcestershire)	
Íralandes Sǣ	Irish Sea
Íralond	Ireland

Kernow	Cornwall
Lygan	River Lea
Lundenburg	London
Mann	Isle of Man
Mældun	Maldun, Essex
Mǣresēa	River Mersey
Meregate	Margate, Kent
Meresai	West Mersea, Essex
Midleton	Milton Regis, Kent
Midweg	River Medway
Neen	River Nene
Nestone	Neston, Cheshire
Norðmanndi	Normandy, France
Norþweg	Norway
Norþ-sǣ	North Sea
Orkneyjar	Orkney Islands
Oxenaforda	Oxford, Oxfordshire
Poole Hæfen	Poole Harbour, Dorset
Portcæstre	Portchester, Hampshire
Readingum	Reading, Berkshire
Sæfern	River Severn
Sceapig	Isle of Sheppey, Thames Estuary
Scir	River Rother
Scirburne	Sherborne, Dorset
Sidyngbourn	Sittingbourne, Kent
Silcestre	Silchester, Hampshire
Shropscīr	Shropshire
Snæland	Iceland
Somersaete	Somerset
Sonwic	Swanage, Dorset
Shropscīr	Staffordshire

6

Stanes	Staines-upon-Thames, Surrey
Sūþburh	Sudbury, near Chepstow, Monmouthshire
Sudwerca	Southwark, South London
Sūð-sǣ	English Channel
Sūþrīgescīr	Surrey
Suth-Seaxe	Sussex
Tamiseforde	Tempsford, Bedfordshire
Tatenhale	Tattenhall, Cheshire
Temes	River Thames
Tenetwaradenn	Tenterden, Kent
Tes	River Tees
Tōfecæstre	Towcester, Northamptonshire
Tomtun	Tamworth, Staffordshire
Tunbrige	Tonbridge, Kent
Uisge	River Great Ouse
Verulamacæster	St. Albans, Hertfordshire
Waie	River Wye
Wælingforde	Wallingford, Oxfordshire
Waras	Ware, Hertfordshire
Watsforde	Watford, Hertfordshire
Wealas	Wales
Werhām	Wareham, Dorset
Wirhealum	Wirral Peninsula
Wiltunscīr	Wiltshire
Wintanceaster	Winchester, Hampshire
Witenestaple	Whitstable, Kent
Whitlond	Isle of Weight
Ynys Môn	Isle of Anglesey, Wales

LIST OF PRINCIPAL CHARACTERS

Historical figures are in bold.

<u>Members of Jørren's Gesith (also called hearth warriors)</u>

Æwulf
Acwel
Arne
Eafer

Eomær
Hunulf
Lyndon
Rinan
Wolnoth

<u>Other Characters</u>

Æbbe – The daughter of Jørren and his second wife Hilda
Ælfred – King of Wessex

Ælfwynn – Daughter of Æðelred and Æthelflæd

Æscwin – Jørren's elder son, now the Abbot of Cantwareburh Monastery in Cent

Æthelflæd – Eldest daughter Ælfred and Ealhswith, later Lady of the Mercians

Æthelhelm – Ealdorman of Wiltunscīr, also the name of the late King Æthelred's elder son

Æthelnoth – Nerian's younger brother, later Ealdorman of Somersaete

Æthelstan – Son of Edward and Ecgwynna, now Æthelflæd's ward

Æðelred – Lord of Mercia

Æðelwold – The late King Æthelred's younger son, a contestant for Ælfred's throne

Anarawd ap Rhodri – King of Gwynedd

Asser – Bishop of Wintanceaster

Bjørn Frami – Danish hersir who joins Jørren's warband with his men

Cei – A former slave belonging to Jørren's family, now the Sǣ Hererǣswa of Wessex

Cissa - Ealdorman of Berrocscīr

Cuthfleda – Jørren's eldest daughter

Cynbald – Hererǣswa of Mercia

Cyngils – Ealdorman of Suth-Seaxe

Dudda – Ealdorman of Sūþrīgescīr

Dunbeorn – Jørren's body servant.

Ecgwynna – Jørren's niece, married to Edward the Ætheling in secret

Ealhswith – Ælfred's Mercian wife and Lady of Wessex

Eadred – Ealdorman of Dyfneintscīr and Hererǣswa of Wessex

Edward – The elder son of King Ælfred and the Lady Ealhswith

Eirik Fairhair – Jarl of Myrteland (the Wirral)

Eohric – Danish King of East Anglia

Fróði – One of the leaders, with Hæsten, of the Viking invasion of Cent in 892

Guðred – King of Northumbria

Hæsten – Commander of the Viking invaders

Halig – Leader of a group of Mercian scouts

Hilda – Jørren's second wife

Hywel ap Cadell - nephew of King Anarawd ap Rhodri Gwynedd

Irwyn and Godric – Hæsten's sons

Jerrik– A Jute, Cei's deputy and commander of the eastern fleet

Jørren – The protagonist and narrator, Ealdorman of Cent

Kjesten – Ywer's twin sister and wife of Odda, Eadred's eldest son

Nerian – Ealdorman of Somersaete

Oswine - Jørren's stepson, Thegn of Ægelesthrep and a member of Edward's gesith

Plegmund – Archbishop of Cantwareburh

Sigehelm – Shire reeve of Cent

Sigfrith – King of Northumbria after Guðred

Sigurd – A Danish hersir, sworn enemy of Jørren

Skarde – Half-brother of Jarl Eirik Fairhair

Uhtric and Leofwine – Two former urchins, now physicians employed by Jørren

Ulfbjørn Bearslayer – Hæsten's deputy

Ywer – Jørren's second son and twin brother of Kjestin

GLOSSARY

ANGLO-SAXON

Ænglisc – Old English, the common language of Angles, Saxons and Jutes.

Ætheling – literally 'throne-worthy. An Anglo-Saxon prince

Avantail - a curtain of chainmail attached to a helmet to cover the throat and neck

Birlinn – a wooden ship similar to the later Scottish galleys but smaller than a Viking longship. Usually with a single mast and square rigged sail, they could also be propelled by oars with one man to each oar

Bondsman – a slave who was treated as the property of his master

Braies – underwear similar to modern undershorts. Worn only by males

Bretwalda – overlord of some or all of the Anglo-Saxon kingdoms

Bryttas – Britons, essentially the inhabitants of Cornwall (Kernow), Wales (Wealas), Cumbria and Strathclyde at this time.

Burh - fortified settlement

Byrnie - a tunic of chain mail, usually sleeveless or short sleeved

Ceorl – a freeman who worked the land or else provided a service or trade such as metal working, carpentry, weaving etc. They ranked between thegns and villeins and provided the fyrd in time of war

Cyning – Old English for king and the term by which they were normally addressed

Danegeld - a tax levied in Anglo-Saxon England to bribe Danish invaders to leave

Ealdorman – The senior noble of a shire. A royal appointment, ealdormen led the men of their shire in battle,

11

presided over law courts and levied taxation on behalf of the king

Fyrd - Anglo-Saxon army mobilised from freemen to defend their shire, or to join a campaign led by the king

Gesith – the companions of a king, prince or noble, usually acting as his bodyguard

Hearth Warriors - alternative term for members of a Gesith

Hereræswa – military commander or general. The man who commanded the army of a nation under the king

Hersir – a landowner who could recruit enough other freemen to serve under him

Hide – a measure of the land sufficient to support the household of one ceorl

Hideage - a tax paid to the royal exchequer for every hide of land

Hundred – the unit for local government and taxation which equated to ten tithings. The freemen of each hundred were collectively responsible for various crimes committed within its borders if the offender was not produced

Larboard – Archaic term for port (as opposed to starboard)

Pallium - an ecclesiastical vestment bestowed by the Pope upon metropolitans and primates as a symbol of their authority

Reeve - a local official including the chief magistrate of a town or district, also the person manging a landowner's estate

Sæfyrd – Members of the fyrd (q.v.) who served at sea

Sæ Hereræswa – Commander of the King Ælfred's navy

Seax – a bladed weapon somewhere in size between a dagger and a sword. Mainly used for close-quarter fighting where a sword would be too long and unwieldy

Settlement – any grouping of residential buildings, usually around the king's or lord's hall. In 8th century England the term town or village had not yet come into use

Shire – an administrative area into which an Anglo-Saxon kingdom was divided

Shire Reeve – later corrupted to sheriff. A royal official responsible for implementing the king's laws within his shire

Skypfyrd – fyrd raised to man ships of war to defend the coast

Thegn – the lowest rank of noble. A man who held a certain amount of land direct from the king or from a senior nobleman, ranking between an ordinary freeman, or ceorl, and an ealdorman

Tithing - a group of ten ceorls who lived close together and were collectively responsible for each other's behaviour, also the land required to support them (i.e. ten hides)

Wergeld - the price set upon a person's life or injury and paid as compensation by the person responsible to the family of the dead or injured person. It freed the perpetrator of further punishment or obligation and prevented a blood feud

Witan – meeting or council

Witenaġemot – the council of an Anglo-Saxon kingdom. Its composition varied, depending on the matters to be debated. Usually it consisted of the ealdormen, the king's thegns, the bishops and the abbots

Villein - a peasant who ranked above a bondsman or slave but who was legally tied to his vill and who was obliged to give one or more day's service to his lord each week in payment for his land

Vill - a thegn's holding or similar area of land in Anglo-Saxon England which would later be called a parish or a manor

VIKING

Bóndi - farmers and craftsmen who were free men and enjoyed rights such as the ownership of weapons and membership of the Thing. They could be tenants or landowners. Plural bøndur

Byrnie - a tunic of chain mail, usually sleeveless or short sleeved

Helheim – the realm in the afterlife for those who don't die in battle

Hersir – a bóndi who was chosen to lead a band of warriors under a king or a jarl. Typically they were wealthy landowners who could recruit enough other bøndur to serve under their command

Hirdman – a member of a king's or a jarl's personal bodyguard, collectively known as the hird

Jarl – a Norse or Danish chieftain; in Sweden they were regional governors appointed by the king

Mjolnir – Thor's hammer, also the pendant worn around the neck by most pagan Vikings

Nailed God – pagan name for Christ, also called the White Christ

Swéoþeod – Swedes, literally Swedish people

Thing – the governing assembly made up of the free people of the community presided over by a lagman. The meeting-place of a thing was called a thingstead

Thrall – a slave. A man, woman or child in bondage to his or her owner. Thralls had no rights and could be beaten or killed with impunity

Valhalla – the hall of the slain. It's where heroes who died in battle spend the afterlife feasting and fighting according to Norse mythology

LONGSHIPS

In order of size:

Knarr – also called karve or karvi. The smallest type of longship. It had 6 to 16 benches and, like their English equivalents, they were mainly used for fishing and trading, but they were occasionally commissioned for military use. They were broader in the beam and had a deeper draught than other longships.

Snekkja – (plural snekkjur) typically the smallest longship used in warfare and it was classified as a ship with at least 20 rowing benches. A typical snekkja might have a length of 17m, a width of 2.5m and a draught of only 0.5m. Norse snekkjas, designed for deep fjords and Atlantic weather, typically had more draught than the Danish type, which were intended for shallow water.

Drekar - (dragon ship) larger warships consisting of more than 30 rowing benches. Typically they could carry a crew of some 70–80 men and measured around 30m in length. These ships were more properly called skeids; the term drekar referred to the carvings of menacing beasts, such as dragons and snakes, mounted on the prow of the ship during a sea battle or when raiding. Strictly speaking drekar is the plural form, the singular being dreki or dreka, but these words don't appear to be accepted usage in English.

INTRODUCTION

We often talk of the Anglo-Saxons but in reality the inhabitants of the kingdoms that made up England at the time of King Ælfred (Alfred the Great) consisted of three different peoples - the Saxons predominated in the south, Anglians in the north and the Jutes in Kent and the Isle of Wight.

In 892, when this novel starts, Mercia was divided between territory ruled by the Danes and that part of the former kingdom controlled by Æðelred, the Anglian Lord of Mercia. The Danish part of Mercia consisted of the Five Boroughs, which began as the fortified burhs of five Danish armies who settled in the area and a number of more or less independent Danish jarldoms stretching from St. Albans in the south to just south of Stamford in the north and from Cambridge in the east to Northampton in the west. This whole area was part of the Danelaw, the area of England where the Danes ruled and where their native laws and customs were observed by all including the Anglo-Saxons who lived there.

The Danelaw consisted of the Kingdom of East Anglia - ruled by King Eohric after the death of his father, Guðrum, in 890 - the Five Boroughs, the independent jarldoms and the Kingdom of Jorvik (see below).

Each of the Five Boroughs was ruled as a Danish Jarldom, controlling lands around a fortified burh, which served as the centre of political power. These rulers were probably initially subject to their overlords in the Viking Kingdom of Jorvik and cooperated militarily in alliance with the rulers of their neighbouring lands. The Danish jarldoms to the south of the Five Boroughs were governed by jarls who had looked toward East Anglia, rather than Jorvik, for leadership in the past.

The Five Boroughs were based around (Saxon names, modern names in brackets):

- Lindocolina (Lincoln)
- Snotengaham (Nottingham)
- Deoraby (Derby)
- Ligeraceastre (Leicester)
- Steaneforde (Stamford)

The other independent jarldoms in the remainder of the Danelaw were based around:

- Huntandun (Huntingdon)
- Grantebrycge (Cambridge)
- Snotengaham (Northampton)
- Bedaforde (Bedford)
- Tamiseforde (Tempsford)

The boundaries of East Anglia corresponded roughly to those of the modern counties of Norfolk, Suffolk and Essex.

The Danish Kingdom of Yorvik (York) - ruled in 892 by Guthfrith, a Christian Viking - consisted of the southern half of the former Saxon Kingdom of Northumbria and extended from the Rivers Mersey and Humber, which formed the southern border, to the River Tees in the north.

The land between the Rivers Tees and Tweed was called Bernicia and was an independent Anglian realm governed by an Anglian ealdorman (later earl) from Bamburgh (Saxon Bebbanburg).

London (Saxon Lundenwic), on the boundary between Wessex and East Anglia, had originally been a Mercian settlement, although not located in the Roman walled city of Londinium but further to the west. It was controlled by the Vikings for a time until King Ælfred captured it in 886 and then made Æðelred, Lord of Mercia, its governor. Within ten years, the settlement moved within the Roman walls and was renamed Lundenburg. The old walls were repaired and the defensive ditch was re-excavated. These changes effectively marked the beginning of the present City of London, the boundaries of which are to this day defined by its ancient city walls.

The original settlement of Lundenwic was more or less abandoned and in time gained the name of Ealdwic, 'old settlement', a name which survives today as Aldwych.

The boundary between Anglian Mercia and the Danelaw ran from London in the south-east to the mouth of the River Mersey in the north-west. It was far from a straight line and the border was a little fluid. However, for two thirds of the way it followed the old Roman road we call Watling Street as far as somewhere near modern Daventry before heading north to the River Mersey near Manchester.

This novel is set around the last major Viking invasion of England before the successful invasions of Sweyn Forkbeard and his son Cnut (or Canute) over a century later. The invaders came from the Continent: Hæsten led a force of eighty ships which landed at Milton, Kent, near Gravesend on the Thames Estuary. They came from Boulogne whilst a much larger army under an unknown leader with two hundred and fifty ships invaded the south coast of Kent, setting up a base at Appledore, north of Rye. There followed four years of intermittent fighting which took the invaders throughout Wessex, Mercia, Wales and the Danelaw as far north as York.

This is their story as seen through the eyes of Jørren. It is, of course, fictional but it is based on the known facts.

PROLOGUE

WESTERN FRANKIA

891

Jarl Hæsten stared gloomily into the bowl of broth the thrall had just given him.

'What's this slop, boy? Do I look like a pig that wants to eat swill?'

'N-n-no, Jarl,' the boy stuttered. 'It's all there is. There is no meat left, the barley has mildew and the vegetables are rotting in the store.'

Hæsten got up and threw the contents of the bowl over the boy who screamed as the hot broth scalded his bare skin. He was a Dane, like Hæsten, but he was born in East Anglia and he'd been captured during a raid on his settlement the previous year. He was ten years old and bewildered by what had happened to him. His father was a hersir, a free man who owned a farm and a small longship called a snekkjur. The hersir led thirty other men but Hæsten had come with five longships and slaughtered everyone except those who could be sold as thralls, essentially girls and young boys.

Hæsten hadn't sold this boy but had kept him as his personal slave. It piqued his vanity to have the son of a wealthy Dane as his servant. However, when last year's harvest had failed and raids into the land around his base at Boulogne had yielded nothing worth eating, Hæsten and his men had starved. The boy had even less to eat; merely the scraps and he had to fight the dogs for those. The jarl knew that his very existence as the leader of his warband depended on keeping his men happy - and that was something they definitely weren't at the moment.

The boy slunk off to cry in a corner. His burns wouldn't have been fatal normally but in his emaciated state he was near to death anyway. His spirit had been broken and now he'd lost the will to live. He died that night but Hæsten hardly noticed. He was too preoccupied thinking about solutions to his problems.

'What are you going to do? We can't stay here and starve,' Ulfbjørn asked. 'The men are already saying that you are unlucky and speculating that a change of leader might solve their problems.'

Ulfbjørn had been Hæsten's closest friend and captain for the past dozen or so years. If anyone else had spoken to the jarl in such blunt terms he'd have probably ended up with a knife in his guts for his impudence. Hæsten bridled but he knew Ulfbjørn was right. The question was what could he do?

'Have you got any bright ideas, because I haven't,' he shot back.

'We could try raiding further afield,' Ulfbjørn suggested. 'The Franks around here are in no better state than we are so we need to find somewhere the crops haven't been blighted and where there is more livestock.'

'That's stating the obvious,' the jarl grunted. 'We haven't got enough men or ships to go raiding. We need more men, many more men and the ships to carry them.'

'We aren't the only ones in this situation, Hæsten. Why don't you contact the other jarls in the area promising them food and plunder if they would bind together under your leadership to pillage the Seine valley? We might even be able to sack Paris. The fat burghers of the city always seem to have enough food to eat and they're wealthy too.'

'I'd prefer to go overseas but ships are going to be a problem; we don't have enough for everyone, especially if we're going to take our families with us.'

Usually only warriors went raiding but Hæsten realised that he couldn't leave the women and children behind. They would starve to death if they weren't first killed by the vengeful Franks.

A month later Hæsten had assembled an army of fifteen hundred men from the various Viking settlements along the coast to the west of Boulogne and he advanced down the valley of the River Seine. However, he found every farmstead, village and town he came across pillaged and deserted. Evidently someone else had had the same idea. He sent scouts out to the east and west of the valley but, however far they roamed, they found a wasteland. It wasn't just the failed harvest that had driven the people out, the land had been stripped bare of anything worth having by other raiders.

Hæsten's army was reduced to eating their horses but the meat didn't keep them fed for long. Soon all that was left was the offal, supplemented by what they could gather by the roadside and in the woods.

'Who do you think it is?' Ulfbjørn asked one night as they camped beside the River Seine and dined on a broth made of the last of the offal from the horses, mushrooms and a few wild herbs.

'Ahead of us? No idea, but they don't appear to be that far away now. Perhaps we'll catch them tomorrow?'

When the two men had finished eating they handed the remaining contents of the cooking pot over to Hæsten's two sons and Ulfbjørn's daughter to fight over what was left. Ulfbjørn's wife hadn't survived the birth of his son the previous winter. The latter had only lived for a few days before he too had died. He envied Hæsten whose wife had fiery red hair and a temper to match. He would have given much to have been able to take her to his bed.

Although there were plenty of widows and even a few unmarried girls available, Ulfbjørn now took pretty young thralls

21

to his bed when he wanted to rut. Despite knowing how he dearly would pay later when his wife found out, Hæsten would sometimes join him in bedding a thrall.

It was the following afternoon before they caught up with the other Viking army. At first Hæsten thought that they had halted to face their pursuers but it soon became obvious that their path was barred by a large Frankish army above which the banner of Odo, King of the West Franks, flew.

Many of the first Viking host turned to face the newcomers whilst the rest continued to guard against an advance by the Franks. The latter looked on with bemusement at this turn of events but made no move to attack. Hæsten rode forward with his standard bearer carrying a triangular black flag with a spread-eagled black raven embroidered on it. Ulfbjørn and three of his hirdmen followed him. He stopped halfway between the two Viking armies and waited.

After an interval, just when Hæsten had come to the conclusion that he was being made to look a fool, a large man on a horse too small for his bulk emerged from his own lines with his standard bearer and a small escort. His standard wasn't a flag, it was a half-rotted horse's head complete with flowing mane mounted on a spear. He and Hæsten exchanged greetings and the other leader introduced himself as Fróði, a Norse sea king who had made a name for himself raiding in the Baltic and along the Fresian coast. Hæsten assumed that he was here because, like him, he thought that Paris and its environs was a good place to pillage at the moment.

'Odo can't afford to fight us,' Fróði said confidently. 'He may have more men than we do, even if we unite our forces, but we are tougher fighters and he won't want too many casualties. A number of his lords have changed their allegiance to a rival

22

claimant to the throne. He needs as strong an army as possible if he wants to be able to defeat the rebels.'

'What do you suggest then?' Hæsten asked, somewhat in awe of the Norseman who commanded so many Vikings – more than the Great Heathen Army that had so nearly conquered all of Anglo–Saxon Englaland nearly thirty years before.

'We need food, horses and above all ships so we can leave this cursed place and go raiding overseas,' Fróði replied.

'Then let's negotiate with this king. Perhaps he'll give us all three if we promise to leave Frankia, but where would we go?'

'I don't know about you but I intend to do what Ívar the Boneless and his brothers failed to do – conquer Wessex.'

CHAPTER ONE

October 892

My name is Jørren and I have been the Ealdorman of Cent for more years than I care to remember. I have been other things as well: King Ælfred's hereræswa, the commander of his armies, and the sǣ hereræswa in charge of the fleet of longships that patrolled the coast of Wessex looking for Viking raiders. Now I'm getting older; I'll be forty one this year and am beginning to feel my age. I no longer crave adventure, content to abide with my family in our hall at Cantwareburh, from where I govern my shire. Unfortunately my peaceful life was about to be rudely disrupted.

It was early October and I was out hunting with my second son, Ywer, to fill our larder for the winter when Rinan came looking for me. As a boy he had saved my life at the Battle of Ethendun and I had taken him into my service. Now he was one of my hearth warriors and one of my closest companions.

Ywer and I had been tracking a small herd of deer all morning. When we'd finally caught up with them we hid ourselves downwind in a clump of shrubs. My son cautiously moved to the side of the shrub from where he had a clear shot at a hart. Not only would it provide us with much needed salted meat for the storeroom but it was a good idea to cull the older stags from time to time.

Ywer released his arrow just as Rinan rode up. The hart jerked his head up and jumped to the left before sprinting away followed by the rest of the herd. The arrow missed him by a hairsbreadth and I sympathised with Ywer's frustration. I didn't blame him for cursing Rinan to hell and back.

'I'm sorry, Ywer, but the matter is urgent,' Rinan said as he dismounted.

'Lord,' he said turning to me, 'Cent has been invaded by Vikings.'

'A raid?' I asked, hoping that was all it was.

'No, lord. This looked to be more serious.'

My heart sank. I thought when we had captured Lundenburg and brought the Danish King of East Anglia to heel eight years ago we had seen the last of the Danes' attempts at conquest.

'Where and in what numbers?' I asked, heading back to where Ywer and I had left our horses.

'Early reports are confused but the men manning the watchtower at Witenestaple say that near on a hundred longships passed them early this morning. Other reports say that they sailed into the channel between Sceapig and the mainland.'

That wasn't that far from the burh of Hrofescæstir but the nearest settlement was called Midleton. It was owned by King Ælfred, the rest of his vill being on the Isle of Sceapig. It might just be chance that the Vikings had chosen to land there but, if so, it was doubly unfortunate. Not only had my shire been invaded but Ælfred would expect me to expel raiders from his estate without delay.

However, so many longships could contain anything between twelve hundred and two thousand warriors, depending on the size of the ships. It would take time to muster a similar sized force and, even if I did, the majority would be members of the fyrd – the local militia – and they were far inferior as fighters compared to seasoned Viking warriors. Nevertheless I had to do something, and quickly.

✝✝✝

I kissed my wife, Hilda, and my youngest daughter, Æbbe, before bidding them farewell. Both were tearful and I got the distinct impression that both thought that they were saying goodbye to me for the last time. I found that somewhat unsettling and perhaps I was a little brusque with them as a result. I sighed. I never seemed to part from my wife on the best of terms.

Squaring my shoulders I strode out of my hall, blinking in the bright sunshine and pulling on a pair of stout leather gauntlets. The area between the hall and the palisade was full of men and horses. Servants were loading packhorses whilst my gesith - my hearth warriors - checked that the stable boys had saddled their mounts properly.

Some horses filled their lungs so that their bellies were distended, thus making it impossible to fully tighten the girth – the strap that went under the horse to keep the saddle in place. More than one rider's saddle had slid sideways in the past to dump its occupant unceremoniously on the ground. The trick was to kick the horse in the side so that it exhaled, then you could tighten the girth properly.

Although we didn't expect trouble, the muster point was only a dozen miles from the place that the Vikings had landed and so everyone wore their chainmail byrnies or, for those who couldn't afford one, a stout leather jerkin. However, riding in full gear ready to fight was tiring and uncomfortable and so we would travel with our shields on our backs and our helmets hanging from our saddle horns.

Every one of my warriors, both those in my gesith and the others in my personal warband, was trained as an archer as well as a fighter with sword and axe or spear. Their bows and quivers hung in a leather shoe from their saddles. Bundles of spare spears were tied to the packhorses together with barrels of arrows. I had a feeling that we would be in the field for a long time and we were equipped accordingly.

Normally we would be able to buy provisions from local farmers. However, the Vikings would have sent out forage parties as soon as they landed and any farmer with any sense would have loaded his carts with everything they could carry and driven his livestock inland. We therefore took dried meat and everything else we'd need with us. Perhaps we might be able to supplement our diet with anything we could hunt but that would be a bonus.

I saw Arne chatting to Eomær as he calmed his overeager horse. The former had been my body servant for several years before I rewarded his faithful service by making him one of my gesith – an unusual honour for a former slave, but then Cei – the Sǣ Hererǣswa who commanded King Ælfred's navy – had been a slave at one point. Eomær wasn't well-born either; he was the son of a charcoal burner.

I had replaced Arne, not with another slave, but with an orphan from the streets of Cantwareburh. I had been visiting my eldest son, Æscwin, now the Abbot of the monastery, when one of the monks caught a twelve year old boy trying to steal food from the kitchens. He took him to the prior who had promptly dragged the urchin before the abbot for summary justice. The penalty for stealing was either a hefty fine or enslavement. The waif had stick thin arms and legs and only a torn homespun tunic, long since outgrown, to hide his nakedness. Plainly he was in no position to pay a fine.

Normally I wouldn't have said anything but the boy had spirit and knew more swear words than I'd ever heard my men use. Suddenly he bit the prior's hand, causing him to release the firm grip he had on the boy's shoulder, and the lad bolted for the door. I stuck out my foot as he darted past me and he did a cartwheel ending up in a crumpled heap in the corner of the room.

I hauled him to his feet by his long, greasy hair. He spat at me and howled defiance so I struck him hard across the face with flat of my hand.

'Enough!' I barked at him. 'Now calm down and tell me your name.'

'Dunbeorn,' he muttered resentfully, rubbing his stinging cheek.

It meant dark child and was an appropriate name for this urchin with his black hair and strange violet eyes.

27

'You call me lord, Dunbeorn. Do you have parents or anywhere to call home?'

He shook his head and a few tears escaped his eyes, which he fiercely blinked away. I don't know why I felt sorry for this scrap of humanity – after all there were plenty like him in every large settlement – but I did. In some ways he reminded me of two of my best physicians – Uhtric and Leofwine. Like this boy they had been homeless urchins in Lundenburg. However, they had been the sons of an apothecary. When their father died they were forced to eke out an existence in the streets. However, unlike them, this child had probably been born in the gutter.

'Well, Dunbeorn, what do you think the future holds for you?' I asked him in a kinder voice.

'Death,' he replied. 'It comes to us all but it comes more quickly to the likes of me.'

His reply startled me. Few warriors lived much longer than I had and recently my thoughts had turned to my own demise. I dreaded the thought of turning into a drooling idiot, sitting by the fire to warm my ancient bones and waiting to die and so I tried not to think about it. However, there was a world of difference between someone my age thinking about the approach of death and a young boy doing the same. It showed the despair with which he regarded his prospects.

'If I ask the abbot to give you into my care and make you my body servant, would you serve me loyally or would you betray my trust?'

I think that I had surprised myself by my question as much as I had Æscwin and the prior.

The boy stared at me open mouthed and thought for a while before gently pulling my hand away from the grip it still had on his hair.

'I swear to serve you faithfully if you spare me and give me food every day.'

He looked so serious and solemn as he said this that I instinctively believed him.

'Very well; Father Æscwin, would you allow me to pay whatever fine you deem appropriate?'

'Don't be silly, father, make a donation to the monastery if you wish – silver is always welcome – but the boy is yours. You can take the rest of the rogues and beggars that infest the settlement with you as well,' my son said with a grim smile.

And so Dunbeorn had become my new body servant. As I watched him bringing two horses towards me – his own mare and my stallion, Thryth, there was little resemblance to the scrawny urchin of a year ago. Good food had filled him out and he had grown a good four inches. I always suspected that he was bright and he had a strong personality. I had also discovered that he had a ready wit and charm. Some of the other boys in my hall had teased him at first but, instead of lashing out, he had smiled and made a quip which turned animosity into rapport.

He was as popular with the girls as he was with his fellow boys and I suspected that, even though he'd only just gone through puberty, he might even be responsible for the swollen bellies belonging to two of the servant girls.

Thryth was a recent acquisition, bought when my previous stallion had fallen ill and died suddenly. His name meant strength and he was at least three hands taller than most of the other horses ridden by my warband. He was black all over apart from a white blaze on his nose and so far he had lived up to his name; not tiring when other horses did.

I mounted and led my gesith and the rest of my warband out of the gates and headed north towards the coastal road. The early autumnal day was bright and pleasant but it didn't lift my spirits. My thoughts were focused on the coming conflict with the invaders. Although Wessex had been at peace for the past six years – apart from the odd minor Viking raid along the coast – we had been expecting trouble ever since Guðrum, the Dane who ruled East Anglia, had died two years ago.

His son and successor, Eohric, was young and hot-headed. King Ælfred suspected that he might cause problems but so far he had confined his aggression to eliminating those of his nobles who disputed his position as king and the odd minor clash with his neighbours, the Danish jarls who ruled the area of Eastern Mercia known as the Five Boroughs. With our attention devoted to internal matters within the four kingdoms that made up Englaland, none of us had anticipated a large scale invasion from the Continent.

Before departing I had dispatched messages to Ælfred in Wintanceaster and to my neighbouring ealdormen - Dudda of Sūþrīgescīr and Cyngils of Suth-Seaxe – I had also summoned the Centish fyrd to meet at Favresham, a vill midway between Cantwareburh and Midleton. I couldn't afford to wait for the king to bring the army from middle and western Wessex to my aid; that would mean allowing the Vikings to range far and wide, creating a wasteland out of half my shire. I only hoped that the fyrds of Cent, Suth-Seaxe and Sūþrīgescīr would suffice to clear the heathens from my shire.

Even that hope was dashed when I arrived at Favresham. I was told by several thegns who had already arrived that a second, and much larger, fleet of ships had sailed up the River Scir and had landed at the inland port of Apuldre.

✝✝✝

Wælmær, the captain of my gesith for many years, had recently retired to a vill I'd given him as a reward for many years of loyal service. He'd been replaced as captain by Wolnoth, a Northumbrian who'd joined me when we were both boys and I was searching for my brother Alric, a captive of the Danes.

Other than Wolnoth, the only other member of that original warband still with me was Cináed. He'd been a young Pict who'd been captured by Norse raiders and made to serve as a ship's boy. We'd killed the longship's crew and he had joined us rather than trying to find his way home. Cei and Jerrick had also been members of my first warband but they were now the commanders of Ælfred's navy and I saw less of them than I would have liked.

Two other men who'd been with me for over two decades, although not part of my original warband, were Acwel and Lyndon. They had joined me at aged twelve to be trained as scouts and there was no one who could track or reconnoitre ground unobserved better than those two. They were the obvious choice to lead two groups of scouts: one to observe the Vikings who'd landed at Midleton and the other to ride down to Apuldre to discover what was happening there.

Two days later the fyrd of Suth-Seaxe arrived and I called a meeting of the ealdorman and the most senior thegns. By then Acwel had sent one of his scouts back to say that the reports about the landing at Apuldre were, if anything, understated. He had counted two hundred and thirty two different craft tied up on the wharf, beached along the river bank or moored midstream. The only good news was that there were only a few small snekkjur and two dozen knarrs. The rest were small boats typically used by the Franks for fishing and trading along the coast and up their rivers. It was a pity that the last few days had been relatively calm or many of them might have foundered during the sea crossing.

His estimate of numbers was something in the region of four thousand, which came as a blow. Even the original Great Heathen Army, which had so nearly brought Wessex to its knees a quarter of a century ago, had only numbered two and half thousand.

'What are they doing?' I asked the scout.

'Not much, thankfully. They appear to be in a poor way and at the moment they are just foraging.'

That at least was good news. I'd feared that they might have set out to link up with the other Vikings at Midleton.

Lyndon also sent in a report. He'd counted seventy six masts in the channel between the mainland and the Isle of Sceapig. Again, these were a mixture of longships and Frankish boats. This group of Vikings were more actively scouring the countryside for plunder and slaves as well as food. His estimate of their numbers was in the order of fifteen hundred. I grunted in satisfaction. When the last contingents had arrived I should have something in the order of six hundred skilled warriors and a fyrd numbering nearly two thousand. The fyrd were of mixed quality but they were a lot better trained than had been the case when the Great Heathen Army had invaded.

'We can't take on both heathen hordes,' Cyngils pointed out after my chaplain had opened the meeting with a few prayers. 'We're going to have to wait until the king arrives with more men.'

There was a general murmur of agreement with what the Ealdorman of Suth-Seaxe had said.

'Even then, we'll face an enormous army if the two groups unite,' Dudda said. 'We've got to keep them apart.'

My priority was to confine the damage done to my shire to the minimum until the Vikings could be sent packing. However, I agreed that to allow them to unite would be a disaster.

'We've got the men to defeat the group at Midleton, why don't we start there?'

The speaker was the thegn of a vill near HrofesCæstir. His vill was only a few miles away from Midleton so I could understand his concern.

'We might outnumber them, but these men are Vikings. I'm not sure that we can defeat them in a normal battle,' Dudda pointed out. 'I think our best strategy is to contain them until Ælfred arrives.'

'That might take weeks!' another thegn protested.

'Better to wait until we're certain we can overcome them than risk being defeated,' Dudda retorted. 'If that happens there is nothing to stop the heathens from rampaging throughout our three shires. No, we should contain them until help arrives.'

'We can certainly ambush their foraging parties, but I would like to see if we can come up with a strategy to defeat the Danes at Midleton ourselves, rather than wait for the king. After all, he might well see the larger incursion in the south as the greater priority,' I pointed out.

Several of the thegns from Sūþrīgescīr vociferously disagreed. No doubt they were worried about their vills further to the west of Midleton and thought that containment was the best policy. However, despite his former caution, Dudda now supported me and so eventually everyone agreed to meet again the following evening to see what I could come up with in the way of a plan.

Dudda and Cyngils had deferred to me as the most experienced military commander present but I had no official position outside Cent. I was therefore dependent on the nobles from the other two shires agreeing to my plans. I had to devise something in the next twenty four hours that everyone could support.

By dawn the next day I was on the coastal road heading west accompanied by Wolnoth, Cináed, Dunbeorn and Banan, the scout who'd brought the message from Lyndon. It was a small group and we'd be in trouble if we encountered any Vikings but a larger escort would be more difficult to conceal. Banan led us off the road after a couple of miles and we followed animal tracks into the woods to the south. After an hour, during which time we led our horses rather than ride, we cautiously emerged into a small clearing in the trees on the rear slope of a low ridge.

Lyndon and other scouts had set up camp there and he took me forward to the top of the ridge. The trees were thinner and petered out entirely a little way down the northern slope. We therefore had a good view of the encampment around Midleton. I

33

sucked my teeth when I saw how extensive it was. The invaders had taken over the settlement and were obviously living in the hall and the surrounding huts and barns but there were also numerous tents and makeshift shelters encircling the buildings. There was another settlement called Sidyngbourn just over a mile away which they had also occupied.

Men stripped to the waist were busy digging a defensive ditch and rampart around the main encampment, which I took as a good sign. It could well mean that the Vikings were planning to overwinter there. If so, they wouldn't be marching south to join up with the other army.

There were two enclosures: one for a hundred horses that the enemy had either brought with them or captured locally, and a rather larger one for sheep. Sceapig, the island across the narrow channel in front of us, was essentially one large sheep farm and evidently the Vikings had brought across enough sheep to their camp to feed them for a few weeks. However, the island held at lot more; enough to last them through the winter unless we could cut off their access to Sceapig.

Their longships and other craft were beached on both sides of the channel between Midleton and Sceapig as well as being moored in the channel itself. As I studied the scene below me a plan formed in my mind.

✝✝✝

Work began the next morning with several parties cutting down trees and trimming the trunks for use in building a palisade. Meanwhile I rode to Dofras to explain what I wanted Cei to do.

'But, Jørren, I have few enough ships as it is,' he complained when I said I wanted him to blockade the Vikings ships in the channel between Sceapig and the mainland. 'How many ships is it going to take to do what you're suggesting?'

'The eastern end of the channel is about six hundred yards wide but the western exit is narrower, perhaps two hundred and fifty yards across. However, even at high tide, the mud banks at either end are shallow so the navigable channel is perhaps five hundred and two hundred yards respectively,' I explained.

'Even so, the longest ships I have are seventy five feet long at most, so to seal the channel I'd need to sink between thirty and fifty ships. The whole navy consists of fifteen of the largest type and twenty smaller ships!'

'Yes, Cei, I haven't forgotten,' I replied a little more testily than I had intended. 'But we will only need a few if we stretch chains between them to make booms. In any case I intend to use some of the Vikings own ships if I can.'

'But won't they just come and remove the chains?' he asked, clearly thinking I had lost my wits.

'Not if we build forts at each end and man them with archers who can protect the booms,' I said with a grin.

'What about at night?'

'I'll have a few boats patrolling the outside of the booms containing torch bearers. They can illuminate any attempts by the Vikings to attack the booms.'

However, he still looked dubious.

'Look, we just need to contain the Vikings here until the king's main army reaches us. I daren't try and defeat them with the men I currently have; not with an even larger host at Apuldre. Even if we don't lose a significant number at Midleton, we can't go on and tackle the second army. If they combine, then I'm not sure that even Ælfred can succeed against so many Vikings. The best way to stop them joining forces is to prevent them using their ships.'

'What's to stop the second army, the one at Apuldre, sailing into the Temes and linking up with the one here?'

'Because you're going to bottle them up as well. They made a mistake when they sailed up the River Scir. The area is mainly salt marsh. The thegn of nearby Tenetwaradenn tells me that the settlement at Apuldure is at the end of a spit of land which juts into the marshes. It's unlikely to be where the Vikings have set up camp but there is an area of high ground just to the west of Apuldre called the Isle of Oxney. The river flows around this island and so it's a perfect defensive location and it's less plagued by the insects that live in the marshes.

'Just before the river divides to flow around the isle it becomes quite narrow. I would imagine that the Vikings will want to keep their ships nearby and so they are probably beached or anchored all around Oxney. The thegn says that two or three ships sunk in the river at that point should be enough to block it, even at high tide.'

'Very well, which is the priority?'

'I want you to see to the blockade at Sceapig and send a ship to Portcæstre to brief Jerrick. He can look after bottling up the Vikings at Oxney.'

It was a complicated plan and much depended on it working in the way I envisioned. I trusted Cei and Jerrick more than almost anyone I knew. They were good sailors and brave men, but they thought in conventional ways. This operation depended on flair and probably a certain degree of improvisation. I couldn't be in three places at once and so I had to leave the maritime aspects of the plan to them and hope it all went smoothly.

✝✝✝

The weather suddenly turned cold. There had been a sharp frost the previous night and I had emerged shivering from my tent with an urgent need to relieve myself. I was only dressed in the tunic I wore for sleeping and I shivered in the chill air. I was debating whether my need was so pressing that I didn't have enough time to return for my cloak when Dunbeorn appeared and wrapped it around my shoulders.

With a nod of thanks I hastened towards the latrines. In many encampments everyone pissed wherever the fancy took them; some didn't even bother to go into the woods to defecate, especially if it was dark. However, my two young surgeons, Utric and Leofwine, had convinced me that this led to disease, especially the bloody flux. I had therefore insisted that latrines be dug and that the men use them. Those caught pissing elsewhere in the camp would be fined and anyone caught emptying their bowels would be flogged. After the first two who contravened my order about crapping inside the camp had their backs laid bare by a whip, the message got through.

Once dressed and armed I rode along to where the top of the ridge gave me a good view down into the Viking encampment. Most of the men I could see looked like Danes but there were quite a few Norsemen amongst them. That confirmed my suspicion that they had come from Frankia, not Danmǫrk itself. However, I wanted more information about the leaders, what they intended and how good the morale of their men was. I needed captives who I could question.

When I saw horses being brought in from the pasture land to the north of the encampment I realised that the enemy were about to send out forage parties and I hastened back to my camp, telling Dunbeorn, who had come with me, to stay and see where the enemy were headed.

Wolnoth quickly assembled my gesith and chose fifty other experienced warriors to accompany us. Then I returned to the ridge above the Viking camp. Leaving the rest on the rear slope I went forwards to the edge of the trees.

'Three groups left their camp, lord,' Dunbeorn told me excitedly, 'one headed north on foot and the other two went east and west on horseback.'

'The one heading north presumably intends to cross to Sceapig by ship and collect more sheep,' I muttered to myself before speaking to my servant again. 'In what strength were the two mounted parties?'

'Perhaps two score men and a few boys in each? I'm sorry, lord. I didn't think to count them.'

'Not to worry, Dunbeorn, but next time remember to get as accurate an estimate of numbers as you can; it's important.'

'Yes, lord. Sorry, lord.'

I smiled at him and his contrite expression changed to one of pleasure. He ran to where one of my warriors held the reins of his mare whilst I debated whether to follow the group who had headed east or the one going westwards. What decided me was the fact that our main encampment lay to the east and I didn't want the patrol blundering into it.

They had a start on us but they would be travelling slowly in a long line looking for farmsteads or small settlements to rob. I therefore headed south-east before coming back towards the coast. That way I hoped to get between them and our camp. I deployed three pairs of scouts a few hundred yards ahead of us to give me warning when we got close to the enemy.

I was beginning to think that we had somehow missed the Vikings when Cináed and Banan came cantering back.

'They're raiding a farmstead not half a mile from here, lord.'

'Have they put out sentries?'

'No, lord,' Cináed replied with a grin. 'They're too busy raping the women and pillaging, all except for a few boys on the outskirts of the place who are guarding their horses.'

There wasn't time for me to see for myself so we'd have to go in blind and trust in God that we'd get it right.

'Wolnoth, take twenty men and ride around to the east of the farmstead. Stop any escaping that way. The rest of you come with me. We ride in amongst the buildings and kill as many Vikings as we can,' I told them. 'Lyndon, you take a few men and capture the boys and the horses. I want at least two of the little bastards left alive for questioning, you understand?'

'Yes, lord.'

That left me with fewer men than the enemy but we'd have the advantage of surprise and they'd be spread out. We walked our horses towards the hall and the surrounding huts and barns. It was more like a small settlement rather than a farmstead, but one held by a ceorl, not a thegn. We got within fifty yards of the nearest building when one of the enemy glanced up and saw us.

He was standing with two other men waiting their turn to rape a young girl. His mouth opened in surprise but by the time he had shouted a warning and had drawn his sword I was on top of him. I swung my sword and felt the jar up my arm as the blade connected with his shoulder. Such was its sharpness and momentum that the sword cut halfway through his collar bone. He screamed and fell to the ground, blood pumping from a severed artery.

My next opponent was ready for me. He came out of a hut holding a wicked two-handed axe and, instead of trying to strike at me, he swung it at Thryth's head. My horse was battle-trained and it backed up as the axe came down where his head had been a split second earlier. I knew what was about to happen and I clung onto the saddle horn as Thryth reared up and struck out with his front legs. One iron shod hoof smashed into the Viking's helmet, cracking it like an eggshell and crushing the skull beneath. The other struck his shoulder and the axe dropped from his lifeless hands.

Thryth came down onto four feet with a jolt which nearly unseated me. For a moment I was off guard. A Viking no more than fourteen years old came at me from the side and he would have probably gutted me with his spear had he not made the mistake of yelling. No doubt it gave him courage but it also warned me and I pulled up my shield just in time so that the spear point glanced off it. I pulled my foot clear of the stirrup and kicked out, catching the boy in the centre of his chest. He shot backwards and landed on his arse, his helmet flying off.

39

I swung down from the saddle and brought the pommel of my sword down on his head. At least I had one captive for questioning now. I left him lying unconscious on the ground and remounted Thryth. Looking around for another foe, I realised that it was all over. The raiders were either dead, had surrendered or had fled.

✝✝✝

We had taken eight captives in all. Apart from the youth I had knocked out, there were three of the boys who had been left to hold the horses and four men. They were all Danes and at first none would talk. They didn't know that some of us were fluent in Danish and I understood from what they said that they were all sworn to a man named Hæsten, someone I'd never heard of. I gathered that, not only was he their jarl, but he was also the leader of the invasion force.

The other interesting fact was that two of the boys – the one I'd knocked unconscious and his younger brother, who'd been one of the horse-holders – were the sons of the group's hersir and he was one of those we'd captured. The man had been badly wounded in the right thigh, otherwise I'm sure that he'd had gone down fighting rather than be taken prisoner.

Once we had gleaned as much as we could from eavesdropping I took the hersir and his sons to one side, out of sight of the others.

'Which of your sons do you want to die first?' I asked the man harshly.

'What? How do you ...'

His mouth clamped shut at that point. He had only spoken because he was startled to hear me address him in Danish.

'I'll ask you again, which of your sons do you want to die first?'

He watched me warily, wondering if I was serious, but he didn't reply. I nodded to Wolnoth and two of my men hauled the elder boy – the one who had tried to spear me – to his feet and one of them pressed his seax against the boy's throat firmly enough to draw a trickle of blood.

'Wait!' the hersir yelled in a panic. 'What do you want?'

'Information,' I replied, signalling for the warrior holding the boy to relax the pressure on his neck. 'I gather that your leader is called Hæsten but I want to know as much about him as you can tell me. What are you doing here? Is it just a raid or something more serious? Are you planning to link up with the other horde who have landed on the south coast? You can start by telling me your names.'

The hersir gave me a calculating look and instinctively I knew he was about to lie.

'Don't even consider misleading me. I intend to keep your sons hostage and if I find you have lied to me, or kept anything important from me, they will still die. However, it won't be a quick death but a slow one roasting over a fire.'

The man looked at the ground in despair.

'And if I cooperate?' he asked after a pause, 'will you still kill us?'

'No, I'll give you a choice: you and your sons can become oath-sworn to me and join my warband or you can return to Hæsten with a message from me. I'll still keep your sons and they'll become my thralls.'

'That's no choice. Hæsten will kill me if I return having lost my men and with no plunder. He'll think that I'm trying to trick him because we intended to keep it.'

'Then swear to serve me and you can join us. There is one condition, however. You'll have to convert to Christianity.'

'Accept the nailed god – the White Christ – instead of Thor and Odin?'

He fingered the golden Mjolnir hanging around his neck and was silent for several moments.

41

'That's difficult for me – and for my sons – we believe in the Norse gods and we know nothing of the nailed god save that he preaches peace and is therefore weak.'

'My men and I are all Christians, even the Danes and Norsemen amongst us. Do we strike you as weak?'

'No, but you caught us by surprise.'

He sounded as if he thought we'd behaved unfairly.

'No, it is you who were weak and foolish. You should have put out sentries in hostile territory. Foraging for food, even pillaging for valuables, I can understand. Instead you slaughtered unarmed men, women and children instead of just rounding them up. By rights I should hang all of you.'

Instead of looking me in the eye and defying me as any man of character would have done, the hersir looked shifty and deceitful. In that instant I knew that he would betray me at the first opportunity, oath-sworn to me or not. I made up my mind.

'You had your chance. Instead of taking the opportunity to save yourself and your sons you prevaricated. I don't feel that I can trust you. I won't even send you back to Hæsten with a message. You will hang with the rest of your men as a warning to other raiders. Your elder son can take my message, the younger will become a thrall. Take them away.'

I had enough compassion not to make the two boys watch their father and his companions hang. I sent the elder off on the worst of the horses we had captured from the Danes with a message to Hæsten telling him that he had twenty four hours to leave Cent and return to Frankia or be killed. His younger brother and the other boys we'd taken prisoner would be sent to Dofras and sold to a slave trader.

I returned to our camp at Favresham well pleased with the day's outcome. We had destroyed a foraging party, learned at least a little about our foes and we would all have a little silver to add to our pouches once the slaves were sold. I hadn't learned the names of the hersir or his sons but I would have cause to rue

42

sparing the elder in due course. As I found out later, his name was Sigurd.

CHAPTER TWO

November 892

I was hardly surprised when Hæsten ignored my warning and, instead of leaving, sent out foraging parties numbering hundreds rather than scores. For the next week or two I contented myself with ambushing as many of these raiding parties as I could. We suffered some casualties but the Vikings usually came off worst.

The weather grew more miserable with each passing day. If it wasn't raining it was foggy; if it was neither the mornings were frosty, or else an icy wind swept over the land. No one day was like the last.

We had moved to the ridge above the Viking's encampment. On arrival we had used the pre-made sections of palisade to erect a wall in less than a day around the area where we intended to spend the winter. By the time that Hæsten's men realised what was happening and attacked us, we were ready for them.

Although there wasn't time to dig the foot of the timbers into the earth, we'd consolidated the structure using props behind each section and lashing the latter together. We had made arrow slits at shoulder height in the palisade when we had pre-fabricated it. It sufficed to protect us whilst our archers poured volley after volley into the enemy as they struggled up the slope towards us. When they withdrew they left a hundred or so dead behind and carried away many more who'd been wounded.

Over the next few days we dug a ditch around the palisade and banked the earth up to bury the feet of the timbers. Then we added a walkway to give the archers added height and so that we could defend the palisade against an assault using scaling ladders.

Once that was completed we started work on the huts which would replace our tents. Unlike us, the Vikings had no access to timber and so the majority continued to live in the tents they had brought with them.

My main problem was the fyrd. As days became weeks and weeks turned into a month they began to slip away. They were concerned for their families and wanted to make sure enough provisions were laid by for them to survive the winter. I couldn't blame them but it threatened to leave us numerically inferior to the enemy.

My plan to trap the enemy fleet in the channel between Sceapig and the mainland worked better that I dared to hope. Cei blocked both entrances with sunken ships and stretched chains between them. As a temporary defensive measure he'd anchored several of his longships manned by archers and other warriors the other side of the two booms to prevent the enemy from unfastening the chains. After several futile attempts to do so they gave up.

Once the main camp was fortified I sent men down to join Cei. He transported them to Sceapig where they erected a small fort at the end of each of the two booms to take over the task of defending them from the ships.

There was little we could do to stop the Vikings from sending men over to Sceapig to bring back sheep at first but, once the forts were finished, I was able cut off this source of supply. My first thought was to attack the foraging parties but that would risk men's lives, so instead I sent Cei around to the far side of Sceapig. They landed and rounded up as many of the remaining sheep as they could and carried them away. Eventually most of the flock found their way into my camp to supplement our rations. That way we dined on mutton whilst our foes starved.

✝✝✝

Messengers had kept me apprised of events elsewhere. The boom across the River Scir had also worked and now the second pagan horde had been contained as well. Ælfred had mustered a strong force to confront them and his son, Lord Edward, had been

45

entrusted with leading it. He had the heræswa, Eadred, to advise him but, even so, I wondered at the wisdom of giving the command to an eighteen year old.

The next surprise was the arrival of the king himself at our camp. At least we had some warning; a messenger had cantered in a few hours before Ælfred appeared at the gates. I was there to greet him, not a little puzzled about his decision to come to see the smaller of the Viking encroachments instead of going to the Isle of Oxney with his son.

'What do you know about these invaders?' he asked me without preamble once we were seated in the small wattle and daub hut which served as my quarters for the time being.

'The leader is a man called Jarl Hæsten. He's a Dane but a fair number of his men are Norsemen. He appears to have gathered together several bands of starving Vikings from the north of Frankia. Their motive seems to be a desire to conquer and settle here instead of Frankia, where the harvest has failed. This is, of course, rather more worrying than if they were merely intent on raiding.'

The king grunted and gazed into the fire burning merrily in the central hearth for a while.

'And he has two and a half thousand seasoned warriors with him?' he asked.

'I would say that is an over-exaggeration, cyning. My estimate would be around fifteen hundred warriors plus a few hundred boys, thralls and the like.'

'Really? Eadred told me that there were some eighty longships and that each would have carried a crew of at least thirty.'

'I fear that the heræswa is misinformed, cyning,' I replied, choosing my words carefully. 'Whilst it's true that there are some eighty ships bottled up in the channel south of the Isle of Sceapig, many of these are small Frankish craft evidently supplied to Hæsten by King Odo to rid his kingdom of this Viking horde. Their fleet also includes knarrs used to transport horses and

46

equipment. Less than a third of the total are what we would call longships.'

Ælfred seemed annoyed that he'd been misinformed.

'You seem to have bottled them up well,' he commented and I detected a note of criticism in his voice.

'Yes, I didn't want them raiding my shire. They arrived half-starved and my intention is to further weaken them before any conflict takes place between us.'

'But you've cut off their escape by sea as well. Surely it would have been better to allow them to set sail once more, having cut off any forays into Cent and the rest of Wessex? Having failed here they may well have returned whence they came.'

'I doubt it, cyning. Hæsten would lose face if he merely turned tail and retreated to the Continent. His men would probably have killed him and replaced him with another jarl had he suggested it. Had I allowed him to leave by sea he was more likely to have tried his luck somewhere else along the coast. He might even have sailed around to join up with his fellow Vikings in the south of Cent.'

Ælfred glared at me when I'd contradicted him but, after he'd thought about what I'd said, he nodded in agreement.

'You might be right I suppose. Well, I want rid of him and his raiders so I had better ask him to meet me so we can come to some agreement.'

'You intend to pay him Danegeld, cyning?' I asked, appalled at the notion.

Danegeld was a special tax levied on a man's hideage – the value of his land. It was unpopular and it merely bought time; it didn't solve the problem. The last time the king had levied the tax and paid an army of Danes to go away they hadn't kept their side of the bargain and Ælfred had very nearly lost the support of his nobles, and consequently his throne.

He gave me another sharp look.

'Just arrange the meeting. I will decide the basis for the negotiations, not you,' he snapped.

I realised that I was treading on dangerous ground. To try to interfere with whatever Ælfred had in mind would not only be foolish but any opposition would probably make the king even more determined to have his own way.

'Of course, cyning. I'll send someone to the Danes' camp immediately,' I replied in what I hoped was a placatory tone.

At first my attempts to negotiate a meeting were frustrated. My first messenger was sent back with a flat refusal to meet with the king. A day later the second came back naked and on foot, Hæsten having decided to keep his clothes and his horse. Ælfred was furious but I knew that the Vikings' leader was playing to the crowd. By treating the priest I'd sent with the king's letter in such a manner, the Hæsten had increased his popularity by humiliating us.

'By heavens, I'll have him dangling from the nearest tree with a rope around his neck for such an insult,' Ælfred fumed.

'I think he needs to be taught a lesson,' I said grimly.

'What do you suggest?'

So I explained my plan.

✝✝✝

My son Ywer had been a warrior in my gesith for the past three years. However, he was impatient for responsibility. I understood that but I was determined that he wouldn't receive preferential treatment just because of his birth. Anything worthwhile had to be earned if it was to be valued.

I'd been born the third son of a ceorl who rented a small farmstead from his elder brother – the local thegn. The coming of the Great Heathen Army nearly thirty years ago had ironically led to an improvement in all our fortunes.

48

My eldest brother, Æscwin, after whom my first-born son was named, had become thegn when both our father and our uncle had been killed at the Battle of Salteode – the first encounter between the invading Danes and the men of Wessex. My other brother, Alric who, at fourteen, was a year older than me had also fought in the battle and had been captured and enslaved.

I had spent the next three years gathering a band of orphans, freed slaves and even a few captured Danish boys. I had managed to find and free my brother and, in the course of fighting our way through the length and breadth of East Anglia, Mercia and Northumbria, I had accumulated enough wealth from those Danes we'd killed to buy a vill for myself. And so I'd become the Thegn of Silcestre. My good fortune didn't end there. I'd come to the notice of the Ætheling, Ælfred, the brother of the King of Wessex at that time and eventually, after he became king, he'd made me an ealdorman.

I'd fought for and I'd earned what I now had. In much the same manner my elder son, Æscwin, had risen through inborn ability from a novice monk to become the Abbot of the monastery at Cantwareburh. I had no intention of letting Ywer think that all he had to do to become ealdorman in due course was to sit idly by and wait for me to die. He would also have to earn his preferment by proving himself worthy.

The appointment of ealdormen - the governors and chief magistrates of each shire - was officially a matter for the Witenaġemot, the supreme council of the kingdom. In practice, the nobles and the senior prelates who made up the council tended to approve whoever the king proposed. Although it wasn't always the case, sons tended to follow their fathers as ealdormen. They were usually the richest and most influential men in their shire and to appoint anyone else would disturb the natural order of things and lead to trouble.

It had happened, of course. In my own case I had been presumed to have been killed in Mercia when I was the

Ealdorman of Berrocscīr, appointed at a time of crisis when a strong military leader was required. Ælfred had chosen another to replace me as my sons were infants when I'd disappeared, and he wasn't about to depose my successor when I turned up alive after all.

However, he'd promised to find me another shire when one became available. In due course I married my second wife, the widow of the recently deceased Ealdorman of Cent and, as their only son, Oswine, was an infant, I was chosen as the new ealdorman.

I freely admit that I had been fortunate but luck and the king's favour were far from the only reasons I had risen to become, not only ealdorman of one of the most important shires in Wessex, but also at various times commander of Wessex's army and later her navy. I don't think I'm being vain when I say that my military ability played a bigger part in my advancement than mere good fortune had.

However, I had seen too many scions of noble houses think that their birth gave them a God-given right to rule and to command men. Arrogance was the one characteristic that a good leader should never display. Consequently I was determined that Ywer should earn his place, first as a warrior and then as a leader.

When he'd been abducted by agents of one of my enemies at the age of nine, Ywer had displayed both courage and fortitude. I would never wish the treatment he suffered at that time on anyone but he had undoubtedly benefitted from the experience. Hardship had helped mould him into the young man he was today. Consequently, I was now prepared to take a risk and give him command of part of the operation against the Viking encampment. It was a vital part. My life and those of my archers would depend on Ywer performing his part correctly as well as displaying good leadership. Men will fight to the death for a leader they believe in. Just being the son of a noble wasn't enough – not by a long way.

We crept forward towards the Viking camp with white blankets over our cloaks so that we blended in with the freshly fallen snow. Although it was the middle of the night, there were few clouds in the sky and the new moon bathed the white blanket that covered the ground in an eerie light tinged with pale blue.

The Danes had built an earth rampart to protect their winter camp but, lacking timber, it offered a poor defence compared to our fortifications. All the same it would be costly in terms of casualties to assault, but that wasn't my intention.

As we moved towards the enemy camp the wind picked up and it felt as if someone was sticking ice cold needles into the exposed skin of my face. I was glad of my wolf skin cloak and for the padded leather jerkin I wore underneath it. However, my hands were chilled to the bone and I hoped that the cold wouldn't interfere with my archers' use of their bows.

When we were a hundred yards from the ramparts I held up my hand and we halted. Still there was no indication that we had been spotted. I had espied the odd head peering over the top of the earth bank from time to time but its owner did no more that give the surrounding land a cursory glance before ducking back into the sheltered interior of the enclosure.

Each group of five men had a fire pot: an earthenware jar with small air holes in the side in which small pieces of wood blazed merrily. They were virtually invisible from more than a few yards away but they sufficed to ignite the oil-soaked rags which had been wrapped around the shaft of each arrow near the point.

A minute later the first volley of fire arrows sped up into the night sky and dropped towards the centre of the Viking encampment. Five more volleys followed before the sound of the ensuing tumult reached me. It was chaos. Men ran hither and thither seeking water and something to carry it in so that they could extinguish the flames as the oiled leather and woollen tents caught fire. Others tried to beat out the small fires with cloaks, blankets or anything else that came to hand.

I waited patiently as another fifty points of light arced into the sky to bring yet more chaos down onto the camp. Surely someone would have the common sense to send warriors out to confront the source of the fires – my bowmen? Then I heard it – the sound of spears and axes banging on shields as several hundred armed Vikings appeared through the narrow gap in the ramparts and charged towards us. I prayed that Ywer remembered to do exactly what I'd told him.

I ordered my men to change target and they sent one last volley at the oncoming Vikings before slowly withdrawing. The arrows with their burning points struck torsos, limbs and shields. It didn't really matter where the arrows lodged: men oiled the covering of their shields to keep the leather from drying out and splitting. Many also greased their bodies to keep out the cold. Whether the arrows caused any real wounds didn't matter, it was the burnt skin and hair that did the real damage.

The Vikings howled with rage as more than a score of their fellows burst into flames. They stopped to roll them in the snow and their attack lost all cohesion. The archers and I beat a hasty retreat and I prayed that Ywer wouldn't let us down. He didn't. As some four hundred Vikings chased after us, he and his men appeared in a wedge formation out of a hollow depression on the enemy's right flank.

The Danes and Norsemen were strung out in a disorganised mass. Ywer's spear-point formation cut through them like a knife slicing an apple. The bewildered Vikings didn't realise what was happening at first and the leading two score or so continued to hare after us. The others turned to confront this new menace but found it difficult to attack the tight formation with its interlocked shields.

Those on the right hand edge of Ywer's wedge carried their shields on their right arms. Their task wasn't to cut down the enemy, just protect their fellows. The rest hacked, thrust and slashed at the Vikings as they forced their way into their midst.

52

Meanwhile my archers had deposited their bows in leather sacks held open by boys and servants at the edge of the trees and collected shields, spears, axes and swords from them. A minute passed and, satisfied that my fifty men were now ready, I yelled for them to form a shield wall. We advanced at a steady pace so as to keep our formation and met the leading Vikings as they charged up the slope towards us.

It was like the sea crashing against a stout cliff face. The first few were cut down as soon as they reached us and, as we kept up the advance, more and more were killed. The only real defence against a good shield wall is another but the enemy were too disorganised to form one. When they tried we broke through it and slaughtered them. Of the forty men who stood between us and the conflict between Ywer and the main body of the enemy scarcely ten can have survived.

When we reached the rest of the Vikings those to the south of Ywer's force found themselves caught between his men and mine. They did the only sensible thing and broke off the engagement. Now they were fighting just to get clear so that they could flee. The Vikings between Ywer's wedge and their encampment had already decided that they had lost the fight and were streaming back towards the gap in their ramparts.

Five minutes later my son and I were left in possession of the field. However, our moment of triumph was short lived. We had lost perhaps a dozen killed and twice that number wounded. The rest of the Vikings – those who had stayed to put out the flames – now erupted from their camp intent on revenge for their humiliation. There must have been over a thousand of them and we numbered scarcely a third of that. It was time for a strategic withdrawal.

There was never any danger of Hæsten's men catching us before we re-entered our fortress but, such was the enemy's fury over what had happened, that they tried a foolish assault on our palisade. It was between twelve and fifteen feet in height and,

53

even with two men lifting a third up, few could reach as high as that, let alone lift themselves up far enough to climb over. A few hands managed to grasp the top of the wooden wall but a swift axe blow or chop with a sword sent them tumbling back down again minus their fingers.

Common sense soon prevailed and the Vikings gave up and slunk back to their encampment, calling down the fury of their gods upon our heads.

It had been an extremely satisfying skirmish. Ywer had proved himself, not just in my eyes but in the eyes of the king as well. We had slain or wounded at least two hundred of the enemy, perhaps more, and we had made Hæsten look like an incompetent fool in the eyes of his men.

CHAPTER THREE

December 892 to March 893

The cold snap in November hadn't lasted long and it was soon replaced by warmer weather and almost continuous rain. It made the roads neigh on impassable and conditions in the camps, both in ours and in Hæsten's, had become increasingly wretched.

Ælfred had hoped that the losses the Vikings had suffered might have forced Hæsten to the negotiating table but the defenders had thrown spears at the priest who the king had sent to request a parley. The man came running back, his grey habit flapping around his legs and causing him to stumble in his haste to get away. It was evident that the man wasn't yet ready to consider a truce. The king returned to Wintanceaster at the end of November saying that he would come back in the spring when he hoped that the Vikings might be more prepared to talk.

The tidings that reached us from the Isle of Oxney weren't much better. The Vikings there had tried to break out of the place three times in all but the combination of the wasteland called the Romney Marshes and Edward's counter attacks had defeated them each time. Those who tried to find their way out through the marshes got lost or were cut off and slaughtered by Edward's men, guided by local men who knew the marshes. The one success that they did have was to break the boom. Some forty ships had escaped before Edward had managed to sink some of their ships in the channel and prevent any more leaving.

We feared that the forty ships that had got away, which might well have carried a thousand warriors or more, would attack elsewhere in Wessex but they had seemingly vanished. Perhaps they had returned to Frankia or even sailed further afield to Danmǫrk or to Íralond? I didn't care just so long as they didn't return to Wessex.

I had left my shire reeve – a thegn called Sighelm – in charge of the besieging force at Midleton whilst Ywer and I returned to my hall at Cantwareburh for the Christmas period. Sighelm had been left in charge of the administration of Cent in my absence in the autumn and I thought it was about time he suffered the boredom of siege warfare whilst I enjoyed a few days with my family. I can't say that he was overjoyed when I asked him but he couldn't very well refuse my request.

I was cold and wet when my hall on top of the hill to the north of the settlement, with its monastery and sprawling maze of huts and other buildings, came into view. We rode in through the gates and stable boys came running to take our horses. Ywer and I dismounted outside the wooden steps that led up to the hall's double doors just as the right hand door opened and Hilda emerged wrapped up in a fur-lined cloak that I'd bought her as a gift the previous Christmas. Even at thirty five she was a fine figure of a woman. Her face was unlined except for the crows' feet around her eyes; however, her hair, once a rich and lustrous brown, betrayed her age. It was thinner now and there were several grey streaks in it.

She greeted me formally but the sparkle in her eyes told me how pleased she was to see me again. I returned the warmth of her greeting and we went into the hall together where I made for the heat of the central fire pit to try and restore some feeling into my chilled frame. She came and took my cloak, handing it to one of the servants, and I took her in my arms, counting myself lucky to have such a wife. Of course we argued, increasingly so it seemed, but I still loved her with all my heart.

When I'd married Hilda she'd been a young girl of seventeen and I'd been a man of twenty three. We'd both been married before and had children: she had a boy called Oswine, who was three at the time we first met, and I already had four. Aside from the two boys – Æscwin and Ywer – I also had two daughters from my first marriage. Cuthfleda, my eldest child, was the head of the household of King Ælfred's daughter, Æthelflæd, the Lady of the Mercians. My other daughter was Ywer's twin sister, Kjestin, the wife of Odda, the eldest son of Ealdorman Eadred - the hereræswa. Hilda and I also had a daughter, Æbbe, who was now twelve. She was too young to be betrothed in my view but my wife had other ideas.

I knew that her son, Oswine, was discontented with his status as Thegn of Ægelesthrep. His father had been my predecessor as ealdorman and, now that Oswine was a man, he held a grudge against me. He believed that it was his right to become the ealdorman, as his father had been. He didn't wish me ill personally - in fact there had been times when he had saved me from harm – but I had reason to suspect that he resented my position as ealdorman.

I also knew he disliked Ywer. The likely reason for that was his position as my heir. My eldest son, being a monk, couldn't inherit my lands or my position as ealdorman and so it was almost inevitable that Ywer would do so. Thankfully Oswine was a close companion of Edward's and a member of his gesith, which kept him out of my hair most of the time.

I knew that Hilda had some sympathy with her son's position, although she was never tactless enough to say that to my face. However, I did detect a slight cooling of the relationship recently. I suspected that her son's relatively lowly status as a noble made her even more determined that her daughter should make a good match. She raised it with me the first night after my return and I confess that it took some of the shine off my homecoming.

'You need to talk to the king about her,' she coaxed as we lay in bed after making love.

'Why? It will be several years before she needs to be wed,' I replied somewhat grumpily.

'That doesn't mean she can't become betrothed. Cissa's eldest son is ten. He would make a suitable husband when they are both a little older.'

57

'The boy's simple in the head. The king would never let a dimwit succeed Cissa; besides the boy's father is in his late thirties. He could live for a couple of decades yet.'

I quite liked Cissa, the Ealdorman of Berrocscīr, but I could never forget that he had only become an ealdorman because I was presumed dead. I had held Berrocscīr before him but I had been sent to negotiate an alliance with King Burghred of Mercia. I was too late; he had already surrendered to the Danes and I was lucky to escape with my life. I had to lie low for months before I could safely return to Wessex and by that time Ælfred had given the shire to Cissa.

Hilda sulked in response to my statement of the blindingly obvious. We both knew that there were no other first sons of ealdormen available. Either the heirs were already betrothed or even married, or else the fathers didn't have any living sons. Besides, Æbbe was headstrong and had already told us that she would never wed whoever we – or more accurately, her mother - chose for her. She would only marry for love. Hilda didn't accept this; she was more interested in using the girl to further the family's status – and in particular hers – than she was in our daughter's wishes.

It wasn't a good start to the festivities but worse was to come.

The king's eldest son, Edward, had married my niece, Ecgwynna, and she had given birth to a boy who they'd christened Æthelstan. The marriage ceremony had been held in secret with the priest, Father Tidwold, as the only witness. Tidwold had been banished from Ælfred's court when Edward had unwisely told his parents of the match. I had been forced to hand the baby over to the king and he'd sent Æthelstan to his daughter, Æthelflæd, to bring up in Mercia. Ecgwynna, feeling betrayed by her husband and by me, had become a nun, thus freeing Edward of the marriage.

Ælfred and his son had kept the matter secret and so the only proof that Æthelstan was Edward's legitimate son, and thus

58

Ælfred's grandson, was Father Tidwold and the marriage certificate, which the priest had signed and which Edward had sealed with his ring. I'd been told to destroy it but I hadn't done so. Instead I had given it into the care of my son, Abbot Æscwin. On Saint Stephen's Day news reached me that Tidwold had died. Now the only proof of Æthelstan's royal birth lay in my son's coffers.

Inevitably, rumours had circulated that Edward had sired a son. Æthelstan's very presence as Æthelflæd's ward led to speculation and most of Edward's gesith knew that he'd got Ecgwynna pregnant. However, the rumours also maintained that the boy had been conceived out of wedlock. Now that Tidwold was dead, my elder son and I were the only ones who could offer proof that Edward's son wasn't a bastard. It was not a comfortable position to be in.

I was tempted to ask Æscwin to destroy the document but I didn't. It was to prove a momentous decision.

As the twelve days of Christmas drew to a close I prepared to return to Midleton. Relations between Hilda and I had remained a little frosty; we had argued twice more about Æbbe's future and eventually I had told my wife in no uncertain terms that I planned to talk to the archbishop about endowing a convent over which my daughter could preside as abbess in due course. It wasn't true, of course - the last thing Æbbe wanted was to become a nun – but it was enough to give Hilda pause for thought.

She came to the door of the hall to see me off but turned and retreated from the cold as soon as I had mounted Thryth. I sighed. I loved Hilda but there were times when I could have cheerfully wrung her neck.

The festive season had been wet and dank for the most part. Now, however, the cold weather had returned and as we plodded westwards along Casingc Stræt flakes of snow fell out of the grey sky. The old Roman road along which we travelled was still in fairly good repair, which meant we didn't have to ride through deep mud, but the biting wind from the north seemed to penetrate my wolf-skin cloak, leather jerkin and thick woollen tunic like icy needles.

The cold seemed to affect me more now than it did in the past; perhaps I was feeling my age. I was well aware that I wasn't as fast and agile as I had been when I was younger, but I still wasn't that old. Ælfred was only three years my elder but he looked like an old man. His health had never been that robust, which probably accounted for it. It was said that he only dined on broth now - fare more suited to a bondsman than a king - because he vomited anything else back up.

Of all the ealdormen of Wessex, only Nerian of Somersæte was older than I was being well over fifty. His two sons had predeceased him and so his successor would probably be his much younger brother Æthelnoth. I glanced across at Ywer riding beside me. I hoped that he would be chosen to succeed me. If I fell in the coming conflict with the Vikings it wasn't certain that he would be allowed to. Eighteen was young to be made an ealdorman, although it wasn't unheard of. I had only been nineteen myself when I'd been made Ealdorman of Berrocscīr, but then the circumstances had been unusual. Hopefully I'd survive a while longer, enough for Ywer to gain in years and experience before he needed to take over from me.

I shook off my maudlin thoughts about my own demise and wondered how the Vikings were faring in this weather; not well I hoped.

✝✝✝

Hæsten had at long last agreed to meet King Ælfred and negotiate a truce. January and February had been hard months: the ground had been frozen solid and even the channel between Sceapig and the mainland was covered by a layer of ice inches thick. The Danes couldn't have sailed away, even without the booms in place. It had been too cold to snow for most of February but earlier blizzards had piled it up into drifts.

It was obvious that some of the Vikings had died from the cold or from starvation as, without the timber to cremate their dead or being able to dig graves due to the hard ground, they had laid the dead out in rows on the island. I counted fifty three bodies but there were probably others out of sight from our fortress.

The place chosen for the king and the Viking leaders to meet was halfway between their encampment and ours. I had sent down cooks and spit boys to roast several sheep over fires in the open so that we could all eat before the talking started. Ælfred was dubious about feeding the enemy but I maintained that it would make them more amenable to a sympathetic reception on our terms.

The dozen Vikings who trudged wearily to the meeting place were a sorry looking bunch. They had obviously eaten the last of their horses as they were forced to walk. Their faces looked gaunt and drained. No doubt their bodies were thin and emaciated but it was difficult to tell under the layers of clothes and furs that they wore to ward off the cold.

The weather had improved a week before the meeting in early March but that wasn't saying much. The temperature was now slightly over the point at which water froze but the thaw was slow in setting in. At least the icy wind had died and a watery sun shone down on the tent erected for our negotiations.

The Vikings fell upon the platters of meat and bread offered to them like ravenous wolves. Inevitably, their stomachs couldn't cope and three of them vomited the food back up. Nevertheless they returned for more but this time ate more sensibly, allowing each mouthful to digest before eating the next.

Once they had eaten their fill the king, who's Danish wasn't as good as mine, asked me to translate.

'Jarl Hæsten, you may choose three men to accompany you into the tent to meet with the king and his advisers. The rest will have to wait outside. Those entering the tent must hand their weapons over to my gesith first.'

I relayed what Ælfred had said and it didn't go down well.

'A Dane gives up his weapons to no man,' Hæsten replied furiously, his hand going to the hilt of his sword.

Immediately the king's gesith lowered their spears and pointed them at the Vikings. I sensed that the talks were about to turn into a bloodbath before they'd even started.

'Wait!' I shouted, putting up my hands. 'The king and his advisers will also enter the tent unarmed. It's a sensible precaution in case discussions get heated and someone does something he later regrets.'

The Vikings didn't take their hands off their swords or lower their spears and axes immediately but at least they made no further aggressive moves. Eventually Hæsten relaxed and his right hand fell to his side.

'Very well, we'll leave our weapons outside the tent but we'll hand them to my warriors, not yours.'

Ælfred understood enough of what the jarl had said to get the gist and immediately unbuckled the belt from which his sword and dagger hung and handed it to one of his gesith. I did the same as I was one of the four negotiators. The other two were Bishop Asser and Archbishop Plegmund. I was dubious about including churchmen in military negotiations but the king rarely took any decisions without consulting the clerics with which he surrounded himself. Three other Vikings divested themselves of their weapons and we all trooped into the tent where there was a wide table with four chairs on either side.

When we were seated I studied the men opposite. Two were clearly Danes like their leader but the fourth looked different. His grey beard reached down to the middle of his chest and had been braided into three plaits. The hair on his head and that of his beard was tied around a number of small bones which looked like human finger and toe bones.

Hæsten introduced the other two Danish jarls and then said that the fourth man was a Norseman named Ulfbjørn Bearslayer. It was only then that I noticed the bear's claw hanging from a silver chain around his neck which was partially hidden by his beard. Presumably he had killed a bear singlehandedly and kept it as a souvenir. Bears were now extinct in Wessex and Mercia, although a few still existed in Northumbria and in Alba, but I knew that they were fearsome creatures who could kill you with one swipe of their paw. I was impressed.

'I will allow you to depart Wessex,' the king began, 'on three conditions. You don't ever return to these shores; you and your family convert to Christianity; and you return any plunder and slaves you have taken.'

There was a flinty look in Ælfred's eye and I swallowed before translating, knowing that these terms were non-negotiable as far as the king was concerned.

'King Ælfred is prepared to allow you to leave here with enough provisions to allow you to return to Frankia but he has certain requests,' I said carefully, watching the Vikings for their reaction.

'Go on, what are these requests?' Hæsten asked, his eyes wary.

'You swear not to return to raid Wessex, that means all the land south of the River Temes,' I replied, thinking that the Vikings probably wouldn't know the exact extent of Wessex. 'That you and your family are baptised and become Christians.'

At that point one of the other jarls asked Hæsten a question and a fierce discussion broke out. In essence they were saying that Hæsten couldn't forsake the Nordic gods in order to become a follower of the Nailed God – their name for Christ. His men would never follow him if he did so.

Ælfred asked what was going on and I explained.

'Tell him the third condition,' he snapped at me, clearly annoyed at the heathen's resistance to Christ and the one true God.

I waited for the hubbub to die down. In listening to what Ælfred was saying I'd missed some of the discussion but I gathered that he had reached some sort of compromise.

'There is one further request,' I said firmly. 'You must return to us all the plunder you have taken as well as any thralls you have taken from our people.'

Another argument broke out amongst the four men at this. I couldn't hear all of it but I gathered that two were in favour of outright refusal but Hæsten and Ulfbjørn Bearslayer thought that they could palm us off with a few trinkets, together with the freedom of just a few of the slaves they'd seized, in exchange for food.

The negotiations dragged on all day. In the end a compromise was reached. The Vikings would leave Wessex and promised not to return. As they agreed to swear to this on Christian relics I knew that they had no intention of keeping the promise and told Ælfred so. I advised him to make them swear on the Mjolnirs they all wore around their necks. It represented Thor's hammer and they would keep such an oath – at least for a time – but neither the king nor the churchmen would hear of it.

Hæsten refused to be baptised but he agreed that his two sons could become Christians. He also agreed that he would leave them with us as hostages. They would also return to us the plunder and slaves they'd taken since their arrival in Cent. Ælfred was content with this, although I was well aware that the Vikings intended to trick us and said so.

The following day was wet and miserable but at least the temperature was well above freezing. The Viking leader's two sons were produced and I interrogated them to verify that they were who Hæsten claimed they were. I wouldn't put it past him to fob us off with two urchins of no value. However, I was reassured to see that both had the same distinctive copper coloured hair as their father. They were ten and twelve years old and answered my questions with no hint of guile or deceit; I was as certain as I could be that they were indeed his offspring.

Just as the baptismal ceremony was about to start a group of riders appeared from the west. For a moment everyone stared at the oncoming cavalcade with alarm and a few picked up their shields and hefted their spears but I saw the banner fluttering in the light breeze. It was the white wyvern on a green background of Mercia.

'It's Lord Æðelred, cyning,' I told the king.

'Yes, I can see it is, although I have no idea what he's doing here. However, he seems to have brought my daughter with him so I can't imagine he is the bearer of ill tidings.'

He was quite correct. I could see the Lady Æthelflæd riding beside him and immediately behind her was my eldest daughter, Cuthfleda. I'd always tried not to have favourites amongst my children but the two I was closest to were Cuthfleda and Ywer. It was some time since I'd seen her and my heart swelled with pleasure.

'Good morrow, Ælfred. I was visiting Lundenburg when I heard you were here, so I thought I'd come and see if you needed any help against these troublesome Danes,' he said with a grin.

'I see, and you brought my daughter to help you fight them, did you Æðelred?' the king replied somewhat tartly.

The Lord of the Mercians frowned and muttered something about his wife insisting on coming so she could see her father again.

'Good, I'm pleased to see you looking so well, daughter,' Ælfred said with a brief smile.

'And I you, father,' she replied with a much broader smile. 'And I've brought your grandchildren to see you.'

'What? Grandchildren? Have you had another child?' he asked looking puzzled.

'No, of course not. I mean my daughter Ælfwynn and Edward's son, Æthelstan.'

As she spoke two women descended from a small conveyance called a wheel-bed. This consisted of a horizontal frame above two axles on which four vertical posts were mounted. From the tops of these a padded cloth was suspended on which the passengers lay or sat. Riding in a cart was uncomfortable as anyone in it felt every jolt and bump in the road. I'm told that riding in a wheel-bed was better as the cloth absorbed much of this, although the swaying motion could make you feel quite sick.

The women were evidently nurses. One of them helped the five-year old Ælfwynn out of the carriage. The girl stared about her with interest before running to her mother, who had just dismounted. The other nurse carried the eighteen month old Athelstan. She set him down on his chubby legs in front of his aunt and he toddled into her waiting arms.

Ælfred greeted Ælfwynn warmly, although he was plainly uncomfortable at showing too much affection towards her in front of his nobles and warriors, not to mention the assembled Vikings. He completely ignored the boy.

'You shouldn't have brought the little bastard here,' he hissed at Æthelflæd.

'He's no bastard and well you know it, father,' she shot back at him. 'Father Tidwold swore to me that he had married Edward and Ecgwynna before he died. I'm sure that, as her uncle, Lord Jørren can confirm that she was legally wed to my brother.'

Ælfred had gone red in the face.

'Enough! Be quiet girl, you don't know what you're talking about. Can't you control your wife, Æðelred?' he demanded angrily.

The latter wisely said nothing and the king turned on me, giving me a baleful glare as if somehow this was all my fault. I too

66

had the sense to keep my mouth firmly shut, although I knew that the little boy was his legitimate grandson. Even if Edward had other sons in due course, Æthelstan would still be the eldest and should be classed as an ætheling.

The king had stalked off to join Bishop Asser and Archbishop Plegmund so that the baptism of Hæsten's two sons, Jøns and Guðmarr, could proceed. I saw Asser whisper something to the king, who nodded. One of the priests then approached Æðelred and said something to him. The Lord of the Mercians looked surprised for a moment and then nodded, accompanying the priest back down to the river band where the baptism was to take place.

Intrigued, I walked down to join the small crowd of witnesses who had formed a semi-circle around the clerics and the two boys. An excited whisper ran around the spectators and I gathered that Ælfred would stand as godfather to the elder, Jøns, and Æðelred would do the same for Guðmarr. Ælfred had also been the godfather of the late King Guðrum and, although he hadn't always remained loyal, the Dane had remained a Christian for the rest of his life.

As with Guðrum, the two boys were given Christian names after their baptism. Jøns became Irwyn and Guðmarr was given the name of Godric. Unlike Guðrum, whose Christian name was scarcely used except by the king's immediate circle and churchmen, the two boys would become hostages and live amongst us; they therefore became known by their new names.

Two days later we watched Hæsten and his Vikings sail out of the channel between Sceapig and the mainland and away into the Temes estuary, supposedly heading back across the Sūð-sǣ to Frankia. They were shadowed by Cei's very much smaller fleet. We'd been puzzled by the fact that they had chosen to exit the channel at the western end as Frankia lay to the south-east of us.

The reason soon became clear as the Viking fleet headed north across the estuary instead of sailing eastwards. They were headed for Ēast Seaxna Rīce, the southernmost shire in the Kingdom of East Anglia.

We were furious with the duplicitous Dane and for a moment I thought that Ælfred was about to order the execution of his sons. However, he relented.

'Jørren, get them out of my sight before I change my mind,' he snapped at me.

I took the two young Danes away wondering what on earth he wanted me to do with them. I could, of course, have confined them as prisoners, or even made them slaves, but I had managed to change boys who were former enemies into loyal warriors in the past and I wondered if I could have the same success with these two. Time would no doubt tell.

CHAPTER FOUR

Easter 893

I regarded Oswine in amazement. He'd been sent by Edward to ask me to come and reinforce his army. Unbelievably the ætheling had let Fróði and the second Viking horde escape from the Isle of Oxney through the marshes between there and the vill of Tenetwaradenn.

'How on earth did thousands of Vikings manage to find their way through what were thought to be impenetrable marshes?' I asked.

'They apparently captured some local families and forced the men to help them by threatening to kill their women and children. Of course, when the guides had served their purpose they killed them all anyway.'

'I see. And weren't Edward's men watching the known exits from the marshes?'

'Yes, of course,' he shot back at me with an annoyed frown. 'However, they were heavily outnumbered by the Vikings and wisely withdrew. Anyway, that's not the point; what's done is done. Our task now is to gather our forces again and meet the Vikings on the battlefield before they can do any more damage.'

'Where are they now?'

'When Edward sent me to you they had stopped at Tunbrige to gather more supplies. They are starving and need to forage every day.'

'Tunbrige? That's forty miles from Tenetwaradenn,' I said, horrified at the destruction that such a large force of Vikings must have done to the heart of Cent. 'Why hasn't Edward tried to halt their progress?'

'Because he only has seven hundred proper warriors and fifteen hundred members of the fyrd; the Vikings still have several hundred more than that and they're savage fighters, not farmers and artisans.'

'He must have gathered more than that from the whole of middle and eastern Wessex,' I said, looking puzzled.

'No, he has only been joined by the men from Berrocscīr, Hamtunscīr, Dornsæte and Wiltunscīr. You had mustered the three eastern shires and the ealdormen of Whitlond, Somersaete and Dyfneintscīr claimed that Vikings from Íralond were planning raids on their shires. Wessex has been weakened by the invasion of Cent and it's rumoured that they seek to take advantage of the situation.'

I wondered how word of the invasions of Danes and Norsemen from Frankia had reached Dyflin, the main Viking kingdom in Íralond, but I kept my thoughts to myself. It wasn't Oswine's fault that the western shires had failed to come to our assistance.

'Where does Edward think that this Fróði and his horde are making for?' I asked instead.

'Initially we thought that he would make for the north coast of Cent to link up with Hæsten but he must have got wind of his ally's flight into Ēast Seaxna Rīce and changed his mind. Now he appears to be heading for the south bank of the Temes west of Lundenberg.'

I thought about this. It made sense. The Great Heathen Army had used the River Temes as an invasion route decades ago. In those days they had controlled the river and used it to move men and supplies along its length. Hopefully the fortified burgs we had built at places like Stanes, Wælingforde, Chisbury and Baðum would make this much more difficult. Furthermore the Vikings had been forced to leave their ships bottled up in the River Rother, so they would have to acquire fresh ships if they were to make use of the Temes.

'Where does Edward want me to muster the fyrd of Cent?'

'Edward wants to confront Fróði near Fearnhamme in Sūþrīgescīr so that would probably be the best place for you to meet him. He expects you to bring the forces of Sūþrīgescīr and Suth-Seaxe with you as well, of course.'

'They are not my men to order about, Oswine,' I pointed out. 'Dudda and Cynegils brought their men to help me to defend Cent as a favour to me, not because I had any control over them.'

'Well, Dudda should be keen enough as the Vikings appear to be heading into his shire next,' he said tartly. 'If you can warn him and relay Edward's request that he gathers his men again I'd be grateful. I'll head off down to see Cynegils myself.

✝✝✝

I emerged with Edward and my fellow ealdormen from the small timber church in the settlement of Fearnhamme after hearing mass to celebrate Good Friday. I was annoyed that Eadred, the hereræswa, was no longer there to guide the young ætheling but he had returned to Dyfneintscīr when the rumours about an invasion of his shire had reached him. With a heavy heart I had agreed to the king's request that I take his place as military adviser, although Edward seemed to think he didn't need my help.

The army had mustered on land adjacent to one of the tributaries of the Temes and altogether numbered nearly four thousand men, a thousand of whom were hearth warriors or members of the warbands of various ealdormen and thegns. My scouts had reported that the enemy numbered some three thousand but they were spread out and advancing on a broad front. I was wary of tackling so many Vikings when we were so dependent on the fyrd but Edward had all the brash confidence of youth and accused me of being a faint-hearted old man.

'There is another army approaching from the west,' one of my scouts rode up to report.

71

For a horrible moment I thought it might be Hæsten and the rest of the invaders, then I discounted the idea. He was ensconced in a newly-built fort at Beamfleote, some distance to the east.

'Did you see any banners?' I asked the scout, who was a boy I'd recruited two years ago when he was thirteen.

'Yes, lord,' he replied confidently. 'The white wyvern on green of Mercia,'

'Then why the hell didn't you say so,' I barked at him.

It was unfair of me but I had feared it might be Hæsten.

'Sorry, lord. I didn't think; it's good news isn't it?' he asked looking crestfallen.

'Yes, lad. It's very good news.'

He looked relieved and we waited whilst my horse was brought.

'Wolnoth, let Lord Edward know that Mercian reinforcements are nearing the camp. Tell him that I will go and meet them.'

'Yes, lord,' Wolnoth replied with a grin.

He was well aware that I should have waited for Edward to join me before riding out to greet Æðelred, for I fully expected the Lord of the Mercians to be leading the new arrivals. I thought that it was foolish of me but I half hoped that he had brought his wife and my daughter Cuthfleda with him. Then I saw them riding behind him and I grinned like an idiot.

'Well met, Lord,' I greeted Æðelred. 'Lady Æthelflæd, Cuthfleda,' I added with a nod of the head to the former and a broad smile for my daughter. 'You have come just in time to join us in defeating the Viking horde.'

'I'm only here because Ælfred insisted that I give you my support,' he replied somewhat testily. 'You've heard the news I suppose?'

'No, what news?'

'The reports that the Irish Vikings were planning to attack Wessex in the west weren't exaggerated. Norsemen from Dyflin together with Danes from both East Anglia and Northumbria are besieging Escanceaster.'

My heart sank. This was beginning to look more and more like a concerted attempt to conquer Wessex. It was even more vital that we destroyed Fróði's pagan army now. If he was allowed to link up with Hæsten, Wessex would end up fighting on two fronts and, if our kingdom fell, then the rump of Mercia wouldn't be far behind. So much for Ælfred's dream of re-conquering the Danelaw and uniting the old Anglo-Saxon realms into one kingdom called Englaland.

'How do we defeat this army of Fróði's?' Æðelred asked at the council of war held that evening in the thegn's hall at Fearnhamme.

The place was scarcely big enough to hold those attending and the roof was in a poor state of repair. The rain that was coming down in torrents outside dripped through bare patches in the thatched roof in a dozen places. The dank smell of old, wet straw that covered the floor of beaten earth did little to make us want to stay there any longer than was absolutely necessary.

'We meet them shield wall to shield wall,' Edward replied confidently.

'Really?' the Lord of Mercia asked sceptically. 'Even if we prevailed, which is by no means certain, can we afford the losses that would inevitably follow such an approach? Moreover, if our aim is to destroy the heathens, how do we ensure that they don't just leave the battlefield and move on to Beamfleote?'

Edward didn't reply immediately. Instead he beckoned Oswine to his side and held a whispered conversation with him.

'I'm sorry, Edward,' Æðelred asked, 'but is this the new hereræswa or some ealdorman that your father has appointed as your advisor?'

The ætheling flushed with annoyance.

'This is Oswine, one of my gesith and my most loyal companion.'

73

'Ah, the step-son of Lord Jørren. I would like to hear what the old dog has to say, rather than the puppy.'

Oswine and Edward glared at Æðelred. Both were clearly furious and I could see the council deteriorating into a slagging match if we weren't careful.

'I think what the Lord of Mercia is saying is that we should discuss the enemy's weaknesses first and then see how best we can exploit them,' I said tactfully. 'Then, if I may suggest it, we need to find a suitable battlefield where we can be certain of not only beating the Vikings but causing them the maximum number of casualties in the process.'

'What are these weaknesses?' Ealdorman Dudda asked before either Edward or Æðelred could speak.

I gave him a grateful look and outlined my assessment of the situation.

'So you're saying that we should lure the Vikings in this re-entrant your scouts have found and surround them?' Edward asked incredulously. 'They'll just break through us; our line will be stretched too thin to contain so many of them.'

'No, Lord Edward. We can block their advance with a strong shield wall and hold the sides of the valley with a mixture of archers and shield warriors. If they try to close with us on the hills on either side they will be struggling uphill whilst our archers pour death down on them. If they get too close we just retire up the slope a little way.'

'Even if we succeed,' Oswine objected, 'they'll just retreat back out of the re-entrant and live to fight another day.'

'That's where our mounted warriors come in,' I replied. 'If they retreat, they'll be routed and our horsemen can harry them incessantly, cutting off small groups and destroying them. Where will they flee to? There is no safe refuge for them. We hunt them down mercilessly. Certainly some, perhaps many, will escape but we'll have destroyed them as a fighting force.'

'It sounds like a good plan to me, brother,' a female voice said as I finished speaking.

The Lady Æthelflæd had accompanied her husband into the hall and everyone assumed she was there merely to remind everyone, Edward included, that Æðelred was the king's son-in-law as well as the ruler of Anglian Mercia.

'You aren't a member of this council, sister, so you can keep your opinions to yourself,' Edward snapped.

'Oh, but she is, Edward,' Æðelred retorted. 'I also thought that my wife was fit for nothing but embroidery and being good in bed but over the years I have learnt to listen to her counsel. I find that she has a better head on her than many a man.'

I was amazed. It seemed that the relationship between Æðelred and his wife had undergone a profound transformation over the past eight or nine years. However, Edward's sneer showed that he didn't believe that any woman could think, let alone do so strategically.

'I have always listened carefully to the reasoning behind the decisions that our father made, Edward,' Æthelflæd said frostily. 'I don't presume to understand everything about tactics or military strategy but I do know how good decisions are made and, perhaps more importantly, how foolish ones are arrived at. Your plan of standing in front of the Viking horde and slogging it out is neither logical nor sensible. On the other hand, I cannot fault the logic behind Lord Jørren's proposal.'

When the great majority of the ealdormen present, both Saxon and Mercian, voiced their agreement with my plan, Edward gave in, seemingly with good grace. However, the venomous look he gave me showed that he blamed me, not his sister, for his humiliation.

When Oswine left the hall in the wake of his master, he moved to the left as he passed me so that he could barge me out of the way with his shoulder. It was childish and petty but it told me that, whatever affection he might have had for me previously, he now shared Edward's antagonism towards me.

Perhaps it was unwise of me to have alienated the king's eldest son but the survival of the kingdom was more important than the esteem in which he held me. Even before this incident I was dubious about my position if Edward became king; I could only pray that Ælfred lived a good many more years. I tried to comfort myself with the thought that there would be other contenders for the throne in due course, not least the king's nephew, Æðelwold. However, a struggle for the throne would threaten the very existence of the kingdom when so many enemies surrounded it.

✝✝✝

That evening I was summoned to a meeting in Edward's tent. When I entered I was amazed at the opulence of the interior. My own tent was large enough for meetings but it was decidedly austere. It contained just a table and chair for me to work at, a bed consisting of a collapsible frame and a straw-filled mattress, two plain coffers and a bench for visitors to sit on. The only luxury I allowed myself were duckboards on the floor to stop the ground from turning into a sea of mud.

In contrast Edward's tent had a solid wooden floor, a white cotton inner lining designed to reflect the light from the numerous candles that stood around on tall sconces, a large wooden bed similar to the one I had in my hall and several chairs. In the middle there was a large table on which a crude representation of the proposed battlefield and several carved wooden figures had been placed. There were four large coffers as well as a wooden frame on which the ætheling's byrnie, helmet and weapons hung.

Edward sat behind the table with Æðelred on one side of him and Ealdorman Dudda on the other. The Lady Æthelflæd sat on the other side of her husband together with the Mercian hereræswa, a young man called Wilfrid, the Ealdorman of Hwicce. Oswine and a member of Æðelred's gesith stood behind their respective leaders.

I looked for a spare chair at the table for me to sit on but there was none. Evidently I was expected to stand. It was a petty humiliation and I despised Edward for it. As I approached the table Dudda rose to his feet and invited me to take his chair.

'I'm only here because the battle is being fought in my shire, Jørren,' he said. 'As we seem to have run out of chairs, please take mine. I'm more than happy to stand.'

It was smoothly said but there were two other chairs against the side of the tent. Edward glared indignantly at Dudda who ignored him.

'That's kind of you, Lord Dudda, but there's no need. I can see a spare chair, I'll fetch that.'

So saying I strode over the one of the spare chairs and placed it on the other side of the table from the others. Once seated, I smiled at Edward and waited for him to compose himself. His attempt to humble me had only made him look foolish and discourteous and he was having difficulty in containing his anger.

'Well, you're here so that we can agree the details of the plan you outlined in the war council earlier today,' Edward managed to get out at last. 'Explain what you propose.'

'Thank you, Lord Edward. We need to weaken the Vikings as much as possible before they reach our shield wall, once they are engaged face to face I propose to attack their rear to force them to fight facing both ways. Not only will this reduce the fierceness of their assault on our shield wall but it will also make it difficult for them to escape.

'However, some, perhaps many, will manage to fight their way clear. I propose to keep two hundred mounted warriors back to pursue and slay those who do manage to flee.'

'Surely we'll need those two hundred experienced warriors in our shield wall?' Edward objected.

'I agree that the stronger our front rank of warriors is the better, however our object isn't just to defeat the Danes and Norsemen, it's to eliminate them as a fighting force. To do that, we need to pursue and harry them as far as we can.'

'Who will command the various elements of our army?' Æðelred asked.

'Lord Edward will be in overall command, of course. I suggest you place yourself with your gesith and a small reserve behind the shield wall so that you can reinforce the line wherever it's needed. Lord Æðelred would you command the shield wall itself? Wolnoth and I will lead the two groups of archers, supported by spear warriors, on the flanks; and I'd like my son, Ywer, to take charge of the pursuit.'

There was further discussion on the detail and then the meeting broke up. As I was about to leave the tent Edward called me back. He waited until we were alone, apart from Oswine, before speaking.

'Twice today you have humiliated me. I acknowledge that your plan is a sound one and, naturally, I will do my best tomorrow to ensure it's successful. However, when it's over, I don't want to see your face again.'

'May I point out, Edward, that it wasn't me that criticised your plan to simply meet the enemy head on and slug it out; it was Æðelred. I merely advanced what I thought was a better strategy. As to making me stand when everyone else was seated, that was unworthy of you. I've no wish to antagonise you, but I will never refrain from saying what's on my mind or acting as I think best for my shire and for Wessex as a whole.'

I watched as Edward's face twitched and went red. I braced myself for a tirade but all he did in the end was to tell me to get out of his sight. I left worrying what revenge Edward might take on me when he was able to and, more importantly, whether he was fit to take on his father's mantle in due course. One could only hope that he would learn wisdom with age.

✝✝✝

The day of the battle dawned grey and miserable. Dark clouds scudded across the sky and moisture hung in the air. It had rained overnight and the ground was wet and slippery, which suited us well. Provided it didn't rain to reduce the power and range of my archers' bows I was happy.

We had moved into position before dawn and now we waited. Edward's and Æðelred's men sat or stood in their five ranks arranged across the top of the bare slope that stretched between the woods on either side. Priests moved amongst them saying mass and dispensing mouthfuls of bread and young boys took water skins along the rows of warriors.

Meanwhile my men waited in the woods either side of the re-entrant. The archers' bows were unstrung and their bowstrings were secreted next to their bodies to keep them warm and dry until they were needed. Groups of warriors and the more experienced members of the fyrd stood amongst them chatting quietly, ready to protect them as needed. I had deployed scouts further down the woods just in case the Vikings decided to sweep the woods prior to their advance.

My one fear was that the heathens would evade us and continue their journey of destruction across Wessex. I was therefore relieved when I saw confirmation that the enemy intended to fight when they erupted onto the valley floor below us. They milled about as their leaders rode amongst them yelling encouragement and working their men into a frenzy. This made some of my younger men afraid but I knew it was a good sign; they would be so fired up that they would run up the slope eager to come to grips with us. That meant that they would ignore the woods and, better still, they would be exhausted by the time they reached our shield wall.

Eventually they formed up into rows roughly eight deep and set off up the incline calling on their gods to aid them and uttering all sorts of dire imprecations at Edward's impassive warriors. I drew my sword and picked up my shield before nodding at Acwel. He put a wooden tube to his mouth and blew into it. The sound that emerged was the booming call of a bittern. A horn might have alerted the enemy to our presence on their flanks but the cry of a bird, even one as noisy as the bittern, would attract far less attention.

The archers strung their bows and wetted the feathers of their first arrows ready for the second signal. I waited until the first wave of Vikings had passed us, then, when the middle of the horde drew level, I nodded towards Acwel again. Once more the call of the bittern sounded above the noise of the onrushing Vikings. As the first volley of arrows darkened the sky I prayed harder than I had ever done that my plan would work.

CHAPTER FIVE

12th April 893 - Easter Sunday

The advancing Vikings were so intent on getting to grips with our shield wall at the top of the slope that initially few of them noticed the mayhem on their flanks. Even the men on the left fell in droves. Some still had their shields slung on their backs and others ran with them by their side which meant that their shoulders, necks and heads were unprotected.

I was with the group of archers and spear warriors in the woods on the left hand side of the slope and so I could only imagine what was happening on the right flank. Over there the Vikings would be completely exposed to the hail of arrows. Even on my side the enemy fell in droves as volley after volley tore into them. Of course half of our arrows were stopped by the Vikings' shields but the rest struck their bodies.

Those with their shields still on their backs came off worst as the whole of their torso on that side was vulnerable. Quite a few wore chainmail byrnies but even these didn't completely protect the wearers. The links parted easily on those of inferior quality and the arrow points, although robbed of some of their momentum, penetrated far enough into their bodies to cause serious harm. Even if the chainmail was better made and held together, the power of an arrow fired at close range was enough to fracture ribs.

My archers had managed to get five volleys away before the Vikings realised what was happening. Several hundred warriors on their left flank broke away from the main body and charged towards the woods which concealed their tormentors. If a man holds his shield in front of him so that only the eyes below the rim of his helmet and his shins are exposed it is neigh on impossible for an archer to wound or kill him. However, it is only possible to advance at a walk like that and these Vikings were angry and ran at us as fast as they could.

Another volley struck them and at least two score went down. By now the leading warriors were no more than fifty paces away. I was pleased to see that my archers didn't panic but coolly drew their bowstrings back to the ears once more. Another flight of arrows punched into the screaming heathens and scores more were thrown back into their fellows with arrows embedded in their chests or throats.

I signalled to Acwel and the cry of the bittern rose above the curses of the advancing horde. In response to the signal the archers turned and ran back into the woods. As they did so they passed a long line of my men waiting in the bushes and behind trees armed with everything from axes and spears to swords and seaxes. The Danes and Norsemen blundered into the woods and inevitably they broke up into small groups as they ran around clumps of shrubs and trees. As they came level, my warriors emerged from their hiding places and struck the unprepared enemy down; then they disappeared back into the trees and the undergrowth.

Meanwhile the archers had reached a line of boys waiting with sacks, shields, swords and other weapons. The bowmen dropped their bows and quivers into the sacks and grabbed the weapons. Then they turned and faced the enemy.

I was out of breath having run a good three hundred yards as fast as I could, weighed down as I was by byrnie, helmet, shield, sword and seax. As I drew in great lungfuls of air I peered into the dense woodland. At first all I could see was the double ranks of archers as they formed a shield wall as best they could between the trees. The boys ran past me carrying their sacks and, as they'd been briefed, halted a couple of hundred yards behind me ready to bring the bows forward again should they be needed.

The air in the wood was still and, although it was chilly, I was sweating both from my exertions and from anxiety. The first of the Vikings emerged in ones and twos and halted when they saw the line of warriors waiting silently before them. None now uttered oaths and threats, however the wood wasn't silent. Behind them I could hear the screams of the wounded on both sides and the clash of metal on metal.

I had now recovered sufficiently and I pushed my way into the centre of our shield wall. As we waited more and more Vikings emerged from the wood to join their fellows. I was getting nervous; if we waited much longer they would outnumber us by some margin. It was good news in a way as it meant that a sizeable number of Vikings had broken away to attack us, making it easier for Edward to hold his position on the top of the ridge.

I decided not to wait any longer.

'Ready men? Let's kill the bastards!'

I took a step forward and the rest of my men did likewise. Unlike the Vikings, who bolstered their courage by yelling abuse, we advanced silently and slowly. It must have been unnerving for the enemy, especially in view of the casualties they had already suffered, and a few of them faded back into the wood. However, although their morale must have been low, the great majority stood their ground.

I stabbed towards the Viking immediately to my front and he raised his shield in response. However, instead of completing the move, I turned the point to my left and thrust it into the neck of the man to my opponent's right. At the same time the spearman to my left killed the man to my front.

He fell to the ground and his place was taken by a huge man with a bushy black beard. I scarcely had time to raise my shield before the giant's great two-handed battle-axe struck it, badly jarring my arm and cutting deeply into the lime wood shield. Thankfully the axe blade stuck fast, held in the split wood. The giant tried to pull it free and - such was the man's strength - the shield was pulled off my left arm, breaking the latter in the process.

Pain washed over me but I fought against it. With his axe useless the huge Viking was defenceless and I shoved the point of my sword up under the bushy beard behind his jaw. I kept pushing and the point sunk in deeper, through the upper part of his mouth and into the soft tissue of his brain.

The man gurgled blood and I was soaked in the stuff as he crumpled to the ground, dragging the sword out of his hand as he did so. The pain from my broken forearm now hit me and I was barely able to draw my seax. I was dimly aware of another Viking thrusting his sword towards me when I felt myself being dragged backwards just as someone stepped past me and into the breach caused by my exit from the shield wall. I remembered no more.

†††

I can't have been out for long because the battle was still raging not far from where I lay. I was dimly aware of Dunbeorn kneeling beside me and trying to pour something down my throat.

'It's something Uhtric gave me, lord. It'll dull the pain so I can set the bone.'

Uhtric was one of the most skilled healers in the kingdom and, being the son of an apothecary, knew his potions. I don't know what was in the concoction he'd given Dunbeorn but it was certainly potent. I was aware of the sharp pain as he manipulated the broken ulna back into place but after that I suffered no more than the ache caused by a badly stubbed toe. He splinted my forearm using strips of cloth ripped from the tunic of a dead man tied to several lengths of wood. I was violently sick but felt much better afterwards. My arm throbbed but the pain no longer incapacitated me.

'Help me up, boy. I need to see what's happening.'

'You should rest, lord. We're winning so there's nothing to fret about,' he replied, sounding as if he was trying to calm a child having a tantrum.

'Help me up, damn you,' I said through gritted teeth as I tried to rise using my good right arm.

Reluctantly he got behind me and put his arms around my chest so that he could help lift me to my feet. The boy was right. My spear warriors had evidently driven off the other Vikings in the wood and had then emerged behind the hundred or so still fighting my archers.

Trapped between the two groups of my warriors the Vikings didn't stand a chance. Several tried to surrender but my orders and those of Lord Edward were quite clear. We had to destroy Fróði's army and no quarter was to be given. Having to guard prisoners would weaken us and so the Vikings were forced to fight on until the last man had fallen.

Leaving the spear warriors to kill the wounded and loot the bodies, I led my archers back to the edge of the wood. The boys appeared from wherever they'd been hiding during the fighting and handed them their bows and quivers.

The wood was quiet and peaceful after the dreadful slaughter that had just taken place within it. When I stepped out of the treeline that all changed. The noise of battle filled the slope before me and, despite the fact that the grey clouds had parted to let the occasional shaft of sunlight through, it did little to lift my dark mood.

I stood with my splinted arm strapped across my chest and studied the scene. Evidently Wolnoth had been even more successful on the other flank. He and his men had emerged from the wood and his archers had recommenced the attack on enemy's right flank. As I watched several hundred Vikings broke away and charged the archers but they simply retreated into the trees where the Vikings were loath to follow. Presumably having been given a bloody nose the last time they'd pursued them, they were reluctant to do so again.

Edward and Æðelred were holding firm on the top of the ridge and, as far as I could tell, the Vikings had suffered the worst of the battle so far. There were bodies everywhere and, judging by those I could see and by the number of wounded Vikings who had been carried to the bottom of the hill for treatment, over a third of the enemy were out of the fight.

I should have left elated that my plan seemed to be working but I didn't. I felt a deep sadness at the loss of life. However, this was no time for maudlin thoughts. The battle was still far from won.

There were no Vikings immediately opposite the spot where we had exited the wood and so I led my men uphill just inside the trees. We emerged about sixty yards from the rear of the enemy shield wall and my archers re-strung their bows. Hundreds of arrows fell on the rear ranks of the Vikings before they realised what was happening. By then a sizeable number of them were dead.

The warriors in the rear ranks of a shield wall are always the least-experienced. They are there to push against the backs of those doing the fighting and keep the line firm. In this case they were mainly boys still being trained as warriors and youths who had yet to kill their first man. I had expected them to turn and attack us and I had my spear warriors ready to protect the bowmen but they weren't needed. Instead of attacking us they ran back down the slope, many of them throwing away their shields, weapons and helmets so that they could run faster.

It didn't save them. As they reached a point halfway down the slope Ywer and his horsemen appeared out of the woods on the other side of the open ground and charged into them, cutting them down with little or no opposition.

I almost felt sorry for them at that point, then I remembered the despoiled land, the murdered women and children and the burnt out farmsteads that the Vikings had left in their wake. I hardened my heart and I ordered my archers to fire into the mass of Vikings still fighting.

It was too risky to aim into them at high trajectory; arrows would inevitably fall amongst our own men. Instead they loosed their arrows into the backs of the Vikings that remained. This time the enemy were hardened veterans who turned and charged at us. It was what I was hoping for and the archers faded back into the trees whilst the spearmen delayed the enemy.

The Vikings' rear ranks on the left had broken off the fight and so Æðelred's men were able to push the reminder back. Whilst my warriors fled into the depths of the wood, the Mercian swung his line around until it was at right angles to the men of Wessex on the other end of the line. Now the Vikings were hemmed in and our L-shaped shield wall pressed them into an increasingly confined space.

I wasn't able to see this happening as I was running through the trees at the time, hampered by the sling tied across my chest. As I passed a large oak I saw a man with a raised sword out of the corner of my eye. I moved sideways to avoid the blow and, instead of striking my shoulder the blade struck my helmet. The last thing I can recall was the strange sensation that I was spinning into a void.

ᛏᛏᛏ

When I came to the wood was quiet and it was getting dark. A had a splitting headache and my arm hurt like the very devil but, after a while, I felt well enough to get up. Try as I might I was unable to do so and then I realised that I was trapped under something. It was difficult to haul myself over the moist earth using only one arm and every move I made was agony.

However, I eventually managed to crawl clear of what proved to be the body of a dead Dane. I have no idea how he ended up on top of me but presumably I had been taken for dead, otherwise the Vikings who were pursuing us would have put a blade through me as they passed, just to make sure.

Once clear I lay there to get my breath back; then I gingerly removed my helmet and my leather arming cap so that I could explore the top of my head with the fingers of my right hand, wincing as I did so. There was a lump the size of an egg and a quite a lot of congealed blood, otherwise I seemed to have had a lucky escape.

I studied my helmet. It was made of good quality steel with reinforcing bars; a gash over two inches long had been cut into the steel but the reinforcing bars over the top of the helmet from fore to aft and side to side had held, although they had bent under the impact. I owed my life to the skill of the armourer who'd made it.

I left it on the ground and pulled myself to my feet using the trunk of a tree for support. For a moment I felt faint and I waited until my head cleared, then I staggered back towards the edge of the wood. After twenty yards or so I came across a group of Mercians searching the dead for anything of value. One of them raised his spear and moved towards me as if he was going to spit me with it until I said who I was.

They relaxed and a boy of fifteen or thereabouts offered me his water skin; it was only then that I realised how parched I was. I drank gratefully and handed it back with a word of thanks. He and his companions seemed overawed to be in my company and just stood there gawping until I asked one of them to go and find me a horse.

The boy darted away and a little later he returned with Wolnoth and several of my men. Whilst he was gone I asked them what had happened after we had retreated into the woods. Apparently Wolnoth had led his men across the slope and into the woods on my side of the battlefield. The combined forces of his men and mine had been sufficient to rout the Vikings in the wood. That left him free to attack the rear of the enemy's left flank.

Surrounded on three sides, the last of the Vikings had broken and ran from the field, only to encounter the horsemen led by my son. Ywer had tried to prevent the Vikings getting away but he didn't have enough men. Thankfully the horde of survivors didn't try and defeat the horsemen; they were far too intent on saving their own skins and disappeared northwards as fast as their feet could carry them.

That was all they knew but I later heard from Ywer that he had pursued the fleeing Vikings and had managed to kill or maim another hundred or so before they reached a small river called the Blæcceburn. Once across many of the surviving Vikings had turned to face him. Rather than attack across the river where the enemy waited on the far bank in much greater numbers than he had, Ywer had called off the pursuit. He'd waited until the enemy eventually dispersed and then sent scouts after them to find out where the Vikings had fled to.

In the end it had been a tremendous victory - not least because Fróði's corpse had been found on the battlefield - but the cost had been high. The Vikings had lost perhaps half their number but we had also suffered. Over seven hundred of our men had died and many hundreds more were wounded. It was a high price to pay but at least their leader was dead and the threat posed by his army had been eradicated – or so we thought.

ᛏᛏᛏ

I was still feeling groggy and both my head and my arm hurt so I didn't go to the victory feast that Edward and Æðelred threw that night in the hall at Fearnhamme. I heard later that the Lord of Mercia had made a speech to the ealdormen, thegns and their senior warriors who were present. In it he paid tribute to Lord Edward for his part in the outcome but most of his praise was apparently heaped on me for my tactics as well as my 'heroic deeds' during the battle, as he put it. According to Ywer, who did attend, his praise couldn't have been more fulsome. Unsurprisingly, this did little to endear me to Edward and his friends.

89

Whilst Æðelred was unwittingly increasing Edward's antipathy towards me I was enjoying the ministrations of Cuthfleda. She had come to find me as soon as she heard that I'd been wounded. Even Æthelflæd had come to see how I was and to thank me. Despite his approbation of me, her husband didn't bother to visit me himself. I had a nasty feeling that Æðelred was courting popularity by associating himself with me. If he wanted to gain Edward's friendship he'd miscalculated badly.

Cuthfleda fed me spoonfuls of broth watched by a frustrated Dunbeorn who obviously thought that was his job. Leofwine had come to examine me and to replace the makeshift splint. His brother Uhtric had also visited me to examine my head wound.

'It's weeping blood and pus,' he told me cheerfully, 'but I can't stitch a gash on the top of your head. All I can do is wash it and put a poultice on it to stop infection creeping in.'

I gritted my teeth against the pain as he cleaned it up but the poultice was actually quite soothing. I fell asleep for a while but then I awoke with a jolt. I'd been dreaming about the battle and a thought had suddenly struck me: if the Viking were pursuing us into the wood how had one got ahead of the rest and hidden behind a tree to ambush me? It didn't make sense. Whoever had attacked me had to be one of my own men.

As if that wasn't enough to trouble me, what if it wasn't a man who held a grudge against me but it was someone paid by another to assassinate me? However, I couldn't think of anyone who hated me enough to want me dead. Although Edward and many of his gesith, including Oswine, disliked me I didn't think any of them would stoop to assassination. It was a mystery but not one I was likely to solve lying here in my sickbed. I tried to relax and eventually I drifted into a deep sleep once more.

CHAPTER SIX

Summer 893

I peered ahead as the fishing boat I'd hired was slowly rowed through the reed beds between the inlet known as Beamfleote Hýþ and the marshlands to the east. I'd heard reports that the remnants of Fróði's horde had joined Hæsten at Beamfleote, although some were known to have taken ships in which to sail back to the Continent. However, the capture of the fort guarding the crossing over the Temes at Stanes and the slaughter of its garrison led credence to the fact that most of those who had escaped from Fearnhamme hadn't left the country but had crossed the river into Mercia.

I had returned to Cantwareburh after the battle and both Hilda and Æbbe had fussed over me like a couple of mother hens. For a while I'd enjoyed it but I grew increasingly frustrated with my inability to do anything. Thankfully Uhtric had pronounced himself satisfied that the break in my ulna had mended in early June. However, even when the splint was removed, my arm was fairly useless. The muscles had wasted away due to lack of use and it was several weeks of regular exercise before my left arm was strong enough to hold a shield once more.

I'd received regular reports about what was happening in the wider world during my enforced period of inactivity. Whilst we'd been engaged with Fróði's Vikings, Ælfred and the men of the western shires had to deal with another invasion. The rumours about an attack by the Norsemen from Dyflin had proved to be true.

Unfortunately their numbers had been swelled by young Danes seeking fame and fortune from both Northumbria and East Anglia. How far King Guðred of Yorvik and Eohric of East Anglia were involved wasn't clear. Both were nominally Christians but, whilst Guðred promoted Christianity in his domain, I suspected that Eohric was a pagan at heart and only pretended to be a follower of what pagans called the Nailed God for political reasons.

The combined Norse and Danish forces had captured the burh of Escanceaster as well as Bydeford. Both offered secure anchorages for their fleets and, as one was on the south coast and the other on the north coast of Dyfneintscīr, they could pillage the whole of the shire if they weren't contained. Inevitably the king saw this as the greater threat and he summoned his son and the men of Hamtunscīr, Whitlond and Berroscir to help him. That left the men of Cent, Suth-Seaxe, Sūþrīgescīr and the Mercians to deal with Hæsten.

I was out hawking with Hilda and Æbbe when Ywer rode up with a man I didn't recognise.

'Father, this man has come from Lundenburg with an urgent message for you,' my son said, looking excited.

'Good morrow, Lord Jørren, Lady Hilda, Lady Æbbe. My name is Arlo; I'm one of Lord Æðelred's gesith. I apologise for interrupting your sport but I have an urgent message from my master.'

'What can be so urgent? Is Lundenburg under attack?' I asked crossly. Give it here.' I added, holding out my hand.

I was annoyed that we had been interrupted at the very moment that my daughter had just flown her first hawk and it had made a kill.

'The message is verbal, lord. Hæsten has left Beamfleote and is raiding the Danish jarldoms to the north of Lundenburg.'

'In force?'

'So we are told, lord. As it is well known that you have the best scouts, Æðelred asks if you could send them to ascertain how many of the heathen swine are left in their fortress. He thinks we may never have as good an opportunity to capture the place.'

'Even if it were lightly guarded, it will take time to raise enough men to take the fortress,' I said with a frown.

Then I understood what Arlo hadn't said.

'Ah, he wants me to send scouts into the Danelaw to shadow Hæsten as well?'

'Precisely so, lord.'

Hilda hadn't said anything but I could feel her disapproval from where I sat on my horse several yards away. She knew me too well.

'Don't think of going yourself,' she said sharply. 'You have scouts more than capable of tracking the raiders and of reporting back on the numbers left behind in Beamfleote.'

'Yes, but I need to see the fort for myself if I'm to work out a way of assaulting it without causing us unnecessary casualties.'

That wasn't the end of the matter, of course. My wife kept coming up with good reasons why I shouldn't go myself but my mind was made up. A day later I rode to Witenestaple and crossed the Temes Estuary under cover of darkness.

†††

In addition to the fisherman who owned the boat and his son, I was accompanied by Ywer, Cináed and my former body servant, a Norse youth called Arne.

'There is firm land just ahead, lord,' the fisherman told me. 'Keep heading north and you will see the pagan's fort on top of a hill; you can't miss it.'

'Famous last words,' I thought to myself. I didn't know this area at all; it reminded me of the marshlands around Athelney where the king, a small handful of clergymen, warriors and I had hidden from the Danes after we'd been betrayed by the then Ealdorman of Wiltunscīr. If you made a wrong turn in those marshes, you drowned.

However, the fisherman was right. We made our way north, guided by the sun which had risen due east of us, and emerged from the reed beds not two hundred yards from the fort. We dropped to the ground and I felt the wet slime seeping through

93

the wool of my tunic and linen under-tunic. I was getting too old for this.

I cautiously raised my head and studied the ramparts above us. A sentry was patrolling to and fro but he wasn't looking our way. We edged back on our bellies until we were once more concealed by the reeds.

'Ywer, there's a small hillock covered in gorse bushes to your left. Take Arne with you and see if you can count the number of longships and other craft you can see and note their position.'

He looked at me with dismay; the gorse would rip their clothes and their skin but he nodded, acknowledging that it would have a good view of the creek. When they had left Cináed and I made our way cautiously through the reeds to the east, seeking a way around the fort under cover. Although the tall stalks screened us from view, any unnatural movement of their feathered tops as we passed through them could give us away. Eventually the reed bed ended and we entered an area of scrub land before reaching the woods which surrounded the fort on three sides.

The circular hill on which the fort was built was flat-topped with short but steep slopes around most of its circumference. To the north the slope was more gradual with a well-worn track leading to a set of gates which were the only point of access. The palisade was fifteen foot high and surrounded by a deep ditch. It would be a pig of a place to assault, even with scaling ladders. The more I studied the defences the more it seemed that the only way to take the place without incurring a massive number of casualties was to batter down the gates.

Siege warfare wasn't something that we had much experience of; thankfully neither had the Danes or the Norse. It was said that the only way that the Vikings had managed to take Escanceaster was thanks to traitors. Apparently Danes who had lived in the two settlements for many years had opened the gates to the enemy. The latest reports said that King Ælfred had failed to recapture the burh so far.

94

However, there we had no agents inside the Viking fort at Beamfleote and dragging a battering ram up the slope to the gates would leave the men pushing the ram vulnerable to a storm of arrows on the approach. Furthermore, once they reached the gates and started to swing the ram into the sturdy wooden trunks from which the gates were made, the enemy could rain rocks and even flaming oil or pitch down on top of us.

The more I considered the problem the more depressed I became. Even if the place was only defended by a few hundred Vikings, as appeared to be the case, they could hold out against a force many times their numbers for some time; and I doubted that we had that long before Hæsten returned with the main body of the enemy. If he did we would be trapped between his host and the fort. It was not a risk we could afford to take. No, if we were to capture the fort it had to be done swiftly.

As we watched the gates opened and several carts drawn by oxen lumbered down the slope and then made for the nearest point on the river bank. I could see that there was a break in the reed beds where a short stretch of shingle beach gave good access to water. There were a score of warriors who stood guard as a dozen thralls filled barrel after barrel with water. It took a good twenty minutes for them to fill all the barrels and then the ox carts made their ponderous way back up the incline to the fort.

'We need to make for that stretch of shingle to see if it can be seen from the top of the ramparts,' I hissed at my companions.

Slowly we made our way to the beach trying not to disturb the slender reeds as we made our way through them. Thankfully, the sentries didn't seem particularly alert – indeed most seemed to be more interested in what was happening inside the fort than outside. I was puzzled by this until I heard the faint clash on metal of metal. No doubt those not on watch were honing their weapon skills against each other.

When we reached the strand where the water barrels had been filled I stood up cautiously to see if the fort was in view. A tremor of excitement ran through my body when I realised that it wasn't.

✝✝✝

Æðelred looked sceptical when I explained my plan for capturing the fort.

'It has its risks, of course, husband,' Æthelflæd said, ' but as Lord Jørren has pointed out, there are few other options which don't involve serious loss of life. Even then, there is no guarantee that an assault with scaling ladders or an attempt to batter down the gates would succeed.'

The lord of the Mercians looked pensive as he paced up and down the chamber that served as his office in the building which had once housed the Roman Governor of Britannia. The delicate mosaic floor had patches which had been filled with earth and the centre was scarred by the countless fires that had been lit within a circle of stones in the middle of the floor but you could still tell that it had once depicted a battle between the invaders from Rome and the original inhabitants: the Bryttas who we had later driven into westwards into Wealas and Kernow.

For a brief moment I wondered if our conquest of the land collectively known as Englaland would last or whether, like the Romans, we too would disappear in time.

'Very well,' Æðelred said at last, 'we'll adopt your plan, Jørren, but woe betide you if it goes wrong.'

'It sounds to me as if you are covering your arse, Lord Æðelred. Either you adopt my plan whole-heartedly or I will have to withdraw my proposal. In that case, of course, I will fully support whatever alternative strategy you decide on.'

He glared at me and he was on the point of losing his temper when his wife gently took him by the arm and whispered something in his ear. He shook her hand off but the anger in his eyes had been replaced by a more thoughtful look.

96

'Very well, I'll put your scheme to the war council,' he said at last.

'Our scheme,' I corrected him.

'I'll support it but it's still your idea and I want you to lead the men responsible for infiltrating the fort.'

†††

I was cold and wet hiding in the reed bed near the strand of shingle by the time that the water party arrived, despite the hot summer sun blazing out of the clear blue sky overhead. Ywer and the other forty warriors with me must have been equally uncomfortable but no one made a sound as the thralls started to fill the barrels.

The score or so of Danes guarding them were relaxed and stood around laughing and joking amongst themselves. They were either very young or elderly but that was no excuse for being lax. Some should have watched the thralls to make sure no-one tried to escape by hiding in the reeds and others should have formed a protective screen just in case they were attacked. Of course, it suited me very well that they had done neither.

I felt sorry for the boys amongst the guards – some no older than twelve or thirteen – but they bore arms and they were the enemy. I put my hands to my mouth and imitated the call of the bittern. It was the signal for my men to get ready. I heard a slight rustling as we moved into position but thankfully it wasn't heard by the Vikings – or if it was, it didn't register.

The call of the bittern sounded once more and arrows struck down over a dozen of the Danish guards. Those that were left alive stood dumbstruck whilst two that had only been wounded tried to crawl into the cover offered by the nearby reeds. A few seconds later and the second volley struck the remainder and we swiftly moved amongst the wounded finishing them off.

Most of the thralls had been knee deep in the water when we attacked and they stood panic stricken as we started to strip the Danes of their clothes and helmets.

'Don't worry,' I reassured the thralls. 'We're friends. You are now free but...'

I got no further before they started to babble their thanks.

'Shut up!' I told them in as loud a voice as I dared. 'Do you want to alert the rest of the Vikings to our presence?'

They gathered around me uncertainly.

'What do you want us to do, lord?'

'Wait here; once we have captured the fort someone will come and collect you and escort you to the ships. I will make sure that you are returned to your homes as soon as possible.'

It took longer than I would have liked before we were ready to drive the ox carts back up the slope. I hoped that no-one in the fort was wondering what was taking so long. However, the sentries at the gate and on top of the parapet seemed no more alert than the guards on the water party had been. I thanked the Lord God for giving us such a hot day. All that most people wanted to do was bask in the sunshine.

I had changed my trousers for the more baggy type preferred by the Danes and tied their broader ribbons around my lower legs. I also discarded my expensive chainmail byrnie for a stained leather jerkin. I couldn't find a Danish helmet that fitted and so I chose an embroidered felted hat called a birka.

Despite the borrowed sword and shield I felt vulnerable as I approached the gates at the head of the returning water collectors. The sentry guarding the open gates was sitting in the sunshine with his back against a gatepost. He appeared to be asleep but he wearily climbed to his feet as we approached. He gave us a cursory glance but then his eyes widened and he studied our faces more closely.

We might have been clothed like Danes but he didn't recognise anyone and, furthermore, Vikings and Anglo-Saxons sported different hair styles. Some of the guards we had killed had been beardless boys but older Vikings usually allowed their facial hair to grow long. It was invariably carefully groomed and often they would either plait it or tie rings, small bones and the like into the hair. In comparison, we were clean shaven or wore moustaches with tips that reached the chin. Some, like the king and me, did have a beard but it was kept shorter and was unadorned.

The sentry should have shouted a warning before doing anything else but he made the mistake of reaching for the spear and shield propped up against the gatepost first. A second later Ywer had thrust his sword into his throat and the only sound he emitted was a croak as blood spurted out of both neck and mouth. He collapsed to the ground and I led my men through the gates at a run.

Less than two minutes later we had killed the sentries on the parapet above the gates and Ywer unwrapped my banner from around his waist and hung it from the top of the parapet as a signal to Æðelred that our mission had been successful. The sentries on the other walls had seen what was going on and the alarm bell rang out from the watchtower. Moments later Vikings emerged from huts all over the fort to see what was going on. I noted with concern that many of them were women and children. I suspected that the Mercians wouldn't hesitate to kill everyone inside the fort once they reached it but there was nothing I could do to prevent that. My main concern was keeping the gates open with my handful of warriors against the hundreds of Vikings who were now forming up fully armed in the centre of the stronghold.

†††

My archers managed to keep the enemy at bay initially but we were out in the open on the walkway and vulnerable to those Vikings with bows and throwing spears who had climbed up onto the roofs of the huts nearest to the walls. To have remained on the walkway would have been foolhardy. We retreated into the towers either side of the gate and to those at the two nearest corners of the fort. From there we could look down on the tops of the buildings and, more importantly, behind the tower's parapet we were no longer exposed.

Sadly we'd lost three men killed and the same number wounded before we managed to take the towers. I watched impatiently for Æðelred to appear with the rest of my men and his own army of Mercia. They had waited out of sight around a bend in the Beamfleote Hýþ for my signal that we had secured the gates. That signal – two fire arrows sent heavenwards together – must have been seen by Æðelred over ten minutes ago but the river water remained undisturbed by the bow waves of our ships.

'Send two more fire arrows skywards,' I told Acwel, who I'd put in charge of the archers.

He nodded but I could tell that he thought it was a waste of time and effort. If the rest of our force hadn't seen and reacted to the first signal, why would they do so when it was repeated?

However, this time there was a response. A few minutes later three ships, all bearing my banner at the top of their masts, appeared around the bend and made towards the landing jetty below the fort. But that was all; there was no sign of the Mercians who formed the bulk of our army.

'Where are the rest?' Ywer asked in concern. 'Have we been betrayed?'

I ignored him and cupped my hands before yelling down to the rest of my warband as they hurriedly disembarked.

'What's going on? Where's Æðelred?'

A good breeze was blowing from the fort towards the landing jetty so my voice carried to Wolnoth as he led his men towards the gate but I couldn't make out his shouted reply. I didn't find out what had happened until our two hundred men swarmed into the fort and I had descended to join him.

'Hæsten has returned unexpectedly,' he told me breathlessly. 'One of our ships keeping watch at the mouth of the creek saw his longships coming along the estuary from the east, presumably having been raiding in East Anglia. Lord Æðelred has taken the rest of the fleet back into the Temes to engage him but he sent me to help you secure the fort.'

It was bad news. The Mercian fleet numbered twenty longships and birlinns of varying sizes carrying more than enough men to seize and hold this fort. However, Hæsten was known to have had three or four times that number with him when he left Beamfleote. God knows where he had got his ships from; he would need a lot to carry all his men. I only hoped that he'd come on ahead by sea with the plunder in a few ships and that the main part of his army were returning more slowly overland.

'Do you know how sizeable the Viking fleet is?' I asked Wolnoth.

'No, lord. We were in the vanguard, some way upstream from the junction with the Temes. All I know is what Æðelred's messenger told me.'

I nodded my thanks and turned my attention back to the immediate problem – capturing the fort. Although those left behind to defend it outnumbered us two to one, all my men were seasoned warriors, or experienced members of the fyrd, whereas the Danes I'd seen so far were almost exclusively old men or callow youths. They should be no match for us but there were a lot of women and children as well and I was about to learn how fiercely people could fight when defending their own.

CHAPTER SEVEN

Summer 893

I chased a group of Vikings down a narrow alley. Instead of staying to engage us on the open ground at the centre of the fort, the enemy had split up into small groups and had melted into the labyrinth of huts, storehouses and workshops. In there they had the advantage of knowing the layout and waited to ambush our men as they sought them out.

It was turning into a war of attrition. So far I had been attacked by women wielding everything from butcher's cleavers to pitchforks and by beardless boys with daggers. It pained me to have to kill them but this was no time for sentiment. If I hadn't slaughtered them they wouldn't have hesitated to kill me.

We'd been lucky. So far we'd escaped with minor flesh wounds suffered by three of my men and had slain over a dozen Danes. Unfortunately one of the wounded was my son. A boy no older than ten had jumped down onto his back from a rooftop and had stabbed him in the shoulder before Acwel, who was immediately behind Ywer, had pulled him off and put his sword through the lad's throat.

The young Dane had only been armed with an eating knife with a three inch blade so the wound wasn't deep. I'd quickly cleaned it and bound it with clean linen and then we'd moved on. A minute or two later we reached the outer palisade and I followed it for a few paces before entering another alleyway. As we moved along it Danes emerged from between the huts and barred our way. I glanced upwards. I suspected that there were others on the rooftops. If so, we were walking into an ambush.

'Acwel, take three archers and go into the huts beside us,' I told him. 'Get up onto the roof and kill anyone waiting to attack us from above.'

He nodded and I turned my attention back to the Danes ahead of us. There were at least a dozen of them against the six unwounded men I had left with me. However, although they all appeared to be warriors, the numerical advantage meant little in the confines of the alley. I was sure they were there to keep us from escaping whilst their comrades above us pelted us with rocks and the like. My suspicions were confirmed when several other Danes emerged behind us.

Neither group of the enemy seemed to be in any hurry to attack. Doubtless they were waiting for us to move further into the killing zone they'd selected, which meant that the ambushers above us were a little further down the alleyway. Suddenly there was a cry and a body crashed into the pathway ahead of us with an arrow in his back. Acwel's men had found a way up onto the roof.

A second later another dead man fell to the ground between us and the Danes. That was enough; they charged straight at us. No doubt the group behind us would do the same and so we formed a shield wall across the narrow path facing in both directions. As the group ahead of us reached the midway point between us, rocks crashed down on them, smashing heads – even those protected by helmets – and breaking bones. Of the dozen Danes only five were left unscathed. Acwel had turned the tables on them.

They stopped, stunned by their losses. However, what had just happened only served to madden the group of Danes behind us. They launched themselves at my three men, blocking their advance and I felt the back of one of them pushing against mine as he tried to give ground in front of their frenzied assault.

I turned and pushed as hard as I could against his back to hold him firm, leaving the others beside me to watch in case the other group renewed their advance, despite their losses. However, a second later the warrior I had been holding in place was killed by the thrust of a Viking spear into his neck and I had to let go of him and step forward into the breach.

I jabbed my sword forward into the spearman's guts, twisting it clear as he fell screaming to the ground, trying in vain to prevent his purple guts from escaping the hole I'd torn in his body.

The Dane standing behind him was plainly a woman although she wore a helmet and carried a sword and shield. I was loathe to cut her down and that was nearly my undoing. She chopped clumsily at the junction where my shoulder met my neck and I managed to raise my shield just in time to block the blow with the rim. Her sword bit through the brass rim and chipped the wood before glancing off. This left her torso exposed as her shield still hung at her side. I hesitated to kill her and, instead, drove the point of my blade deep into her thigh. She screamed and dropped to one knee just as Cináed, who was standing to my right, brought his sword around and chopped into her neck.

I was gasping for breath and exhausted by this stage. I sucked in a great lungful of air and readied myself to meet the next attacker but it was all over. Another group of my warriors led by Lyndon had emerged behind our assailants and had made short work of cutting them down. I turned my attention to the first group of Danes but they had disappeared, leaving their dead and wounded behind them.

✝✝✝

It was another hour before we had finally secured the fort and rounded up the remaining Vikings. They were a sorry looking bunch - old women and young children in the main. The rest had gone down fighting. We hadn't escaped entirely unscathed. Of my two hundred and forty men, twenty two had been killed and a dozen of the injured would never fight again. Over thirty more had wounds that should heal in time. The two physicians - Uhtric and Leofwine – had come with the ships and they, together with several monks, treated the wounded of both sides.

The women we'd captured were too old to fetch anything as slaves and so I let them go. Their only real chance of survival was if the Danish settlers in the area took them in but, as Hæsten had raided all of Ēast Seaxna Rīce indiscriminately since his arrival at Beamfleote, I didn't think that there was much chance of that. The children would be shipped off to the slave markets and sold.

We were laying the dead out a little distance from the fort prior to their burial if Christian, or burning if pagan, when several longships appeared around the bend in the creek. For a moment I thought that it was Hæsten but I was relieved to see the Mercian wyvern flying from the mast of the leading ship. Ten minutes later I greeted Æðelred as he stepped ashore.

It seemed that Hæsten had arrived with less than a dozen ships and had beat a hasty retreat as soon as he saw the size of the Mercian fleet. Æðelred had pursued the Vikings but they had faster ships and had disappeared heading north up the East Anglian coast.

'What do we do with this fort?' I asked when he'd finished his tale.

'Tear down the palisade and burn everything. I don't want to risk Hæsten returning and occupying it again.'

The next day I sailed away, leaving the smouldering remains of the fort in my wake, and returned to Cantwareburh and Hilda's arms. Ywer's wound soon healed and we returned to our previous peaceful existence. I knew that Ælfred and Edward were still besieging Escanceaster in the far west of the kingdom and that Hæsten was somewhere in Danish Mercia but it all seemed far away and I foolishly ignored it; besides, I had problems closer to home to deal with.

Sigehelm had been my choice as shire reeve and I was content to leave much of the routine administration of Cent in his hands.

This included the collection of taxes. Aside from the destruction wrought by the Vikings recently, the land was rich and fertile. It was heavily cultivated and included many fruit orchards in addition to the usual arable land and lush pasture for livestock. Consequently it was prosperous and its ceorls and thegns were comparatively wealthy.

This should have been reflected in the taxes collected but of late these had declined. Even allowing for the depredations of Hæsten and Fróði over the past twelve months or so, there should have been much more. I began to suspect that Sigehelm was creaming off significant sums for himself and I fretted about what to do. I had no proof and I wasn't sure how to tackle the problem.

Hilda sensed that something was troubling me almost immediately and nagged me until I told her what it was.

'Send for his accounting books,' she said at once. 'Say the king has ordered you to account for the diminished share you send him.'

I kissed her fervently, much to her surprise. I should have thought of that instead of overcomplicating the problem. She responded to my kiss and one thing led to another. It had been a long time since we'd made love in the middle of the day and it was all the more special because of that.

The next day I sent a messenger to Sigehelm asking him to come to my hall with the account books so that I could examine them and respond to the king's supposed request. At the same time I sent men to the thegns I trusted the most to keep a secret to ask them what taxes they had paid to the shire reeve over the past three years.

A week later my suspicions were confirmed. I asked my elder son, Abbot Æscwin, to conduct the audit and he confirmed my suspicions. Sigehelm had been keeping almost a third of the tax receipts for himself. Unfortunately, he hadn't come himself to present the record books but had sent one of his clerks.

It made things more difficult because his hall was well fortified and I suspected that he had used part of his ill-gotten wealth to recruit more hearth warriors. The last thing I wanted was open warfare between us. It would cost the lives of Kentish warriors unnecessarily and it would make it look as if I couldn't rule my shire properly in the eyes of the king and the other ealdormen. I was particularly anxious not to give Edward the opportunity to accuse me of incompetence.

'Return the books to him with a letter of thanks and invite him and his family here to celebrate All Hallows Eve,' Hilda suggested.

It was now the middle of September and All Hallows Eve was still six weeks away but it was a reasonable excuse. The night had been a pagan festival of the dead before we had converted to Christianity. It was traditionally a night of feasting and dancing when supposedly all those who had died the previous year rose up and joined in the merrymaking. The following day was one of obligation when everyone was expected to attend mass and celebrate the lives of all those saints who had no special day on which they were remembered.

It wasn't as important a festival as Christmas or Easter but it was special enough to serve as an excuse for inviting Sigehelm to join us without arousing suspicion.

At the Feast of All Hallows the hall was crowded. I had invited seven of my more important and influential thegns and their families as well as Sigehelm's. They were there both to allay any suspicion he might have and to witness what was about to unfold. I had also invited my elder son, Æscwin, his prior and his treasurer to the celebrations. These were hardly Christian in character but I needed them to support what I was about to say. I decided to make my speech early on in the evening before everyone got too drunk.

'Lord Abbot, ladies, nobles, warriors of Cent I bid you welcome to my hall on this night of revelry.'

Cheers and ribald comments greeted my remarks and I noticed with amusement the look of disapproval of the faces of the three churchmen.

'However, before we get down to the serious business of enjoying ourselves I have an announcement to make.'

I paused and my eyes swept the room. The mood had changed and, satisfied that I now had everyone's attention, I continued.

'I have become concerned since returning from defeating the Vikings that the revenues due to me and the king seem to have dwindled in recent years.'

At this murmurs grew as those present asked each other quietly where this was going. Some evidently thought that this was the precursor to a demand for more taxes and one or two looked at me belligerently. I glanced at Sigehelm but his face didn't yet betray any anxiety.

'I therefore asked the abbot to look at the record of accounts and advise me on this matter. Lord Abbot...'

'Thank you, Lord Jørren. I asked the prior and the treasurer of the monastery to examine the scrolls on which tax revenues are kept and compare these to the records kept by the reeves serving a number of thegns in the shire.'

I glanced at Sigehelm again and this time his agitation was plain to see. No one wore swords to a feast but he was nervously fingering the jewelled hilt of his dagger.

'I have to report that the two records did not match. I'm not talking about minor discrepancies; the disparity was enormous.'

At this point Sigehelm got to his feet in a rage.

'It's a lie; a blatant falsehood. You're Jørren's son – he's asked you to lie for him. He's the one who's taken any missing funds!'

'I wasn't the one who carried out the inspection of the accounts, Sigehelm. It was the prior and the treasurer,' Æscwin replied calmly. 'I also took the precaution of asking the archbishop to verify the finding and his chaplain concurs that my report is accurate – or are you calling all five of us liars?'

Sigehelm stood still for a moment then, uttering a cry of rage, he lunged at me with his dagger from where he was sitting on the other side of Hilda. I had never thought of Hilda as being brave or as a fighter, unlike my first wife, but she stabbed Sigehelm in the forearm with her little eating knife before his blade reached me. It did little real damage but it was enough to cause him to howl in pain and drop his dagger.

Less than a second later he had been seized by Ywer and one of the sentries standing behind the high table. He slumped in their arms and they turned to take him away when an anguished cry broke the stunned silence.

'Father! No, this can't be happening.'

I had forgotten about Sigehelm's family. He'd been accompanied by his wife, daughter and son. The latter two were sixteen and thirteen respectively. Now, whilst the two females sat motionless, paralysed by shock, the boy pulled out his dagger and rushed to his father's aid.

It had taken everyone by surprise and he'd stabbed Ywer in the chest before anyone could stop him. Another sentry thrust his spear into the boy and he fell to the floor mortally wounded but by then the damage had been done. My son had only just recovered from his most recent wound and now he lay on the floor with his lifeblood pumping out of him.

In the confusion Sigehelm shook off the other sentry and headed for the door. He never got there. Two of the thegns and several of my senior warriors intercepted him and someone – I never did discover who – delivered a fatal wound.

However, I only found that out that a little later. My focus was on Ywer. Thankfully, both of my physicians were present at the feast and Leofwine knelt by son's side to staunch the bleeding with clean linen cloths whilst his brother rushed away to fetch his medical bag.

Hilda and I attempted to comfort each other as we stood watching the two brothers struggling to save Ywer's life. Uhtric pulled out fabric and other foreign material with tweezers whilst Leofwine alternately washed the wound and held a cloth against it to save him losing too much blood. Then Leofwine held the edges of the wound together whilst Uhtric sewed it up with catgut. Finally he put a poultice of moss and honey on it and bound it tight with a bandage.

Hilda, our daughter Æbbe and I followed the stretcher as Ywer was carried to the room that served as the hall's infirmary, leaving the chaos in the hall to be sorted out by others.

✝✝✝

'You're losing your touch, Jørren,' Ælfred told me whilst Edward stood beside him with a sneer on his face. 'Firstly, you recommend a man to the Witenaġemot who proves to be an embezzler, then you confront him in a hall crowded with roistering men and, as a result, both he and his young son end up dead instead of being brought before me for trial.'

He had said nothing about the wounding of Ywer but perhaps that was because the wound had looked far worse than it was. True, he had lost a lot of blood but no vital organs had been damaged and my son was making a good recovery.

'I only found out what he was up to recently, cyning. I expected him to try and defend his actions or confess his guilt, not react the way he did; no one did. He was no warrior.'

'Enough! That is no excuse; you handled the whole matter badly. It has, however, helped me to make up my mind. As you know, it has been the tradition in my family for the eldest of the king's sons to be made King of Cent.'

It was not entirely true. Wessex had taken Cent from Mercia seventy years ago and it was given to the then King of Wessex's son, Æthelwulf, to rule as a sub-king under his father, together with Sūþrigescīr and Suth-Seaxe. However, all three former kingdoms had been absorbed into Wessex shortly after I was born. Since then there had been no separate King of Cent.

The news came as a complete and utter shock. Cent had become a shire within Wessex like any other shire, ruled by an ealdorman who was directly responsible to the king. What would Edward's elevation mean? Would there still be separate ealdorman in Cent and the other two shires or would Edward take on our responsibilities?

'I don't understand, cyning. What does this mean?' I managed to stutter after a moment or two.

'It means that I want my son to learn how to rule whilst I'm still alive. He's proved himself to be a capable warrior and commander; now it's time for him to hone his administrative skills as well. You'll remain as ealdorman, of course, but you will answer to my son in future instead of directly to me.

At least I had the common sense to approach Edward and congratulate him, however insincere my voice must have sounded. He grasped my hand and leaned in close so that only I could hear what he whispered in my ear.

'Your days as ealdorman are numbered, Jørren. One of my first acts will be to restore the shire to its rightful lord, Oswine.'

I left Ælfred's chamber my mind in a whirl. Instead of contemplating a peaceful future living in Cantwareburh with my family until it was my time to die, it seemed that I now faced an uncertain future.

†††

Hilda was as dumbfounded as I was when I told her. For a moment I wondered where her loyalties would lie; after all, Oswine was her son. However, I needn't have worried. They had been very close at one time but that was years ago. She shared my distrust of Edward and consequently disapproved of her son's friendship with him. This had driven them apart and her priorities now lay elsewhere. The chief amongst them being where we would live and who would now marry the only child we had together – Æbbe. The daughter of a mere thegn was a very different prospect to that of a wealthy and well regarded ealdorman.

I held the title deeds to over twenty vills but most of those in Cent had come to me when I married Hilda. Edward was very likely to confiscate them and give them to Oswine as they had originally belonged to his father. That left me with a number of small vills in the shire in addition to my original holdings: Basingestoches and Silcestre, both in Hamtunscīr.

The other problem was my warband. It numbered nearly ninety, including the twenty or so companions who formed my gesith. Not only could I not afford to maintain anything like that number of professional warriors but no thegn maintained a gesith: they were the prerogative of kings, senior members of his family and ealdormen. My men were devoted to me as I was to them. The thought of dismissing most of them was anathema to me.

I had amassed several coffers of silver and one of gold during my lifetime and so I could afford to pay my warriors for a while yet but my wealth would be a diminishing asset if I didn't cut back on my expenditure quite drastically.

If anything, Ywer was even more incensed about Edward's treatment of me than I was.

'It's not right, father!' he fumed, his eyes alight with fury. 'After all you have done for Wessex, this is how you are repaid? You must complain to King Ælfred. He has to force his son to reinstate you.'

'It will do no good, son. Although he said that I would remain as the ealdorman, he can hardly overrule Edward so soon after making him king of the eastern part of his realm. No, we must resign ourselves to accept it, however unjust it may be.'

I could see from my son's expression that he thought I was being weak but he was wrong. I couldn't blame him; it was his inheritance that was being given away, not just my hard-won wealth and status. However, I had learned long ago not to resist the inevitable but to make the best of it.

CHAPTER EIGHT

Autumn 893

Soon after his installation as King of Cent, Edward formed his own witan and invited every thegn in the three shires now under his rule in addition to the three ealdormen and the senior clergy to attend. I made my way to Guilforde, where the witan was being held, with a heavy heart. The black clouds overhead reflected my mood but thankfully the rain held off.

There was nowhere else large enough to hold us all until the new royal hall was built and so the witan was held in the small timber church. The thegn's hall and every spare bed in the huts of the inhabitants were occupied by Edward, his entourage and space elsewhere had been reserved for the other senior men, such as my fellow ealdormen and the senior churchmen. However, no accommodation had been reserved for me or my escort.

My elder son, Æscwin, was one of the churchmen attending and he offered to give up the room he had been allocated in one of the taverns for me. However, word came from the new king forbidding him to do so, not that I would have accepted his kind offer in any case. We were forced to set up camp outside the settlement and put up with the unremitting cold which the walls of our tents did little to keep at bay. It was a foretaste of what was to come.

I thought that Edward was taking a risk by putting my removal and Oswine's election to the vote but it soon became evident that he had prepared the ground well. Cyngils and Dudda came to visit me soon after my arrival to beg my forgiveness. Edward had warned them that, should they decide to oppose his wishes, he would seek to replace them as well. It wasn't the action of a man who wished to gain the loyalty of his subjects but it seemed that the man would stop at nothing to get rid of me. I was willing to bet that he had also threatened or bribed enough of the thegns to make sure the vote went against me.

Shortly after the two ealdormen left Archbishop Plegmund came to see me. The senior clergy had also been told which way the new king expected them to vote but Plegmund refused to bow to pressure. He assured me that he would speak in my favour at the meeting the following day. It was some comfort but not much.

As the witan was being held in his shire, Dudda presided over the meeting with Edward sitting beside him. The archbishop sat on Dudda's other side and began the meeting of the witan with a few selected prayers and a short homily. He prayed for harmony within King Edward's new realm and praised the courage of those present when fighting against the invaders, mentioning in particular my part in the defeat of Hæsten at Midleton and of Fróði at Fearnhamme. He also paid tribute to Edward for his part in Fróði's death, of course, but that did little to dispel the deepening frown on the king's face.

I didn't think that the archbishop was doing me any favours by praising me and, when he went on to imply that it was solely my efforts that had enabled us to capture and burn the Viking stronghold at Beamfleote, it was too much for Edward.

He shot to his feet with a cry of 'enough!' and glared at the archbishop who stood impassively looking at him, contempt etched on his face.

'Your illustrious father would never have ventured to interrupt an archbishop - or any churchman come to that - in the middle of a homily,' he rebuked him, albeit in a mild voice.

'My father never had to listen to the drivel and lies you are uttering,' Edward retorted.

'I do not lie, cyning, and take such an accusation very seriously. It's unworthy of you. The truth is you do not want to listen to anyone except the fawning lapdogs you surround yourself with. I hope that when it comes to a vote later, those present will have the integrity to go with their consciences and ignore whatever threats and promises you have made. I warn you now, King Edward, that you will lose your father's throne when the time comes unless you mend your ways. You have many fine qualities but you listen to the poison that toadies drip in your ears and allow jealousy to rule your mind.'

With that Plegmund picked up his crozier and strode out of the witan leaving behind him a stunned silence and Edward opening and closing his mouth like a carp. After a few seconds Æscwin and most of the other clergy followed him; but not all.

Instead of flying into a rage, Edward sat in brooding silence for some time after the archbishop's exit. I began to hope that Plegmund's words might have had some effect on the young king but my hope was ill-founded. A few brave souls spoke in my defence when Dudda read out the list of appointments Edward proposed to make. He didn't depose me as such, merely listed Oswine as the Ealdorman of Cent.

I didn't wait until the list was voted on but marched out of the church followed by Ywer and others of my gesith who had been standing at the back as spectators. I wrote a tersely worded letter to Edward stating that I had been unjustly treated. I went on to say that I had considered appealing to Ælfred but I didn't want to cause friction between father and son. I added that I would leave the hall in Cantwareburh by the end of the month.

Hilda and I had already decided to move to Silcestre for the time being and were in the middle of making the necessary preparations when two messengers arrived within hours of each other. The first was from Ælfred expressing his regret and sorrow at my dismissal by his son but he went on to say that this placed him in a difficult position. He needed to be seen to support his eldest son, however, he did promise me a pension to be paid annually as long as he lived to reward me for my loyal and valuable service. It wasn't much after all I had done for him and

116

for Wessex but it was something. At least the pension would enable me to retain most of my warband.

The second messenger was from Æðelred and it was both long and unexpected:

To my friend and fellow noble, Jørren,

I was astounded to hear of your treatment at the hands of King Edward. I have no wish to interfere in the affairs of Wessex but it does seem to me to be a poor reward for all you have done for the kingdom during your lifetime. You have my fullest sympathy.

As you will no doubt know, Hæsten retreated further into Ēast Seaxna Rīce after the loss of Beamfleote and most of his ships. He seems to have recruited more disaffected young Danes from East Anglia and the Five Boroughs before skirting Lundenburg to the north and entering Mercia. My hererǣswa, Wilfrid, was killed in August when he tried to halt their advance along the north bank of the Temes.

The heathens constructed a fortress on a peninsula between two rivers – the Sǣfern and the Waie - called Sūþburh. With the aid of several of the local Welsh chieftains, I have constructed defences across the isthmus and we are currently besieging them. We removed all grain stores and as much livestock as possible from their line of march and therefore they cannot have much in the way of supplies with them in their new fort. I intend to starve them out but I suspect that they will make an attempt to break out before long, rather than surrender.

I sent a message to King Ælfred asking for help and he is sending a force from the western shires to support me. However, I need to appoint a new hererǣswa who can help me to devise a suitable battle strategy and also unify our disparate forces. He needs to be an experienced warrior and I can think of no-one more suited to the task than you.

I can offer you land in Western Mercia in return but we can discuss that in due course. If you accept my offer, please bring Hæsten's sons, Irwyn and Godric, with you. They may come in useful if it comes to negotiations.

Your daughter sends her love. Please let me have your response as soon as convenient.

Æðelred
Lord of Mercia

I re-read the letter several times, my mind in a whirl. I was a Jute living in Cent and a subject of Saxon Wessex. I was being offered an important role in our struggle against the Vikings but it meant transferring my allegiance to Western Mercia, the inhabitants of which were mainly Angles. Half of the former kingdom was ruled by Danes and the other half was constantly under threat from them and from the Welsh, even if some of them were currently Æðelred's allies in the face of a common enemy. Whatever estates I was to be given were hardly likely to be anywhere as secure as Silcestre or my other vills in Wessex. It was not a decision to be taken lightly.

'What do you think?' I asked Hilda and Ywer after I had mulled over the offer and failed to reach a decision.

'We need to consider Ywer's future as well as ours,' Hilda said thoughtfully after a pause. 'Ælfred won't live for ever and it is almost certain that Edward will succeed him. He may well leave us alone if we stay in Wessex but Ywer is hardly likely to prosper, nor I suspect is he likely to feel much loyalty to Edward,' she added, giving my son a shrewd glance. 'Furthermore, your eldest daughter holds an important post in the Mercian court. My inclination is to accept Æðelred's offer.'

I looked at Ywer who nodded.

'I agree. I have no wish to serve a man like Edward and, if we stay in Wessex, I would support Æðelwold's claim to the throne when Ælfred dies.'

That was something I had not even considered. If Edward continued to bully his nobles he risked alienating them. They might well then support his cousin's claim to the crown when the time came. Internal strife within Wessex would give the Danes an opportunity to achieve what years of invasion had failed to do. It was not a reassuring prospect. Perhaps Mercia might be a better bet after all.

✝✝✝

It had taken the best part of a week for us to reach Glowecestre, the burh which Æðelred used as his main base. His hall, whilst not comparing in size to Ælfred's in Wintanceaster, had been expanded since I had last been there. Now it filled three sides of a square with a central courtyard. The main hall was built of stone but the buildings on the other two sides and the palisade at the front were constructed in timber.

The gates were flanked by two towers, one taller than the other to serve as a watchtower. I climbed it later and I could see the River Sæfern half a mile away quite clearly. Next door lay the monastery which had an impoverished appearance compared to Æðelred's hall. The monks lived in cells constructed of wattle and daub and even the abbot's hall was small with a thatched roof in need of some repair. The church was also made of timber and scarcely large enough to hold the community it served.

It surprised me that more buildings in Glowecestre weren't made of stone as there was a plentiful supply. Many of the old Roman buildings had been built using stone and the burh was surrounded by the original stone walls dating from the same period. I learned later that Æðelred had ordered that all the stone buildings be demolished in order to provide building material to repair the walls. It was a sensible defensive move but I doubted that it made him very popular with the inhabitants of those houses he had destroyed, especially as he had then used some for the stone for his own hall.

The Lord of the Mercians wasn't there himself, of course, he was across the Sæfern besieging the Viking horde at Sūþburh.

Nor was Lady Æthelflæd present as she was with her husband. However, Cuthfleda had returned from her mistress' side to welcome us. I had thought that we would have to share a cramped guest chamber in the lord's hall but my daughter took us to a separate hall outside the Roman walls. It had its own palisade, warriors' hall and kitchens, as well as a brewhouse and stables. It was large enough for my family, servants and a small guard force.

Hæsten's two sons, Irwyn and Godric, had accompanied us and, although I had seen little of them, I had received regular reports about their conduct. They kept themselves to themselves and spoke as little as possible to their captors. This wasn't difficult as they only spoke Danish and refused to learn Ænglisc or Latin. Some of my men spoke their language, and spoke it well, so it was possible to communicate with them but such exchanges were somewhat one sided.

We had barely settled into our new accommodation when the abbot came to visit me. He was accompanied by his chaplain and a nun whose hand was held by a small child wearing what looked like a miniature version of a novice's habit.

'I thought you would like to see your great nephew whilst you're here,' the abbot said after we had exchanged inconsequential pleasantries.

At first I couldn't think who he meant and then I realised who the little boy was. He was the son of my niece and my nemesis, King Edward – Æthelstan. I had last seen him a year ago when we were negotiating Hæsten's withdrawal from Cent. Then he had barely been able to walk; now he was a boy rather than an infant and looked older than his three years.

I was surprised that someone so young had been left in the care of monks, even if he had a couple of nuns to look after his personal needs. However, with both his uncle and aunt away I supposed that it made sense. What surprised me was the fact that he was already being taught to read and write.

'His father, King Edward, has decreed that he should become a novice and take holy orders as soon as possible,' the abbot explained.

That was typical of the man. By making the boy into a churchman he was making sure that he couldn't challenge any future sons of Edward for the throne when the time came.

All my warband without exception had elected to come with us when I gave them the choice. Many were married with children and, despite the size of the hall, conditions would be cramped and Hilda suggested finding accommodation in the burh for some of the families. However, most of my warriors would shortly be accompanying me westwards to join the Mercian army so I told her to save our money for now.

I bade farewell to Hilda and Æbbe the next morning. My youngest child had asked to come with us, saying that if Cuthfleda could put up living in an armed encampment, then so could she. Hilda was scandalised at the suggestion; she had long ago accepted that her elder step-daughter was very far from her idea of what a lady should be but she wasn't about to let her own daughter emulate her.

It was only thirty miles from Glowecestre to Æðelred's camp but, as we were accompanied by wagons bearing supplies for the army as well as our tents and other equipment, it took us all day to get there. The weather had been kind to us during our trek along the Temes valley but now it changed. The morning had started chilly and overcast and as the day wore on the clouds darkened and the temperature dropped even further. It was still the middle of October but it felt more like January or February.

My scouts returned to say that we were less than five miles away from the Mercian encampment when the heavens opened and we were deluged by a mixture of rain and sleet. The last few miles were miserable and the prospect of having to put up our tents in such conditions was not an appealing one. Furthermore, we would be the latecomers and doubtless all the best spots for setting up camp would be taken already.

I was therefore pleasantly surprised when we arrived and were shown to a site upriver from the main camp where the grass hadn't been trampled into deep mud and the water was unpolluted by those camped below us.

As soon as we had washed the dust from our faces Ywer and I mounted our horses to ride into the main camp to pay our respects to Lord Æðelred. We took Irwyn and Godric with us as Æðelred had asked to see them. However, we had scarcely gone a hundred yards when I saw him riding towards us accompanied by Lady Æthelflæd. To my delight Cuthfleda was riding just behind

Æthelflæd. I dismounted, not without a little pain after being in the saddle for most of the day, and bowed my head to Æðelred and his wife. Cuthfleda had also dismounted and we hugged each other briefly before I led the way back to my pavilion.

I was hardly ready to receive visitors but Dunbeorn managed to produce some mead, bread and cheese from somewhere. Only a table had been unloaded so far, so we were forced to stand whilst we ate, drank and talked. The two Danish boys stood in a corner, as far away from us as possible, and stared at us sulkily.

'Your two hostages don't look very happy,' Æthelflæd remarked.

'They are well cared for but they resent being captives. Although they've been baptised, they refuse to wear a crucifix and won't communicate with anyone. I've never known boys their age to be so stubborn.'

'Thank you for bringing them. They may prove useful if we ever manage to persuade Hæsten to negotiate with us,' Æðelred said.

At that the two boys brightened up but I didn't think there was much chance of their father doing a deal for their release. He had only been forced to talk to us at Midleton when he and his men were starving.

'He didn't seem to care for them that much when they were taken as hostages,' I remarked.

'Why do you say that?' Æthelflæd asked.

'He broke the agreement straight away, lady, even though it could well have resulted in his sons' deaths.'

'Oh! I had forgotten that. It doesn't sound as if they'll be much use to us in that case,' Æðelred muttered. 'I don't understand why Ælfred kept them alive.'

'Because he has a forgiving nature,' Æthelflæd replied, darting a look at her husband which I interpreted as annoyance at the implied criticism of her father.

'The wretched pagans have been reinforced by the Irish Vikings and Northumbrian Danes that Ælfred is busy chasing out of Dyfneintscīr,' Æðelred told me after the two boys had been escorted away. 'Unfortunately they arrived in longships. As I'm trying to starve them out we need to stop them using them to resupply their camp by sea.'

'What about the king's ships? Have you asked him to use the western fleet to attack them?'

'Yes, of course, but Ælfred says he needs them to patrol the coastline of Wessex to stop more Vikings arriving from Íralond.'

'Where are their longships based when they aren't at sea?'

'There is a beach to the east of their fort. Why? Do you have a plan?'

'I'm not sure yet. I need to find a fishing boat so I can see this beach for myself.'

'Excellent! I knew that you were the right man to appoint as my hereræswa. Come, you must meet my ealdormen, the two Ælfred has sent me and my ally from Wealas.'

I was a little concerned at meeting the latter. The last time I'd encountered the present king, Owain ap Hywel, had been outside Abergafenni during a punitive raid to punish his father for raiding into Mercia. We'd hardly parted on friendly terms. If my memory served me correctly, Owain had promised at the time to separate my head from my body the next time we met. However, the Mercians had also been involved in the punitive campaign and, if Æðelred had managed to persuade Owain to join him in a common cause against the Vikings, perhaps he'd tactfully forget my part in his father's humiliation as well.

I needn't have worried. He greeted me affably and behaved as if we'd never met before. I'm sure he remembered me only too well but he had changed from the volatile and impetuous youth I'd encountered then. I fleetingly wondered if Edward would gain in wisdom and political acumen with age, as Owain appeared to have done.

I had met the two ealdormen from Wessex, Æthelhelm of Wiltunscīr and Æthelnoth of Somersæte, before but I didn't know them well. My old friend Nerian had died recently and his brother, Æthelnoth, had succeeded him. He looked like Nerian when he was much younger and we got on well from the start. His fellow ealdorman was a different proposition. Those that knew him better than I did said that he was vain, arrogant and one of those men who thought that because he was rich he knew everything. He was in his early thirties and so he should have learned more sense by now.

Our first problem was to deal with the longships who were raiding the coast of Wealas for supplies. Just north of our camp limestone cliffs rose up and lined the Sæfern for a little way.

124

When the river became accessible again further north the area was marshy. I had to go some distance north-eastwards along the peninsula before I found what I was looking for - a fishing hamlet.

The inhabitants had either been killed by Hæsten's men or had fled because the only signs of life amongst the mean huts were the rats. Thankfully the fishing boats were still there and, as far as I could see, were quite useable. They were of a type typically used by fishermen in Wealas, although we were still in Mercia - the border being the River Waie at this point.

The craft were called coracles: oval in shape, they consisted of a willow frame covered in tarred leather. Some were evidently intended for one man but many were large enough for a crew of three or four. They appeared far from sturdy but they would suit my purpose well enough, provided the weather didn't deteriorate. Unlike the day of our arrival, of late it had been fine and rather warmer than was usual at this time of year.

Owain found me two men who were adept at rowing these strange boats using a single paddle and the three of us set out just after dawn the next day to travel down the river towards the Viking fortress. When we reached the cliffs I could see the stony beach near the end of the peninsula ahead of us. There were four longships beached there – a large drekka, two smaller snekkjur and a knarr. I had expected more but no doubt the rest were away foraging.

As we rowed back against the current I noticed a piece of flotsam drift past. I watched it idly as it continued on its way and was surprised to see that the current took it in towards the beach and it struck the hull of the nearest of the Viking ships. It gave me an idea.

It took several days for us to gather enough coracles for what I intended. By the time that I was ready there were eleven ships of varying sizes beached near the end of the peninsula. As dawn broke we set two dozen of the craft free two miles upriver from the beach, each loaded with dry kindling, tar soaked logs and cordage. As they gathered speed my archers sent several volleys of fire arrows into them. Some disappeared into the water with a hiss but enough struck the coracles to ignite the contents.

As they travelled downstream with the current they gathered speed and, at the same time, the flames took hold and turned them into floating infernos. Three missed their targets and carried on but the rest lodged against the Viking ships. Two escaped unharmed but the others were set alight, the fire spreading along the wadding soaked in pitch pine used to seal the gaps between the strakes of the hull. Soon the tarred cordage caught fire and then the furled sails.

The hulls were charred rather than burned but the masts blazed merrily, as did anything combustible on board. The ships weren't utterly destroyed but it would be a long time before they could put to sea again. When they were repaired, or when new ships arrived, we would just send more blazing coracles into them.

✝✝✝

Disappointingly the Vikings weren't that stupid and the next day we watched them haul the charred hulks around the end of the peninsula and into the mouth of the River Waie using two longships which had returned that morning. There were mud flats either side of the smaller estuary at this point, which meant wading through the thick, cloying muck knee deep to reach the water, even at high tide. It was presumably why they didn't beach their ships in this, the more sheltered area, in the first place. Before they could start work on the ships they would need to construct wooden jetties and sinking the necessary piles into the mud would take time.

'Why don't you float your little fireships down and set fire to them before the heathens can repair them?' Æthelhelm asked at our nightly council of war.

'Because the tide runs differently,' I explained patiently. 'That in the Sæfern sweeps around the shallows and sandbanks, taking anything floating on the water in close to the shore. The tide in the Waie remains in the centre of the estuary.'

'There must be a way of bringing them into the shore where the boats are,' he said glaring at me as if the behaviour of the river was somehow my fault.

'Well, I can't think of one. If you can I would be glad to hear it,' I retorted.

'I think we can forget the longships for the moment,' Æðelred said tactfully. 'Without them the Vikings have no access to food, unless they eat their horses. They will be loath to do that as that would restrict their future mobility. Furthermore, grass is poor fodder for their animals at this time of year. My expectation is that they will be forced to break out of their fort soon and we must prepare for that.'

Æðelred was correct but the Vikings caught us by surprise all the same. We had dug a defensive ditch across the narrowest part of the isthmus – a distance of no more than three hundred yards. We had mounted a palisade on top of the ramp constructed from the spoil from the ditch and filled the latter with sharp stakes. We had taken the ends twenty yards into Sæfern and well into the mud flats bordering the Waie. We were therefore confident that the Vikings couldn't get around our defences without ships.

We watched as they spent days constructing sections of walkways out of the trees that were left on their portion of the peninsula, but there was no sign of them sinking piles into the mud to which the walkways would be attached. I was so focused on the idea that they needed to repair their ships and provide jetties where other longships and knarrs could berth that I never considered any other possibility. To be fair, I wasn't alone. All the leaders of our army thought the same.

The weather changed at the end of October. The wind now blew from the north and, as well as being much colder, it brought rain and sleet with it. Perhaps that's why the sentries missed the Vikings until it was almost too late.

The first I knew of their attempt to break out of the peninsula was the clash of arms, shouts and screams that could only mean that they were attacking our defences. Dunbeorn awoke from the corner of the tent where he slept and helped me into my byrnie and boots before handing me my helmet, shield and weapons. I rushed towards the ramparts but I was suddenly conscious of men running at me from my right. Somehow the Vikings had got into our camp and chaos ensued.

I yelled for men to gather around me and a few did, but not enough to hold off the score of the enemy now rampaging through our camp. Thankfully Ywer had realised what was going on and brought the majority of my warband to my aid. From chaos order slowly emerged. Things were still confused but, thanks to the light given off by the few campfires that still lit up the stygian darkness, we were able to see enough to form a shield wall to oppose the Vikings already in the camp.

Other warriors, both Mercians and Saxons from Somersaete and Wiltunscīr, came out of the gloom to reinforce us. It was impossible to be certain as to the number opposing us but they seemed to be growing all the time. No sooner had we managed to extend our line to hold the Vikings at bay than they were joined by reinforcements, putting us under renewed pressure.

I faced an axeman at one point who raised his double-handed battle-axe on high to cleave my body in two. There was nothing I could do to defend myself as I had brought my shield across my body to block a spear that had been thrust towards my guts. My seax was similarly engaged beating away a sword blow on the other side.

I was in despair when I felt something brush past my legs. A moment later the axeman let out a howl of pain and sunk to his knees, the axe falling harmlessly to the earth. Someone else had stabbed the swordsman to my left and I managed to thrust my seax into the spearman's neck. As soon as I'd pulled my blade clear I cut the throat of the crippled axeman and realised that those facing me hesitated to attack after seeing their companions' fate.

I glanced down to see who my saviour was and was greeted by the grinning face of Dunbeorn as he cleaned the dagger he'd used to hamstring the axeman on the dead man's trousers. A second later he'd disappeared behind me again.

I dimly saw hundreds more of the enemy appear from our right and I groaned. Our luck had run out. The two hundred or so men I had gathered would be overwhelmed by the new arrivals. I offered up a prayer for my soul as I was convinced that we were all about to die.

Moments later someone ordered every single Dane and Norseman away, presumably to attack our defences from the rear instead. We raced after them and arrived at the ramparts a minute too late. The Vikings who had managed to infiltrate our camp had surprised our defenders and opened a breach through which the rest of the heathen horde were now rushing.

It was past dawn by now but the light cast by the sun through the dark clouds only dimly illuminated the battlefield. I was suddenly conscious that it had started to rain as droplets of icy water stung that part of my face not protected by my cheek guards and nasal. I watched in horror as hundreds of Vikings raced towards me and yelled for the warriors around me to form a shield wall but I was too late. The man beside me was killed by an axe blow and he cannoned into me as he fell. I lost my balance and that probably saved my life. I fell to the ground and the dead man ended up on top of me. He was a big man and his dead weight pinned me underneath him.

It seemed an age until someone lifted him off me. By then I was exhausted and had long ago given up the struggle to get free of him. I looked up and was delighted to see Ywer's relieved face looking down at me.

'Thank God, father. I thought you must be dead when I couldn't find you anywhere,' he said lifting me up and crushing me to him in an embrace.

'I will be if you don't let go,' I managed to utter as I struggled for breath.

'Sorry, father; I was just so relieved to find you alive,' he said as he let go.

'What happened? Did we defeat the Vikings?'

'In a way, I suppose. We were left in possession of the battlefield and they lost many hundreds of men, but the rest got away. Most were on foot, although they did manage to capture a few of our horses.'

'Why aren't we pursuing them? We can't let them get away to start pillaging all over again.'

'We also lost a lot of men, father. We need time to recover and deal with the countless wounded. Æðelred has sent scouts after them to track them to see where they're headed.'

I nodded and then I had a thought. All the time I was fighting something was nagging away at me. How had the Vikings managed to get into our camp, so I asked Ywer, who grunted and spat.

'All the time we thought that the heathen bastards were constructing a jetty to repair their ships they were, in reality, making duckboards so that they could use them as a walkway over the mud and around our defences. Furthermore, they managed to free Irwyn and Godric and take the boys with them.'

Perhaps I'd been wrong to assume that Hæsten didn't care about his sons after all.

CHAPTER NINE

January/February 894

'We should have finished Hæsten off when we had the chance,' Ywer complained as he sat nursing a headache after celebrating the start of 894 a little too boisterously.

My son was now in his twentieth year. Like all young men, he found the winter months interminable. Whilst I was happy to spend time with Hilda and my family in our hall at Glowecestre and have a rest from fighting the wretched Vikings, Ywer found that the days and weeks dragged. The snow was too thick on the ground to go hunting and so there was little for him and his friends to do other than get drunk and try and get the prettiest of the servants into bed.

We had hounded the Danes and their Norse allies all the way back to the border with the Danelaw. Once they had entered the Five Boroughs we gave up the chase and returned home. Æðelred was pleased by the outcome of the campaign and I think he'd fooled himself into thinking that he'd taught Hæsten a lesson he wouldn't forget in a hurry. I wasn't so sure that we'd seen the last of him and his army but, with winter upon us and the first snow of the year having fallen, there was no point in worrying about it until the spring. Later we heard that the Vikings had erected a fortress where the River Temes joined the Norþ-sǣ in which to overwinter.

'We did our best, Ywer,' I replied with a sigh. 'At least they've got a many fewer men than they had a year ago.'

'Maybe, but the young Danes of Northumbria still seem all too keen to join him.'

'I'm sure it's a lot more exciting than farming but Viking leaders need to be successful and reward their men with silver and slaves. Hæsten has hardly been able to do much of that recently.'

One would have expected his men to have drifted away from Hæsten, given his ill-fortune recently. It was true that no more Danes had come from the Continent to join him and those in the Danelaw seemed to have turned against him, probably because of his raids into their lands in search of forage and loot. Nevertheless, the Northumbrian Danes still seemed all too eager to join him and plunder their fellow countrymen. One reason could be that King Guðred was said to be dying and the land lacked strong government.

Guðred called himself King of Northumbria but in reality he only governed the southern part of the kingdom. The land to the north - between the River Tes and the Firth of Forth - was effectively an independent realm ruled by the Lords of Bebbanburg. The Danish settlers south of the Tes, remnants of the Great Heathen Army of a quarter of a century ago, had intermarried with the original Anglian inhabitants and were Christians in the main. However, many still clung to their Viking heritage.

Ywer got up from his seat and began to pace to and fro in the chamber which my family occupied. Although my son slept in the warrior's hall and spent most of his time there, he often joined the rest of the family for an hour or two each day. He particularly enjoyed playing me at tæfl. It was played on a chequered board with two armies of uneven numbers. The king with the fewer pieces had to move from the centre to the edge of the board without being captured. It was a good way of learning strategy and Ywer was able to beat me more often than not these days.

'Why don't we attack them now, when they'd least expect it?' he asked suddenly.

'Because the fyrd have dispersed to their homes and winter is not the time to march right across the country from the west coast to the east,' I pointed out.

'Are we at least watching them?'

'No. Don't forget that they are ensconced in East Anglia. I don't suppose King Eohric would agree to grant Mercian scouts safe passage through his kingdom.'

He ignored my sarcasm and continued to expound his plan.

'We don't have to approach their camp along the north bank. We could cross from Witenestaple or one of the other settlements on the north coast of Cent.'

'I know that Wessex is supposed to be our ally, but have you forgotten that Edward is King of Cent and Oswine is the ealdorman. He is hardly likely to welcome you or any of my men.'

'But I could travel with a party of Mercian scouts. I'm sure that Edward would agree if Æðelred asked for his permission.'

'No, it's foolhardy. You'd still have to travel across country on horseback to get to Witenestaple and the roads are neigh on impassable.'

I thought that was the end of the matter but I should have known that my opposition would make Ywer all the more determined. We played tæfl the next afternoon but after that I didn't see him for a couple of days. I didn't think much about it, assuming that he was drinking with his friends and visiting the whores in Glowecestre but when he hadn't appeared for four days I sent for him.

An embarrassed looking Wolnoth came to tell me that he couldn't find Ywer anywhere; in fact, he hadn't seen him for a couple of days.

'Do you know where he is?'

'I believe that he went riding with some of the Mercian scouts,' he said, looking at the ground.

'Wolnoth, what is it that you're not telling me?'

'I believe that he put a proposal to Lord Æðelred.'

133

My heart sank.

'What proposal?' I asked, already knowing the answer.

'That he take a small party of scouts into Cent and cross the estuary of the Temes to reconnoitre Hæsten's camp.'

I was furious, mainly with Ywer, but also with Æðelred for not having consulted me. Hilda begged me to wait until I'd calmed down but I didn't listen and set off for his hall immediately. Thankfully he was engaged in hearing various lawsuits and so I was forced to cool my heels until he'd finished. I'm sure that saved me from falling out with my new lord.

'But he told me that it was your idea!' Æðelred protested when I finally managed to see him. 'Ywer plainly lied to me.'

It was evident that my son had sunk in Æðelred's estimation. I was furious with him but I had a sneaky admiration for his courage and determination all the same. Evidently I was not alone in this.

'I'm sure that his motivation in keeping an eye on that snake Hæsten is praiseworthy, husband, even if what he did was reprehensible,' Æthelflæd said soothingly.

'Like father like son,' Cuthfleda muttered giving me a dark look. 'You would have done the same at his age, father. Indeed, I seem to recall you telling me you left your vill without permission having stolen supplies, two horses and a slave.'

'That was to go and rescue my brother; it was entirely different,' I replied huffily.

Both Æðelred and Æthelflæd smiled at her riposte. It was true. At the tender age of thirteen I had set out to rescue my brother who was a prisoner of the Great Heathen Army. I had been a lot more foolhardy then than Ywer was being now.

'I suggest that you set off yourself and bring your errant son back here,' Æðelred said after a pause. 'If you manage to find out anything about Hæsten and his future intentions at the same time,

134

that would be useful but I don't need to tell you not to take any risks.'

Two hours later I set off accompanied by just four companions – Wolnoth, Eomær, Cináed and Dunbeorn. To take more would have attracted undue attention and that was the last thing I needed when I entered Edward's realm. In any case, there was only room for us, our mounts and a packhorse on the knarr I'd chartered. I hadn't a hope of catching Ywer and his Mercian companions by road. Provided we didn't run into any storms, I hoped to arrive in Witenestaple before they did.

†††

We would be extremely lucky to avoid bad weather during the long voyage around the Kernow peninsula and along the whole of the south coast of Wessex. Wisely the captain of the knarr insisted on putting into harbour or a sheltered cove each night. It was prudent but the weather stayed fair and I fretted at the time we lost by doing so.

If it hadn't been for my concern about my son, I would have enjoyed the passage. It was good to be at sea again, even if the knarr did wallow a lot more than a longship. The conditions were good for early January, if somewhat cold. The wind blew from the south-west for most of the way and rarely exceeded a stiff breeze. Although the tops of the waves were adorned with wind-driven white spume for most of the time, they never grew to a size which might threaten the ship.

We had scarcely seen another sail the whole way. It wasn't the season for Viking or Frankish pirates to be abroad and only a few merchantmen braved the winter seas. That changed when we turned and tried to head westwards into the estuary of the Temes. Not only was the wind against us and we had to tack but we encountered three longships almost as soon as we had cleared the most easterly point of Cent.

I had hoped that they would ignore us but they immediately turned and bore down on us. The captain breathed a sigh of relief when he saw that they were flying the banner of Wessex but I wasn't so happy. In these waters they probably belonged to King Edward.

'Raise the Mercian banner,' I yelled across to Dunbeorn.

He nodded and ran to my chest before swarming up the mast to affix the green cloth with its white wyvern motif. Both Wessex and Mercia used the wyvern – a type of dragon with two legs – as their symbol; in Wessex's case it was a gold beast on a red flag.

As soon as they saw the Mercian symbol the three ships changed back to their original course and I breathed a sigh of relief. I didn't think that Edward would have given orders to detain me, had he found out that I was on board; that would have been petty and unjustified. However, I wasn't entirely sure as I'd heard that he was furious when I'd taken service with Æðelred.

According to the reports which had reached me, he had asked his father to deprive me of my vills in Wessex but Ælfred had refused. Nevertheless it was going to be difficult, if not impossible, for me to collect the revenues from those located in Cent.

We landed at Witenestaple only to find that we were just too late. Ywer and the Mercian scouts had crossed the Temes to the opposite shore earlier that day. Luckily the knarr's captain had part of his cargo to unload and so he hadn't departed for Lundenburg before I found out. For an extra pouch of silver he agreed to take us across to Ēast Seaxna Rīce.

We sailed north-west and landed on a beach just north of a large island. It was well away from any habitation, which was just as well as it took some time to coax our horses down the narrow gangplank and onto the sand. By the time we set out heading eastwards it was late in the day and darkness wasn't far off. We planned to camp beside a small river that ran into the Temes but found that the water that close to the estuary was saline. We followed its course inland until the water tasted sweeter and lay down wrapped in thick blankets and fur lined cloaks for the night.

We took it in turns to stay on watch and sometime after midnight Cináed shook me awake. I had already stood my watch so I was annoyed with him until he whispered that he'd heard a horse whinny faintly somewhere to the north of us.

He woke the others and we spread out in a line, crouching close to the ground as we made slow and careful progress towards where Cináed thought the horse was. After about a quarter of an hour I spotted a man sitting at the base of lone tree. He was difficult to make out but the pale moonlight glinted off his polished helmet when there was a brief break in the cloud cover.

We crept closer. If this was a Danish patrol they would certainly outnumber us but I didn't think that they would spend the night in the open when they were so close to their winter encampment. However remote a possibility, my hope was that we had stumbled across my son and his companions.

We edged around their camp to where the horses were tethered. There were nine animals, which tallied with the number which had left Glowecestre – the mounts for Ywer and six Mercians plus two pack horses.

Leaving the other three I returned to where the sentry was sitting slumped against the tree. I crept up behind him and found that, if he wasn't actually asleep, he was less than alert. I clamped my hand over his mouth at the same time as I put my seax across his throat. Then I noticed he wasn't dressed like a Dane.

'Who are you?' I hissed at him after cautiously removing my hand.

'Beadurof,' he stuttered.

I relaxed. He was one of the men with Ywer.

'I should kill you for failing to keep a proper watch,' I told him. 'Had we been Danes you would all be dead by now.'

'I'm sorry, lord, please forgive me.' Beadurof said miserably.

'You know who I am then?'

'Yes, Lord Jørren. But what are you doing here?'

'Good question,' a voice said from behind me. 'What are you doing here, father?'

Ywer and the Mercian scouts had appeared behind me and a second later my three men joined them.

'I came to stop you doing anything foolish, Ywer. I am deeply disappointed that you left without my permission and Lord Æðelred is furious that you deceived him. No doubt, he will be having a word with you too, Halig,' I added, addressing the leader of the Mercians.

'Your son has misled me too, lord,' Halig said, giving Ywer an angry look. 'He assured me that you knew that he was coming with us.'

'Very well but now is not the time for recriminations,' I said quietly. 'I suggest that we join you for what's left of the night and then discuss our plan of action in the morning.'

✝✝✝

The Viking encampment looked deserted. We'd watched it for most of the morning and we'd seen no sign of life: no sentries on the ramparts or comings and goings through the open gate.

'The Vikings might have planned to spend the winter here but they're certainly not here now,' Halig muttered.

'No, I fear you're right. Come on, we have to make certain.'

I led my little group of eleven men through the gates and into the camp. Behind the earthen ramparts lay a muddy expanse of nothing. You could see where the tents had been pitched and crudely made duckboards still lay along the walkways between the places where they had stood but there was nothing else, except the usual detritus that every army leaves behind.

'Halig, who's your best tracker?' I asked.

'Probably Beadurof; he may be a useless sentry but he can follow the faintest of trails.'

'Right, he can lead with Cináed. Let's see where Hæsten and his heathens have disappeared to.'

''You think that they've left here for good then?' Ywer asked.

'Yes, why else would they have taken their tents, their families and everything they own with them? They left them behind last year.'

'Yes, it seems a strange thing to do, especially in the middle of winter. If the snow and ice comes, they could all perish.'

It was a fair point. Although it was cold, the sun shone in a sky dotted with white, puffy clouds at the moment. However, such fine spells seldom lasted for long at this time of year so I didn't imagine that Hæsten would stray far from the main roads. What puzzled me was why he would risk going anywhere with women and children in tow in January. The only explanation I could come up with was that, unlike the previous year, he didn't intend to return.

The trail took us north-west away from the coast and we camped for the night beside a stream. I estimated that we were between fifteen and twenty miles from Lundenburg now but that couldn't be Hæsten's destination, surely. The old Roman walls had long since been repaired and, even with so many warriors, the Vikings had little chance of capturing the place.

For the next few days we followed the trail to the north of Lundenburg and as far as Verulamacæster. The weather had continued to be fine until the last day. When we awoke that morning the temperature had dropped and the sky was full of dark clouds. I had given up using Cináed and Beadurof as scouts. Even a blind man could follow the tracks of several thousand people, some mounted, and numerous carts. Now we took it in turns to ride point in pairs.

One of the Mercians, a boy of fifteen called Osric, accompanied me as we rode ahead of the others along the rutted track. After a while it met an old Roman thoroughfare which had to be Casingc

Stræt. From the tracks it seemed that the Vikings were now headed north-west along the dividing line between Æðelred's Mercia and the Danelaw.

'Where do you think they could be going, father?' Ywer asked when the rest had caught us up.

'Well, as we all know, Casingc Stræt leads to Wrocensaete eventually', I replied thoughtfully.

Wrocensaete on the River Sæfern had been an important Roman town on the border with Wealas. Now it was no more than a minor settlement in Mercian Shropscīr, the most northerly of the shires ruled by Æðelred. I didn't believe that it could be Hæsten's final destination. For him to risk a march right across the country in winter there must be a greater prize at the end of the road.

We camped for the night just to the south of the old road and we sat around the fire deliberating on where the Vikings might be making for. It was Halig who suggested that their destination might be Cæstir. It was an old Roman legionary fort near where the borders of Northumbria, Wealas and Mercia met. However, a combination of raids by the Welsh from Gwynedd and the arrival of Norse settlers who'd been driven out of Íralond had driven out the Mercian inhabitants in recent years.

I'd been instrumental in helping the Mercians recapture Cæstir a decade before but now the place was more or less a ruin and the whole area lacked any sort of central government.

Using it as a base, Hæsten could raid the surrounding area with impunity. The Norse who had settled along the coast to the north of Cæstir might provide him with more recruits as well. The more I thought about it, the more likely it seemed.

'What do we do, father?' Ywer asked. 'Carry on to confirm where Hæsten has gone?'

'No,' I shook my head. 'We are too small a force to traverse the edge of the Danelaw. It serves as a useful boundary but Danes

140

regularly cross it. It's not worth the risk. We need to return to Glowecestre and let Lord Æðelred know what is happening.'

The next day saw a further deterioration in the weather. We were awoken by a shower of hail and two hours later it began to rain. As the day wore on the rain turned to sleet and finally to snow. By then we had turned off Casingc Stræt heading for Wælingforde on the River Temes, one of Ælfred's fortified burhs. I knew that it was roughly fifty miles over poor roads but, depending on the conditions, we should be able to reach there in two days. Thankfully the snow stopped falling after a while and the going underfoot wasn't as treacherous as it might have been.

I was still riding ahead of the others with Osric when the virgin snow that covered the road up to that point became muddier thanks to the passage of several horses.

'How many do you think, Osric?'

The boy dismounted and studied the churned up track.

'At least a score, all mounted,' he replied after a minute or so.

'Very good,' I said with a smile. 'Now a more difficult question. Are they Saxons or Vikings?'

'Oh, I don't know. How can you tell?'

'Look at the size of the individual hoof prints you can see. Do you notice anything about them?'

'They are different sizes,' he said with a grin.

'And what does that tell you?'

'We all ride horses roughly the same type, all from breeders who specialise in war horses. The Vikings ride whatever they can steal, from plough horses to ponies.'

'And so?'

'The riders ahead of us are likely to be Vikings.'

'Very good.'

I was so engrossed in getting the young scout to think through the evidence that I forgot what we were there for. I paid the penalty a second later when four arrows hit us. Two struck Osric, killing him instantly, another wounded his horse in the rump and the fourth struck my byrnie and glanced off. Poor Osric's horse gave a squeal of agony and it bolted up the road the way we'd come.

I went to mount my horse but, before I could do so, I was surrounded by Danes.

'Well, well. Lord Jørren, I never thought that we would have the pleasure of meeting again,' one of them said giving me an evil grin. 'I don't suppose that you remember me. My name is Sigurd Eriksson. You hanged my father and sold my younger brother into slavery two years ago in Cent.'

I remembered him then. He had filled out, grown taller and he now had a beard of sorts but I vaguely recognised him. I never knew his name, nor that of his father – a hersir leading a pack of Vikings who'd been engaged in pillaging a farmstead when we'd come across them. We'd killed most of them and hanged the rest, only sparing the hersir's two sons. The younger had ended up in the slave markets and I'd sent the elder back to Hæsten with a message. It seemed that I might be about to regret my clemency.

'I've always promised myself that one day I'd seek you out and hang you the way you hanged my father. I never dreamt that you would walk into my clutches with only a boy as companion. What was he?' he asked spitting on Osric's corpse. 'Your servant, or perhaps your catamite?'

He was trying to goad me but I wasn't about to react to his taunts.

'Instead of talking through your arse, why don't you get off that farm horse and fight me like a man – if that's what you are,' I said scornfully.

For a moment I thought that he was going to do just that, then he laughed.

'Very good. You'd like that, wouldn't you? Why should I give you a chance? You hanged my father when he was wounded and a captive and I intend to do the same to you; except I won't just wound you before you die. I intend to geld you.'

142

Sigurd was an arrogant young man and that was his downfall. He hadn't bothered to strip me of my sword and seax; nor had he drawn his own sword. I suppose that, having surrounded me with his men he was confident that I posed no threat to him. He was wrong.

I was stiff from riding and far from as agile as I'd been when I was younger but I was still able to duck down swiftly whilst drawing both my blades. Before Sigurd knew what I was about, I drove my seax into his horse's chest. The beast reared up, upset by the sudden pain, and Sigurd was thrown off. He landed heavily on the muddy road and the wind was knocked out of him with an audible whoosh.

Before he could get his breath back I pushed the point of my sword into his throat. His men had been taken by surprise but now they levelled their spears and swords at me.

'Back!' I shouted in Danish, 'or Sigurd dies now.'

They hesitated before a few did as I'd commanded. The rest continued to threaten me and then one of them kicked his horse forward and lowered his spear again.

'Let Sigurd go or you die now,' he barked.

I had been buying time, hoping against hope that Ywer and the rest of my men would be able to do something to help me. They would have to know something was wrong as soon as they saw Osric's horse. I was beginning to think that I'd gambled and lost when the man threatening me suddenly fell off his horse with an arrow in his back. Several more arrows struck the Danes and two more men and a couple of horses were hit.

The remaining dozen or so milled about in confusion before a couple of them decided that discretion was the better part of valour and fled. When my men emerged onto the roadway the rest turned their horses and followed them.

A minute later the wounded Danes had been killed together with one who'd been trapped under his horse. The other rider whose horse had been killed tried to make a run for it on foot but

Halig rode after him and hit him with the flat of his sword. He tumbled to the ground and, before he could get back to his feet, the Mercian had leant down and thrust the point of his blade through the Dane's neck.

'Well, Sigurd, it seems the tables are turned,' I said as soon as he'd been disarmed. 'Tell me, what are you doing here? You're someway from Casingc Stræt.'

He gave me a startled look. No doubt he was surprised that I knew where Hæsten's army was.

'Just kill me; you'll get nothing out of me,' he said defiantly.

'It's true. I'll not make the mistake of letting you go again. But tell me what I want to know and you'll die with your sword in your hand. Keep silent and I'll cut off your right hand first.'

As I'd hoped, Sigurd was a firm believer in Valhalla, the home for dead heroes. If I cut off his sword hand and sent him to the afterlife weaponless he'd end up in Niflheim, the land of primordial ice and cold.

'What do you want to know,' he asked sulkily after a moment's thought.

'Two things: what are you doing here, well south of your line of march, and where is Hæsten heading?'

He sighed and then shrugged.

'We're short of food; we were sent out to forage but we got lost when the snow started.'

If that was true, Sigurd was more of an incompetent fool than I had thought. I had to smile at the thought of him blundering around getting further and further away from the rest of the Vikings.

'And your ultimate destination? Why would Hæsten set off right across the country in winter?'

'Because King Eohric had got fed up with us. At first he was prepared to put up with us raiding his territory because he thought we'd be able to defeat Wessex and Mercia and he could expand his lands. He had an agreement with Jarl Hæsten that we'd settle in the west and he'd absorb the eastern half of Wessex into his kingdom. When we came back a few months ago he and Hæsten fell out. Had we not left we suspected that he would attack us himself in the spring.'

I suspected that it was an empty threat. Eohric could probably call upon two or three thousand men but many of them would be farmers and the like, similar to our fyrd. They'd be no match for the Viking horde. The truth was probably that Eohric's Danish jarls and Anglian thegns had got fed up with the depreciations of Hæsten's men and had given their king an ultimatum. What surprised me was that Hæsten had taken the possibility of an attack by Eohric seriously but then he hadn't shown much sound judgement in the past.

'So he's headed for Cæstir?' I asked.

I could tell by the look on Sigurd's face that I'd guessed correctly.

We left him hanging from a tree but I'd given him back his sword and sat him on his horse first. The blade dropped from his grip when the horse was led forward and the rope around his neck jerked tight, so perhaps he didn't actually die with it in his hand, but I'd kept my word.

We set off again for Glowecestre richer by everything of value we'd taken from the dead Vikings, including several horses. However, I'd been shaken by the encounter with Sigurd. I'd forgotten all about him until I'd met him again. It reminded me that I still didn't know who the traitor was who'd tried to kill me in the wood at Fearndune. A cold shiver ran down my back which had nothing to do with the weather.

'You're absolutely certain that Hæsten is making for Cæstir,' Æðelred asked yet again.

'You know as much as I do, lord. What do you think?' I asked.

'There's only one way to find out,' Æthelflæd said impatiently, 'and that's not by sitting here going over things again and again.'

Æðelred bridled at her tone for a moment, then sighed.

'You're right, my love. We need to send men there to find out the truth.'

He paused and then looked me in the eye.

'When you joined me I promised you land,' he said. 'Cæstir and the shire which surrounds it has become a lawless wasteland in recent years. If the Vikings have seized it we need to drive them out and restore it to Mercian rule once more. Once we've achieved that I'll make you the Ealdorman of Cæstirscīr.'

I was furious. He had promised me lands in Mercia but instead he was trying to palm me off with an area which I'd have to master first and then hold, even after Hæsten's Vikings were removed. I'd need a lot more than my own warband to do that. If ever there was a poisoned chalice, this was it.

'We can discuss that later, husband,' Æthelflæd interrupted, giving me a warning look. 'First we need to find the Vikings and deal with them once and for all.'

I nodded my thanks to her. Had she not spoken first I'd have said something I'd later regret.

'As usual you are right. Lord Jørren, I want you to go and find out what's happening in Cæstir. If Hæsten isn't there, I need to know where he is.'

'You want me to set out now?' I asked incredulously.

Since we'd returned to Glowecestre winter had hit us in earnest. The snow now made most roads impassable and the cold sapped one's strength if you spent too long outside.

'No, obviously not,' he snapped. 'But I want you ready to go as soon as conditions improve.'

'Cæstir lies not far upriver from the coast, if I remember correctly,' Cuthfleda said, speaking for the first time since I'd entered the chamber. 'It might be quicker and safer to travel there by sea,' she suggested.

It would certainly be quicker, I thought to myself, but not necessarily safer. Not only could we be caught in a storm but, once the weather improved, there was always the danger of running into Norse pirates. That meant taking a small fleet and Mercia didn't have many warships. However, my daughter was right. It might well be better than trying to get there overland as the direct route lay along the border with Wealas.

'I'll leave the details to Lord Jørren, but I need to know the exact situation as soon as possible.'

I bowed and left the room, wondering when exactly I would be able to relax and enjoy my advancing years in peace.

CHAPTER TEN

Spring 894

We set out in three birlinns and a Danish skeid which the Mercians had captured at Beamfleote the previous year. The skeid had eighty oars and Æðelred had renamed her Byrnsweord – Flaming Sword. It was crewed by my gesith and the rest of my warband whereas the smaller, slower and clumsier birlinns contained Mercians under the command of three of Æðelred's favourite thegns.

Perhaps they were good at fighting on land but none of them showed much prowess as seafarers. In the end I put a warrior who had considerable experience of sailing on each ship to help them. It probably wounded their pride and so I doubt that it endeared me to them but at least we were now making faster progress.

We eventually entered the estuary of the Dēvā, the river which led to Cæstir. Shortly afterwards we saw a sandy beach with a few fishing boats drawn up on it. There were several men, women and children repairing nets but they fled up a path which led to the top of a small ridge as soon as they saw our ships. The keel of Byrnsweord ploughed into the soft reddish sand and, before it had come to a complete standstill, a few of my gesith and I leapt onto the beach and gave chase.

When we reached the top of the ridge we could see a small settlement less than half a mile away. The inhabitants were busy collecting what they could and then they drove their livestock before them, heading into the hinterland. I wasn't interested in their scrawny animals or poor possessions; what I needed was information.

Then I spotted a boy who was limping and trying to keep up with the rest. He kept looking behind him as the rest of them drew further and further away from him. I gave chase and soon caught the crippled boy.

He was so frightened that he'd wet his ragged trousers in fear. I soon realised that he only spoke Norse so Arne, a Norseman who had been my body servant before he joined my warband, took him to one side and spoke quietly to him.

'He says he's never been as far as Cæstir, lord,' he said when he returned. 'However, he heard his father and his uncle discussing a great Danish host who had arrived there a few weeks ago. They were worried that they would raid their settlement but so far they have only plundered the lands to the south.'

I was extremely relieved that my gamble had paid off. I would have lost all credibility with Æðelred and the Mercian nobility in general if Hæsten and his men hadn't been at Cæstir.

'Did he say what this place is called?'

'Yes, he said it was called Dingesmere.'

I let the crippled lad go and he limped off after the others. I was looking forward to sleeping in a dry hut but there were only poor hovels to be found and they stank of rotted fish, animal faeces and urine. I was amazed that the Norse inhabitants, who normally took a pride in cleanliness, lived in such squalor. However, these were poor people, unlike the Norse warriors I'd encountered before.

We returned to the beach to camp for the night and discuss our plans for the morrow.

We had only managed to bring three horses with us. Warships are not designed to carry animals and I didn't want to be delayed by bringing a knarr; sailing with the birlinns was bad enough and Æðelred had made it very clear that he wanted my report as soon as possible so that he could plan a spring campaign.

I took Wolnoth and the senior of the three Mercian thegns with me. I would far rather have taken Ywer or one of my scouts but the thegns would have been affronted. As it was, they tried to say that one of them should accompany me instead of Wolnoth. I placated them by leaving one in charge of the camp and suggesting that the other take some of his men and scout the area around Dingesmere. I didn't think there was any danger nearby but I quietly asked Ywer to make sure that the camp was properly guarded and that a lookout was kept along the estuary, just in case we were caught off guard by Viking ships.

We had ridden for three hours before we saw the fort ahead of us. We had been going cautiously with Wolnoth riding a few hundred yards ahead of us to make sure we didn't stumble upon a party of Vikings and so I suppose we must have covered perhaps ten miles or so in that time.

The last time I'd seen those walls was ten years ago when I'd helped the Mercians re-capture the place from the Norse. I'd been badly wounded during the assault on the walls and my son Ywer, then only nine, had been kidnapped. After I'd rescued him I'd returned home hoping never to see the place again, yet here I was.

On that occasion a man called Durwyn had been left in charge with a garrison of five hundred men. He'd been ambushed and killed two years later whilst out chasing bandits, together with his shire reeve and a score of his men. Æðelred had appointed the captain of the garrison as governor pro tem, whilst he found a replacement for Durwyn, but he had other things to worry about and so Cæstir had been forgotten. It was a great shame after the trouble we'd taken to capture the place.

I could only assume that - if Hæsten had indeed led his army here - the garrison, the monks in the monastery and the rest of the inhabitants had all been killed or enslaved because no word of any survivors had reached the rest of Mercia.

The land around Cæstir was flat for the most part and so there was no vantage point from which to observe the fort. However, there were clumps of trees and so we made our way to one of those. We dismounted when we got there and cautiously crept

150

towards the front of the copse from where we could see the western walls. Unlike other old Roman towns and cities I'd seen, the stone used here was a reddish brown. When I was last here I'd noted that it appeared much more weathered than the grey walls that existed elsewhere and I'd concluded that the stone used here must be softer.

Ten years ago parts of the walls had collapsed and had been replaced with timber to make the settlement secure. Now there were great gaps where more stone had crumbled away and some of the timber palisade had been removed. No doubt both had been used by those who lived nearby to construct their settlements and farmsteads. As we watched gangs of men, women and children laboured to repair the walls. They were obviously slaves but they were guarded by Vikings. I felt a sense of elation. I'd been correct; these had to be Hæsten's men.

Others were digging out the ditch in front of the wall and yet more were building a wharf along the river bank under the southern wall. Half a dozen longships were moored out in the river and three knarrs were tied up alongside the part of the wharf which had been completed.

Although much repair work remained, there was no doubt in my mind that the defences would be completed long before Æðelred's army could get here.

As I watched all this activity Wolnoth nudged my arm and indicated something over to our left with his head. We weren't the only ones interested in what Hæsten was up to. A dozen mounted Norsemen had appeared from the north and sat on their horses observing the activity. Suddenly we saw a score of mounted Danes emerge from the north gate and ride towards the Norsemen. The latter immediately turned their horses and rode away.

'At least we can be grateful for one thing, the Danes don't seem to have allied themselves with the local Norse,' the thegn muttered.

'Perhaps,' I replied warily.

Privately I thought that it was a bit of a leap to assume that from this one encounter. Just because one group of the local settlers didn't seem well disposed to the newcomers didn't mean that all the jarls hereabouts felt the same.

I needed to find out more; in particular would the Norse settlers join an alliance to oust the Danes? I doubted very much if they were happy about the presence of such a large army close to them. There was no one leader in the vast tract of land north of Mercia. Officially it was part of Northumbria but nowadays it was composed of disparate parts, even if the Dane sitting on the throne in Eforwic claimed otherwise.

Guðred, King of Northumbria, held sway over what had once been Deira in the south-east of the once great kingdom whilst the land between the Tes and the border with the Kingdom of Alba was ruled by the Lord of Bebbanburg, an Angle called Eadwulf. The western half of Northumbria from the Dēvā to the border with Strathclyde was a lawless land fought over by the Britons of Strathclyde, the Angles of Northumbria and the Norse invaders who'd been driven out of Íralond by the resurgent native inhabitants.

The shire of Cæstir, which Æðelred had promised me, was scarcely in better state. Since the death of Durwyn the Mercians who lived there had been raided by the Welsh, the Danes living in the Danelaw and the Northumbrians. The population had dwindled and much of the shire was little better than a wilderness. Even if I succeeded in bringing it under my control, it would hardly yield enough in its present state for me to afford the warriors necessary to protect it. It was a dismal prospect but before I could even lay claim to the title of ealdorman I had to defeat Hæsten.

'There's a large group of horsemen approaching, lord,' Eafer, called down from the top of the cliffs. He was now one of my best warriors but when I'd found him he'd been a feral boy who managed to survive by eating wild berries and the flesh of dead animals.

'Any banners?' I asked as I took my helmet from Dunbeorn and belted on my sword and seax.

'No, lord. Just a ram's head on a pole.'

'Norsemen then, not Danes,' I muttered to myself as I climbed up the steep incline from our camp on the beach. I was followed by dozens of my men.

I stopped at the top of the cliff to get my breath back after the climb. The three Mercian thegns joined me and I took my shield from Dunbeorn. Our warriors spread out behind us ready to form a shield wall if necessary.

'Unfurl our banners,' I told Eomær and the Mercian standing beside him.

I had abandoned the white horse of Cent when I had been deposed. Now my banner was a severed horse's head dripping blood embroidered in white and red on a black background. Hilda had been against the design, saying that it would only serve to further antagonise Edward. I agreed that he wouldn't miss the symbolism – that was the idea - but I insisted and so she and Æbbe had reluctantly embroidered it for me. The banner of Mercia flying beside it showed a white wyvern on a green field.

There were over a score of riders, enough to be a jarl's escort but not enough to threaten us. I assumed, therefore, that they had come to talk, not to fight. I stepped forward accompanied by the three thegns, Arne and Ywer and waited whilst an equal number of Norsemen dismounted and walked towards us.

'Who are you who dares to invade my land?' a young man with golden hair demanded.

He was dressed in expensive scarlet trousers tied with broad yellow ribbons below the knee, a blue tunic embroidered at the hems with gold wire and he wore a chainmail byrnie that had been burnished until it shone like silver. The red stone on the pommel of his sword sparkled in the weak sunlight and so I suspected it was a large ruby. He was bare-headed but both his hair and his beard were elaborately plaited. If most of the shire was impoverished, it didn't look as if this man's land fell into that category.

'The last I heard this peninsula was part of Mercia and therefore belongs to Lord Æðelred, who we serve. Who do I have the pleasure of addressing?'

'My name is Eirik Fairhair, Jarl of Myrteland and all the land to the north,' he said in Norse.

Myrteland meant place of the myrtle, presumably their name for the peninsula between the Rivers Dēvā and Mǣresēa which we called Wirhealum.

'All the land?' I asked using Arne to translate. 'As far as Strathclyde?'

He flushed in annoyance.

'Not quite all, but much of the coast hereabouts.'

'So you are the leader of the Norse settlers?' I probed.

'The more important of the jarls, yes,' he said in a tone which defied me to contradict him.

Both the Norse and the Danes were fond of boasting of their fame and exploits and exaggerating their importance to impress others and so I took his claims with a pinch of salt.

'He could be a useful ally, father,' Ywer said quietly. 'Perhaps it would be good not to antagonise him.'

My initial impression of Eirik wasn't favourable, however, my son was correct. This man might prove to be better as a friend than an enemy.

'Very well,' I said with a smile. 'I assume that you are as keen to get rid of the Danes who have captured Cæstir as we are?'

154

'That depends,' Eirik said cautiously.

'On what?'

'On what replaces them. The few Mercians who held the place before the coming of Hæsten left us alone. They didn't trouble us and we didn't trouble them.'

'Perhaps that's a discussion for another time? For now my interest is solely to defeat Hæsten and re-capture Cæstir.'

'You still haven't told me what your name is.'

'It's Jørren, Hereræswa of Mercia.'

'I've heard of a Jørren who was an ealdorman of Wessex. My uncle said he was killed leading the army that took Cæstir from my people ten years ago.'

'As you can see, I'm far from dead.'

He looked at me speculatively.

'So what happened? You used to be an important man in Wessex from what I've been told. I don't know much about the south but Mercia is not Wessex.'

'Let's just say don't put your trust in kings,' I said, beginning to feel uncomfortable under this young man's scrutiny.

He smiled broadly.

'That's why we don't have them. Most of the Norse settlers here fled from one king or another who all claimed the throne of Dyflin. Come, we have much to discuss I think. Accompany me back to my hall and we'll talk further.'

It had begun to sleet and it made sense to seek shelter but I didn't trust Eirik and he must have sensed this.

'Bring a score of warriors with you if you don't yet trust me but I swear on my mjolnir I mean you no harm,' he touched the Thor's hammer he wore around his neck. 'I'll even leave my brother here until you return. Come here, Skarde.'

A boy of about twelve dug his heels into his horse's flanks and rode up to his brother.

'You will stay here as a hostage to ensure this lord's safety,' he told the boy.

155

My Norse wasn't nearly as good as my Danish, which was why I used Arne as an interpreter, but it was good enough to translate what Eirik had said without Arne's assistance. I also got the gist of the boy's furious reply which roughly translated as an extreme reluctance to stay with what he described as turds who'd just dropped from a cow's arse.

'You'll do as you're told or I'll leave you with them as a thrall,' Eirik replied furiously, glaring at Skarde.

They looked nothing like each other. Whereas Eirik was tall, fair haired and well-built, his brother was distinctly skinny, had black hair and a cleft-chin - which is what Skarde meant in Norse. I guessed that they were half-brothers, or even step-brothers. If so, Skarde wasn't much of a hostage. I doubted if Eirik cared anything about the boy's fate. In fact, he might even be glad to be rid of him.

However, if I declined the jarl's invitation, the slight would not be forgiven and I would have made an enemy. I gave more weight to the oath sworn on his mjolnir than I did to having a hostage. Although many Christians gave no credence to pledges sworn on pagan symbols, I knew that the opposite was true. Those sworn on a saint's relics or on a crucifix meant nothing to them, however much Ælfred and Æðelred liked to think otherwise.

I chose Wolnoth and Arne to accompany me. Although Eirik said that I could bring more I felt that taking just two companions showed my trust in him; besides, we only had three horses.

We rode through the sleet and, as I had the hood of my cloak over my head, I could see little of the countryside through which we rode. Nevertheless, I got the impression of good pasture land in which flocks of sheep huddled together for warmth. There was the odd small wood and the land undulated but there were no tall hills. At last the sleet abated and I looked about me as we rode. We had crested a low ridge and there in front of me was another estuary, this one was much narrower than that of the Dēvā but I knew it had to be the Mǣresēa.

There was a hall in the centre of the settlement towards which we were headed and from the latter's size I guessed that it held perhaps two to three hundred people. That probably meant that Eirik had no more than forty or fifty warriors. Doubtless there would be other small settlements and farmsteads which recognised him as their lord but, even so, he probably couldn't muster more than a hundred fighters, and some of those would be boys and old men. It was something of a disappointment; I was hoping for many more.

'We call this place Grárhöfn,' Eirik told me proudly.

It meant grey harbour and I could see a wooden jetty jutting out from a beach of grey pebbles. There were two snekkjur and a knarr moored to the south side of the jetty and several fishing boats drawn up onto the shingle. Surrounding the settlement there were several fields which had been ploughed ready for sowing crops in the spring. The huts looked in good repair with duckboards between them to stop people sinking into the mud and the hall was one of the more ornate examples of Viking timber buildings.

As I drew closer I could see the barge boards at each end had been intricately carved and ended in representations of snake's heads which looked at each other with open mouths showing their fangs. They looked for all the world as if they were about to bite each other. The building was constructed of smooth planks and had an open undercover walkway which ran all the way around the hall. Supported on wooden pillars, I assumed that the thatched roof over the walkway was intended to protect the window openings from the weather.

The front gable displayed two oversized shields which looked as if they had been freshly re-painted. One featured a red dragon's head on a black background whilst the other was green with a red wolf's head. Above the roof of the hall was another structure. This looked like a small pitched roof supported on short pillars but, instead of being thatched, it was covered in wooden shingles.

157

Smoke was whisked away from this structure by the wind and I realised that it was a covered opening above the fire pit below. It was an impressive building and I resolved to incorporate some of its clever features in my new hall in Cæstir, if I ever got to build one. The roof over the smoke hole was a particularly good idea as rain and snow had often dampened the fire in my old hall in Cantwareburh.

There was no palisade; I supposed that all the available timber nearby had been used for the buildings. Instead there was a deep ditch and an earthen rampart all around the settlement. The only access was over a wooden bridge which could presumably be quickly removed in case of an attack. I later learned that it was retracted on rollers at dusk and replaced at sunrise.

We rode over the bridge and entered the settlement. All those we passed stopped to stare at us. It was obvious that we weren't Norsemen or Danes; our different trousers, leg ribbons, helmets and shields marked us out as Anglo-Saxons. We dismounted outside the hall and boys came running to take our horses. They were dressed in nothing but homespun tunics with an iron collar around their necks. They were thralls and, I suspected, had been enslaved during raids into Mercia and Wealas. Two spoke to each other in a language I didn't recognise but which was probably Goídelc – the version of Gaelic spoken in Íralond. The wind off the estuary was icy and I shivered despite my wolf-skin cloak. The young thralls were blue with cold and I felt some sympathy for them.

We entered the hall and I was glad to be in the warm, if smoky, interior. The cold didn't use to bother me so much; perhaps I was getting old.

The settlement might be small but it was evident that Eirik wasn't poor. His hall was lavishly fitted out with good quality furniture and the sleeping areas were all equipped with furs. I doubted that he had acquired his wealth from farming and fishing. He was obviously a successful raider as well. The question was

158

where did he go for his plunder? I hoped it wasn't Mercia but, if he used the two longships in the harbour, it was more likely to be Wealas, the west coast of Northumbria and perhaps even other Viking settlements.

We were invited to sit on a bench by the fire and Eirik sat opposite with two of his warriors. Young female thralls appeared with horns full of ale and platters of bread and cheese. We ate and drank companionably for a minute or two before Eirik spoke.

'What is your plan for getting rid of the Danes?'

'I've taken Cæstir before - ten years ago when it was held by your countrymen,' I replied. 'Then we attacked using scaling ladders and a battering ram but it was costly in terms of casualties. I'm hopeful that this time we can starve the enemy out.'

'Those Norsemen were nothing to do with me or my family, of course. Many fled back to Mann, Orkneyjar and Íralond. I heard that some even went west to Snæland. They didn't remain here in any event.'

I wasn't sure if that was the truth or whether Eirik was just trying to convince me that he and his fellow Norse jarls weren't my enemies. It seemed more likely that many had gone back northwards to the western coastal area of Northumbria. Whatever the truth, I sensed that in reality he was as eager to get rid of Hæsten's Vikings as we were and would therefore co-operate with us if he could.

'How many men has Hæsten got in Cæstir?' I asked, taking a swig of the strong ale and smacking my lips appreciatively.

'It's difficult to be precise, although we have watched them ever since they arrived,' Eirik said cautiously. 'We think that there are perhaps four thousand Vikings in all, mostly Danes but there are few Norsemen as well. If we assume that every male between thirteen and fifty is a warrior, then I suppose he might have as many as fifteen hundred.'

'That tallies with what we know. We believe that he had two thousand or so at Sūþburh and we counted over six hundred dead after the battle. It's possible that a few disaffected Danes from East Anglia and Northumbria have joined him since but I doubt that very many have.'

'I'm surprised that any have,' Eirik grunted, spitting into the fire to show his contempt for Hæsten. 'He is both unsuccessful and unlucky. I find it surprising that more of the men he brought from Frankia haven't deserted him.'

'Where would they go?' I asked. 'Everyone's hand is against them, except for Guðred of Northumbria perhaps.'

'You haven't heard? Guðred is dead.'

'I knew he was sick but not that he'd died. Who has replaced him?'

'Sigfrith, or so it is rumoured,' Eirik said with a shrug.

'Sigfrith? The only Sigfrith I know was one of the leaders of the Northumbrians who King Ælfred drove out of Escanceaster, but I thought he'd gone to Dyflin.'

'Yes, he did, and tried to take the throne. When he failed, he returned to Yorvik and made himself king there. There is talk that he may have hastened Guðred's end. Moreover, Guðred's two sons seem to have vanished.'

'If I remember correctly they weren't very old.'

'Fifteen and thirteen; old enough to be rivals for the throne.'

It seemed that we had replaced an ineffectual ruler in the north for one who was an enemy, and a ruthless one at that. It wasn't good news.

I sat for a moment, letting the news sink in and speculating about the implications.

'I suspect that Sigfrith may prove to be a more effective king than his recent predecessors.'

'You're thinking what I'm thinking? That he may try and impose his rule on the west of his realm?'

Eirik nodded.

'Then it is imperative that we oust Hæsten and forge a strong alliance between Mercia and the Norse settlers along the coast between here and Cumbria.'

'That would mean you don't oppose us as settlers. Do you have the authority to agree to that?' he asked sceptically.

'Lord Æðelred is a pragmatist. Provided you are prepared to recognise him as your lord, I'm fairly certain that he will grant you the land you now occupy.'

'Which means paying him taxes for it?'

'Naturally, but in return he will make this part of Mercia strong again, which will enable us to resist encroachment by Sigfrith, or the Welsh, or indeed by fresh Norse invaders from Mann and Íralond.'

'I will think on what you have said and discuss it with my fellow jarls,' Eirik promised. 'However, we came here to be our own masters and not the subjects of some foreign king.'

'Æðelred is not a king and paying a few taxes in order to gain a powerful ally to help you keep your land seems a small price to pay,' I pointed out.

Arne had been acting as translator throughout our discussions but, as I got up to leave, Eirik bid us farewell in excellent Danish. I left feeling that I may have misjudged Eirik initially. He was a vain man but he was also clever and wealthy. I had a feeling that he could be very useful to me in the future.

CHAPTER ELEVEN

May/June 894

'This can't go on much longer,' Æðelred told his nobles. 'The fyrd are deserting a score at a time but, with summer coming, you can expect scores to become hundreds.'

It was the perennial problem for Anglo-Saxon armies. Most thegns relied upon the freemen of their vills to provide fighting men when needed. Only a few could afford to maintain warriors on a permanent basis. Even ealdormen didn't keep more than a few score of them. King Ælfred had several hundred and his son mustered a force of just over a hundred but Mercia wasn't anywhere near as rich as Wessex. The combined warbands of Æðelred and the nobles of Mercia numbered less than four hundred.

The fyrd assembled for the siege of Cæstir provided another fourteen hundred but, as Æðelred had pointed out, that number was shrinking. Thankfully my efforts to win Eirik Fairhair to our cause had borne fruit. Not all the Norsemen on the nearby coast of Northumbria had joined him but three hundred had. However, they were also getting bored sitting outside the walls of Cæstir, and blockading the Dēvā, in the hope of starving Hæsten's Vikings into surrender.

'I agree,' I said, getting to my feet to address the assembled ealdormen, senior thegns and Norse jarls. 'The Vikings must be very short of food by now and I'm betting that the infants and younger children are dying. Nevertheless, Hæsten is a stubborn man. He knows that the fyrd need to get back to the land or their families will starve this winter.

'So far Hæsten has refused to negotiate but lack of food will have weakened his warriors as well as his women and children. I suggest the time has come to assault the walls and batter down the gates. That's how we captured Cæstir ten years ago.'

There were general nods of agreement from those standing in Æðelred's tent. Only Æthelflæd looked unhappy.

'Assaulting the walls will cost many lives,' she pointed out. 'Can we at least attempt to get Hæsten to negotiate one more time?'

'The last time I sent a priest forward to offer talks he was lucky to escape with his life,' Æðelred reminded her.

'That was two weeks ago,' she replied. 'Since then he has had no fresh supplies and, judging by the smoke coming from the centre of the fort, he is having to cremate his dead more and more frequently. Even if he's a stubborn old fool his men might persuade him otherwise.'

'Perhaps if we sent a warrior to offer terms instead of a Christian priest he might have more success?' Ywer suggested.

'Are you prepared to risk your life to find out?' one of the Mercians sneered.

'Yes, if it will save lives. Are you?' my son retorted.

I looked at him in alarm. The Vikings had shot at the priest in response to his offer of talks and he was lucky to escape with just a wounded arm. To get within hailing distance of the walls meant going within bowshot. The Vikings didn't have many archers but the few they did have were good with a bow.

'It's worth a try,' Æðelred said, 'that is, if Lord Jørren agrees?'

I was tempted to say no; the thought of Ywer putting himself in very real danger horrified me. However, I would lose any credibility I had gained amongst the Mercian nobles if I did that. My nomination as their hereræswa had been less than universally popular. I was an outsider and regarded as a Saxon, who many Mercians still thought of as their enemy. The fact that I was a Jute, rather than a Saxon, was a distinction that most ignored. Only my reputation as a warrior and as a leader had prevented some from openly opposing my appointment.

'I agree, lord, but I suggest that I should be the one to go and make the offer, not my son.'

'Father, no!' Ywer blurted out.

'Quiet!' I told him sternly before addressing Æðelred again. 'I carry more weight than a youth that the Vikings have never heard of.'

Æðelred looked alarmed. In the few months I had served him he had come to rely on my advice nearly as much as he did on his wife's. Plainly he thought he might lose me, not only as

hereræswa but also as the Ealdorman of Cæstirscīr. Who else would take on the thorny problem of the most northerly shire if I perished?

'Very well,' he said reluctantly, 'but stay at a safe distance.'

It was a platitude. He knew very well that I needed to be fairly close to the walls if I was to make myself heard.

I walked forward dressed in byrnie, helmet and carrying my shield but I discarded my sword and seax two hundred yards from the fort's east gate to show my peaceful intentions. I carried the branch of a tree, clad in new leaf, in my right hand but I was certain that my shield would offer better protection than the symbol of peace.

'That's far enough,' a voice called in Danish when I was a hundred yards from the wall. The wind came from the north and easily carried his voice to me. I would have to shout against it and I suspected that they wanted to keep me at a distance to humiliate me. If I stopped there they would claim that they couldn't hear me, and with some justification, so I kept walking.

'I said that's far enough,' the voice on the wall called again.

'What? I can't hear you,' I yelled back.

I advanced another few paces until an arrow struck the ground close to my feet.

'Can you hear me now?' I called.

'Yes, say what you have to say and go before we kill you.'

'Am I talking to Jarl Hæsten?'

'Who wants to know?'

'Hæsten will know me. My name is Jørren, the architect of his defeat at Midleton in Cent.'

'I know who you are, Jørren,' another voice called down.

Even at this distance I recognised the speaker from his stocky build and helmet of polished steel with its gold circlet and eye protectors. I also recognised the two boys standing by his side - Irwyn and Godric. The woman with red hair standing with them had to be his wife.

'Jarl Hæsten; we meet again. Greetings. I'm pleased to see your family is well.'

It was a lie. Even Hæsten and his wife and children looked thin and gaunt.

'What do you want, Jørren? If you have come to offer us terms you are wasting your time.'

'How much longer can you hold out against us, Hæsten? Judging by the cremation pyres which increase in intensity and frequency each day, there won't be anyone for you to lead soon.'

I had wondered where the wood was coming from for the pyres but I suppose he was tearing down buildings as the numbers needing to use them as shelters grew fewer and fewer.

There was a long pause whilst several of the warriors close to Hæsten spoke to him. Judging by their gesticulations I felt certain that they were urging him to talk to me.

'Come into Cæstir, Jørren, so we can meet face to face,' he said once the argument had ended.

Although he might have been persuaded by his men to negotiate in good faith, I half suspected that he would kill me, perhaps after torturing me first, and then display my head on the ramparts. However, it was a risk I was prepared to take if it led to the end of this stalemate.

They put a hood over my head as soon as I entered the gate so I couldn't see what sort of state the inhabitants were in but the place reeked of death and disease. I was led along for what seemed an age before it was removed. I was in what had once been a large villa, most likely that of the Roman fort's commander, which Hæsten was presumably now using as his hall. The walls had crumbled away in places, to be replaced by timber, and the roof was newly thatched. Nevertheless enough of its former glory remained in the form of mosaics on the floor and murals on the walls to indicate what it must have been like centuries ago.

Hæsten had a reputation as a heartless and vicious killer who didn't let scruples get in the way of what he wanted, so I had grounds for concern about my treatment at his hands. However, he treated me honourably, his sons offering me ale and bread before we sat down to talk. Either he didn't have servants or he didn't want them to overhear our conversation.

'We'll leave here provided you allow us to go where we want,' Hæsten said without preamble.

I knew he was a man of few words but I hadn't expected him to say what he wanted quite so bluntly.

'That rather depends on where you want to go. If your intention is to raid Mercia, then the answer is no.'

'Do you think I'm a fool?' he asked, his eyes betraying his annoyance. 'Of course I realise that is unacceptable. No, our families will return to Ēast Seaxna Rīce with enough warriors to protect them; the rest of us will be raid the land you call Wealas. We need food to survive and plunder to keep my men happy.'

My immediate reaction was favourable. Anarawd ap Rhodri, King of Gwynedd, had long been a thorn in Æðelred's side, raiding northern Mercia for years. There was personal animosity between them as well. Anarawd had defeated Æðelred when he'd invaded Gwynedd on a punitive expedition thirteen years ago. Therefore I was fairly certain that the Mercians would wholehearted support the raid that Hæsten proposed, provided they weren't seen as complicit in it. The last thing that Æðelred needed at the moment was a war with Gwynedd and its client kingdoms of Powys and Ceredigion.

'I'll take your proposal back to Lord Æðelred and return with his answer,' I said, getting up to leave, but Hæsten put his hand on my arm.

'We want food and medical help before we leave,' he said.

'I'll see what can be done.'

Then I had a thought.

'We can't just let you leave to attack Gwynedd straight away. Anarawd would think that we were behind the raid. You'll need to travel part of the way with your families and then break away to enter Wealas.'

Hæsten thought for a moment before nodding his agreement.

'Before I go back, the Mercians will want to know what happened to the inhabitants.'

'The inhabitants? Ah, you mean the people who were living in Cæstir when we arrived. They became thralls - that is the ones who survived the fighting; many died opposing us.'

'Yes? And where are they now?'

'They all died subsequently. It's your fault. You deprived us of food. What was I supposed to do? Let our people die so that thralls could live?

'So you let them die of starvation?' I said, unable to hide my anger.

'No, I'm not a monster. We killed them quickly and cleanly and then burnt their bodies in the Viking way.'

'But they were Christians!' I protested. 'They should have been buried in hallowed ground.'

167

'I don't know what that is,' he said with an impatient shrug. 'Besides the ground was too hard to dig graves.'

I returned to our encampment with mixed feelings: elated at my success in bringing matters to a successful conclusion but sick at heart knowing that the siege had meant the death of hundreds of my fellow Christians.

✝✝✝

I sat on my horse watching the long column of men, women, children and wagons as it wound its way out of Cæstir and headed south-eastwards. They were escorted by several hundred Mercians to make sure they didn't make any mischief on the way.

We had insisted that they leave their few ships behind and, after a long and bitter argument, Hæsten had agreed to exchange them for the carts, a few horses and enough supplies to last all the way back to East Anglia.

The plan was for Hæsten and six hundred of his warriors to steal away from the column one night. The Mercians would make a desultory pursuit for appearances sake and then return to Cæstir, leaving the rest of the Vikings to make their own way back to Ēast Seaxna Rīce. However, they had agreed to travel via Northumbria and East Anglia to make sure they didn't pillage Anglian Mercia on the way. Inevitably their passage would be opposed by the Danes living en route but that wasn't our problem.

Surprisingly the Vikings adhered to the agreement and I heard later that the main body had reached a place on the coast of Ēast Seaxna Rīce called Meresai and constructed a fortress there ready for the winter.

We heard reports of Hæsten's progress from time to time but I had other matters to occupy me so I didn't pay much attention to

168

them. Lady Æthelflæd had her own warband and, much to my surprise, she elected to stay and add her fifty warriors to mine when her husband disbanded his army and returned south.

She volunteered to supervise the re-building of Cæstir, especially the monastery, which the Vikings had all but destroyed. It would need to be re-consecrated, of course, especially as we had found the abbot's body crucified on the cross hanging above the altar. We may not have been able to bury the other victims but at least we could lay the poor abbot to rest in the monastery's graveyard.

My first task was to appoint a shire reeve. I was tempted to choose someone I knew I could trust and the obvious candidate was Ywer. However, the politically sensible choice would be one of the local dignitaries. I therefore asked Eirik, who was delighted. He might claim to be the most powerful Norse jarl in the shire but others would have disputed it. Now he became what he'd claimed.

When he accepted he made a strange request of me.

'I'd like you to take my half-brother into your household and train him to be a warrior.'

It wasn't a problem but I was curious as to the reason for it, so I asked him. He chewed his lip for a moment. Plainly it wasn't something he really wanted to talk about but eventually he told me the tale.

'I'm the bastard son of a thrall who my father fell in love with. She died giving birth to me and my father raised me as his son. A few years later he married Skarde's mother and my brother was born when I was six. His mother always hated me but my father loved me and when he died his men chose me as the next jarl.

'Skarde feels that he's been cheated of his inheritance. The truth is, even if my father hadn't made it clear I was to succeed him, Skarde was too young to become jarl. That was a year ago and he has stirred up discontent ever since. I need to get rid of him and either he is trained by you to become one of your warriors or .....'

169

He left the sentence unfinished but it was clear what the alternative was. His half-brother would either be killed or sold into slavery. I had a feeling that Skarde might bring trouble with him but I decided to give the boy a chance.

'I'll take him but if he proves to more trouble than he's worth I'll have to send him back to you.'

Eirik nodded and the next day a sulky Skarde joined several other boys I'd enlisted locally for training as scouts and warriors.

Whilst work to repair Cæstir went on I decided to visit every settlement and farmstead in the shire. I needed to obtain the fealty of the thegns and jarls but I also wanted to assess the defences. Ælfred had made it almost impossible for Hæsten's horde to raid with impunity by building burhs. They served as bastions to protect the local population and, because they were interconnected by good roads, troops could be moved swiftly from one burh to another to counter Viking raids. I intended something similar for Cæstirscīr. Even without the threat posed by Hæsten, should he return, I needed to protect my people from raids by the Welsh and from across the border with Northumbria.

The first place I visited was Wirhealum. Eirik's wasn't the only settlement on the peninsula. There were five others as well as numerous farmsteads. Two other settlements further up the coast were Norse and three inland had remained Mercian, although some of the outlying farmsteads had been taken over by Norse families. I thought that there might be ill-feeling between the two, especially as Mercians were invariably Christian and the Norse pagans, but they seemed to have reached an amicable arrangement whereby they each got on with their separate lives in peace. They didn't mix much though, which probably explained why Eirik and his people spoke little Ænglisc, the common language of the Saxons, Angles and Jutes.

I had taken forty warriors with me, not so much for protection, but to impress the local people and to assure them that I was capable of defending them against their enemies. I had also asked Eirik to accompany me.

The nearest settlement to Cæstir was Nestone. It was one of those still held by a Mercian thegn – a man called Pybba. The settlement lacked a palisade, making do with thorn bushes planted in a circle around the hall, huts and hovels. Its purpose was to keep animals out rather than act as a defensive barrier. People tending the fields ran for the nearby trees as we approached and mothers grabbed small children and locked themselves in their homes.

I reflected that it might have been wiser to have left most of my escort at a distance and gone to see the thegn with a few men but it was too late now. We filled the open ground in front of the small hall as the thegn emerged with three other men, all carrying swords and shields but not wearing chainmail or even leather jerkins. Pybba was in his late forties or early fifties and the men with him looked like younger versions – evidently his sons.

'Greetings Thegn Pybba. You may sheath up your swords; we mean you no harm. This is a courtesy call, nothing more. Wolnoth, take the men outside the settlement. Jarl Eirik, please remain with me.'

I turned back to Pybba and his sons.

'Forgive our intruding on you unannounced. My name is Jørren, Ealdorman of Cæstirscīr, appointed by Lord Æðelred and the Witenaġemot of Mercia.'

The latter part wasn't strictly true. Those nobles present at the siege of Cæstir had supported my appointment. I think my success in ending the siege without bloodshed might have had something to do with that. It still had to be formally ratified by the next meeting of the full witenaġemot but that appeared to be a formality.

'Welcome, Lord Jørren. I thank you for ridding us of the heathen Danes.'

171

His voice was friendly enough but he kept casting suspicious glances at Eirik.

'I'm surprised to see Jarl Eirik Fairhair with you though,' he went on. 'We get along well enough but we aren't in the habit of visiting each other.'

'Cæstirscīr is a part of Mercia but one which has been neglected ever since Ealdorman Durwyn was killed. I intend to restore the shire's prosperity but it is underpopulated. We need to encourage settlers to come and rectify that and to make us strong militarily. I don't care if they are Saxons, Angles, Norsemen or even Danes provided that they are prepared to swear fealty to me and to Lord Æðelred. It's not enough to live in peace but separately. We must all work together to ensure that the shire thrives again.'

One of Pybba's sons whispered something in his father's ear and immediately the old man looked contrite.

'Forgive me, lord. My son has just reminded me of my manners. Please come into my hall and take some refreshment.'

He paused before continuing, obviously a little reluctant to do so.

'Jarl Eirik, please join us.'

'Eirik Fairhair has consented to act as my shire reeve,' I told Pybba once we were seated on benches arranged around the central hearth.

Pybba opened and closed his mouth in surprise whilst his sons muttered to each other.

'Half the population of the shire are Norse and so it makes sense for them to be properly represented in its governance,' I went on before anyone could make an unfortunate comment.

'You're not a Mercian, Lord Jørren,' Pybba said after an uncomfortable silence.

'No, not even an Angle, which means that I can be seen as impartial when it comes to disputes.'

'You're a Saxon then?' one of the sons said contemptuously.

'No, I'm a Jute,' I replied staring him in the eye. 'And you address me as lord.'

He dropped his eyes to the floor muttering an apology.

'How exactly do you intend to make us strong enough to resist the depredations of the Welsh, the Northumbrians and even the Norse from the coast of Cumbria,' another of the sons asked, hastily adding 'lord.'

'Well, I have a highly effective warband and I'm already recruiting more boys to train. The Lady Æthelflæd has remained in Cæstir with her own warriors for the time being. That coupled with the hearth warriors of the various thegns and jarls will give us the nucleus of a strong force when required. The fyrd must be re-formed and trained properly. Furthermore Jarl Eirik, my son Ywer and I will provide the leadership that has been so lacking in recent years.'

Pybba nodded which I took to be approval.

'You mentioned re-population. How will you achieve that, lord?'

'There are some forty to fifty vills which have disappeared over the years. The land is still there but it needs the people to cultivate it. Lord Æðelred has given me the deeds to all of them and I will appoint reeves to re-establish these settlements and farmsteads. As for the people to work the lands, there are always younger sons seeking land of their own. I will send messengers far and wide to encourage settlers to come.'

'From Mercia, lord?'

'From wherever, but I only need people who will be loyal and work hard. I will form the shire's witan shortly which will include every thegn, jarl and senior churchman to help me to vet the applicants.'

'Senior churchmen? There is scarcely a priest or monk in the whole shire, lord. They have either been killed by the pagans or have fled,' Pybba said, giving Eirik an accusatory look.

173

'Lady Æthelflæd and her chaplain are seeking a suitable candidate to appoint as the new Abbot of Cæstir. I'm told that there are a number of monks from Glowecestre and elsewhere in Mercia who are willing to form a new community here. Once it is established, I'll discuss the founding of other monastic houses with the new abbot and also encourage the building of churches in the major settlements.'

'You'll expect to collect taxes from us, I suppose, lord.' One of the other sons asked. 'We are a poor vill with little to spare, even in good years, and recently there have been few of those.'

'Lord Æðelred is lending me a steward until I can find one of my own. It will be his job to visit every vill and assess its value and to decide what it can afford to pay in the way of taxes. I'd remind you that I'm paying for maintaining my warband for your protection and for the restoration of both Cæstir and the shire for now but there is limit to how much I can afford to pay out of my own coffers.'

Silence greeted my remarks. I wasn't surprised. Taxes are never popular.

'However, you will gain in other ways. I intend to recruit men with expertise in agriculture, breeding horses and other livestock and in fishing. They will visit you and help you to improve the efficiency of your harvests, your breeding methods and storage of food for the winter.'

A stunned silence greeted this announcement. I doubted that any thought had gone into the growing of crops or storing supplies for the winter and a breeding programme was evidently a strange concept. Things had doubtless always been done a certain way and no-one saw any need to change. I suspected that there was no system for breeding; animals were just left to do what comes naturally. I was no farmer but I had been brought up on a farmstead and even I could see that agriculture here was inefficient and unproductive.

I left Pybba and his sons with a lot to think about. I was under no illusion; changing the habits of a lifetime was going to be an uphill struggle but unless they produced a surplus each year I would soon be penniless.

My visits to other vills were similar to that to Nestone but I found that the Norse jarls were more interested in my ideas for improvement. From what I'd been told many had been born in Norþweg, a land of fjords and mountains with little in way of arable land or good pasture for livestock. They had left and settled elsewhere because they wanted an easier life. The land of northern Mercia gave them the good land they craved and if it could make them prosperous there was far less need to go raiding for what they needed.

The deserted vills were more problematic. The buildings were dilapidated ruins and the arable land was overgrown. Re-building the huts and storage sheds would take time and money and reclaiming the land for crops and pasture would be laborious. Nevertheless, it had to be done.

My other problem was defence. I had intended to copy Ælfred's strategy and build burhs but I lacked the money, the labour and the warriors to garrison them. In the meantime I rode out to visit the rest of the deserted vills. One lay in the valley of the Dēvā seven miles south of Cæstir and was, so I was told, called Fearndune. It meant the hill of ferns and the low rises on both banks of the river were covered in ferns. The remains of the settlement were located at the top of the rise where the ground was relatively flat.

I had ridden out with Wolnoth and a small escort to view the place.

'It would make a good place to put a fort from which to patrol this bank of the river, lord,' he said after we had explored the place.

'I agree, which is why I want you to establish a settlement here within a strong palisade. There is a ford here which the Welsh will otherwise use to cross and raid us. There are other fords, of course, so you'll need to patrol the river frequently.'

'Me, lord?'

'Yes, it's time I rewarded your long and devoted service. I want you to set up home here with your family. I'll also send ten of the older married warriors to help you get started and I'm hopeful that other families will come and join you if you offer them land to farm.'

'You want me to become a reeve, lord?' he said dubiously.

'No, Wolnoth, I want you be the thegn.'

The look of astonishment on his face was priceless. He was nearly as old as I was and had joined me with several other young scouts when his former lord, Edmund of Bebbanburg, was killed by the Great Heathen Army at the battle outside Eforwic thirty years ago. Now the only other one left from those far off times was Cináed.

'Thank you, lord. I don't know what to say.'

'Don't thank me. Your deserve it and it's not exactly a great favour. Guarding the east bank of the river will be taxing. I'll give you Hrodulf and Oscgar. As Mercians they might be useful to you in recruiting ceorls to join you.'

I'd rescued them both as boys when they'd been thralls captured by the Danes and they'd proved to be excellent swordsmen and even better archers.

'Who will you select to replace me as captain?'

'I'm not sure. Cináed is the most senior and he's been with me since I was a boy but he's as old as I am. Perhaps he also deserves to be given a vill?'

'I'm not sure he'd thank you. He'd think he was being put out to grass!'

'I hope that you don't think that.'

'No, I know that the task you've given me won't prove to be an easy one. I don't think that he'd want to be your captain either.

What he would be good at is training the boys you're recruiting to be scouts.'

'Yes, you may be right. I was thinking of Acwel or Lyndon for that role.'

'Those two like working together. They've even married two sisters. They won't want to be separated.'

'Who would you choose as your replacement?'

I already knew who I wanted to appoint but I was interested in what Wolnoth thought and why.

'The three obvious candidates are Rinan, Eafer and Eomær. Rinan has been in your gesith the longest and you and he have had a special bond ever since he saved your life at the Battle of Ethunden.'

That took me back two decades. After Ethunden I'd found him living wild, surviving on berries and any small game he could trap. His father and uncle had been killed during the battle and his thegn had abandoned him to get his hands on his family's land. Subsequently he had been one of my few companions when we had scoured Daneland for the traitor Wulfhere. He had saved my life a second time when Sexmund, the son of Edda who had tried to have me killed, had attacked me at a feast. I owed him a great deal and, as Wolnoth said, he and I were very close. That didn't mean he would make a good captain, of course, but he was a good scout and a fearless warrior. He was also cunning and intelligent.

'There are others,' Wolnoth continued. 'Eomær and Eafer were both your body servants at different times and you also have a close relationship with them. Both are excellent warriors and respected members of your gesith. Eafer is the younger, of course. I think anyone of them could do well as your captain.'

'But you think one would make a better leader than the other two?'

'Yes, and I think you know who that is without me telling you,' Wolnoth said with a grin.

'You're right, of course. I'll talk to Rinan when we get back.'

We mounted our horses and set off back to Cæstir, where a surprise awaited me.

✝✝✝

I dismounted outside the villa which Hæsten had used as his hall and which was now mine. I was looking forward to washing the dust from my face and to a tankard of mead and so it took me a moment to realise that it was Hilda who waited in the portico to welcome me.

'Hilda!' I exclaimed in delight, 'and Æbbe! When did you arrive?'

'We came with the new abbot,' she replied with a twinkle in her eye after I'd given both my wife and daughter a hug.

'Good afternoon, father,' a voice said from behind me.

I turned to find my elder son standing there.

'Æscwin? What on earth are you doing here?'

Then I realised what Hilda had said; she'd called him the new abbot.

'Why have you left Cantwareburh? Have you fallen out with Archbishop Plegmund?'

'No, not in the least. In truth, he was against me coming here. However, my work there was almost entirely administration and I didn't become a cleric to do that all day. Here I can serve God better by establishing a new monastery and by converting the pagans, especially the Norsemen, to Christianity.'

He hesitated, then continued.

'The fact that I'm your son didn't endear me to King Edward and that made relationships between him and the Church a little difficult.'

I couldn't believe that the man was still being so petty but Edward was a stubborn man and once he got an idea in his head there was no shifting it. He'd taken against me and evidently that wasn't going to change. It presumably meant that he would never look favourably on Ywer either.

'Well, I'm delighted to see you and to have my family all back together again. Cuthfleda is here too, with the Lady Æthelflæd, although I don't suppose it will be long before she needs to return to Æðelred's side.'

'I'm glad that they are reconciled,' Æscwin remarked.

For a moment I had to think, then I remembered that the Lord of Mercia had thought Æthelflæd was stubborn and had ideas improper to a woman when they were first wed. He'd even beaten her and raped her. That had all changed later once he realised how valuable his wife was to him. The rape had resulted in the birth of a daughter – the Lady Ælfwynn – who must be about six. Afterwards it was common gossip that, however closely the couple worked together, Æthelflæd had never allowed her husband into her bed again.

It meant that Æðelred would never have a son to succeed him. I wondered about that but then I had a thought. King Edward wanted his son, the four-year-old Æthelstan, to enter the church. As a monk or a priest he wouldn't be a contender for the throne of Wessex if Edward had other sons. However, he was also Æthelflæd's nephew. Whilst she appeared to accept Edward's decision about Æthelstan's future, I couldn't help wondering if the boy's aunt might have other plans for him.

The next morning Æscwin and I accompanied Æthelflæd to the north-west corner of the old fort where she proposed to site the monastery she was endowing. I welcomed her generosity but I didn't feel that I could contribute much to discussions about where the church should be sited or the size of the dormitory. I was far more interested in the opposite end of the settlement.

There was an old Roman bridge, now in ruins, which crossed the river opposite the southern gate. The old road from there led into Gwynedd. I would need to rebuild the bridge in timber and place a fortified gateway at one end to defend it, but I wanted to establish a trade route into Wealas. If my new shire was to prosper we needed to attract artisans and merchants to settle here and that meant access to markets wherever they could be found.

My problem was money. I had brought several coffers of silver and one of gold with me from Cent but they seemed to be emptying at an alarming rate. We'd allowed the Vikings to leave Cæstir peaceably, consequently there was no Danish plunder for us to share out. We also needed slaves to help work the farming land I planned to reclaim from nature, to construct buildings and defences and to improve the roads in the shire.

The solution to both my problems lay in raiding. The question was where? As soon as Rinan became my captain I called a meeting to discuss it with him, Eirik and Ywer. When my shire reeve arrived at my hall it was the first time he'd met Hilda and my youngest child, Æbbe. She seemed fascinated by the handsome young Norseman and, to my consternation, he seemed equally taken with her. They couldn't take their eyes off each other.

The meeting was inconclusive. Eirik thought that a raid to replenish my coffers and add to his was a splendid idea. At first he suggested a foray into Gwynedd but, although Hæsten's continuing depredations were keeping the Welsh occupied for now, I didn't want to antagonise my neighbour across the river. In fact, I wanted to try and reach an agreement with their king, Anarawd ap Rhodri, to our mutual benefit.

We met several times after that and each time I was conscious of the growing attraction between my shire reeve and my daughter. At first I was alarmed and I wasn't alone. Hilda liked the young jarl well enough but that was a very different matter to allowing the only child we'd had together to become romantically entangled with him. For a start he was a pagan.

Now that I was an ealdorman once again, Hilda had visions of Æbbe marrying a son of another Mercian ealdorman. However, the only suitable candidate was Ludeca, the fifteen year old son of the Ealdorman of Shropscīr. My daughter was now fourteen and therefore it might seem like an ideal match. However, Ludeca had been present with his father when we besieged Hæsten and I'd thought him an arrogant prig with few redeeming qualities.

He liked to boast about his military prowess. However, I'd heard what happened when he'd come across a raiding party when leading a patrol along the border with Gwynedd the year before. He'd deserted his men and fled as soon as they encountered the Welsh. His patrol had outnumbered the raiders and soon made short work of them but few had a good word to say about Ludeca after that.

'You can't be thinking of encouraging a match between our daughter and that pagan,' Hilda chided me that night, after I'd said that Æbbe could do a lot worse than Eirik. I'd had time to think about it and I'd come to the conclusion that he might make a suitable husband after all. He was relatively wealthy and, as shire reeve, had status above other thegns and jarls in Cæstirscīr.

Against that, he was a Norseman and wasn't a Christian. He was learning Ænglisc, just as I was improving my Norse, but his people would seem alien to my daughter when she went to live amongst them. It wasn't just the language, the culture was different, especially their attitude to women.

A Norse woman was, by law, the property of her husband. She had only limited freedom to dispose of any property which belonged to her without his permission. She was prohibited from participating in most political activities. She couldn't act as a witness and couldn't speak at a thing – the Norse word for an assembly. Above all, she was forbidden to carry weapons or become a leader.

Æbbe wasn't like Æthelflæd or Cuthfleda, however much she admired them, but she had a strong personality and I couldn't see her being as subservient as she would need to be as Eirik's wife.

That said, I knew of Viking women who'd flouted convention and had even become notable warriors. I'd once heard a skald sing of Lagertha the Shieldmaiden, wife of the infamous Viking king, Ragnar Lodbrok, who's death at the hands of the Northumbrians had led to the invasion by the Great Heathen Army three decades previously. She had been almost as famous as a warrior and a leader of warriors as her husband.

I'd come to the conclusion that, should they be serious about one another, I would have to talk to him and ascertain what degree of freedom he'd be prepared to allow his wife. It was with this proviso in mind that I'd inadvertently indicated to Hilda that betrothal to Eirik might not be out of the question. Of course, I now regretted not keeping my thoughts to myself until after I'd spoken to him.

'We don't even know how serious their evident infatuation with one another is,' I said, trying to placate my scandalised wife. 'It may come to naught.'

I climbed into bed and reached out for Hilda.

'Just make sure it does,' she said, turning her back to me.

I sighed and went to sleep grumbling to myself that I had enough problems without adding to them by falling out with Hilda.

✝✝✝

Once we'd discounted raiding Wealas the other options were Ynys Môn, Mann, Íralond or Northumbria. However, much as I needed more funds and slaves, I couldn't bring myself to raid people with whom I had no quarrel. Naturally, Eirik didn't see it that way and I was beginning to think I'd have to ignore my scruples when the solution to my problems presented itself. A messenger arrived from Anarawd of Gwynedd.

He wasn't what I was expecting. The inhabitants of the northern part of Wealas who I'd encountered so far had been uneducated peasants who spoke a garbled version of the Brythonic tongue. This young man wouldn't have looked out of place at Æðelred's court, or indeed at King Ælfred's.

He was dressed much the same as any young man from a noble house in Wessex or Mercia except that he wore no ribbons around his calves. The other distinction was his trousers, which were multi-coloured and rather garishly so. He had been escorted into my presence by two of my warriors, one of whom whispered in my ear that he'd arrived by ship and asked to be taken to see me.

The man was obviously nervous in case he'd done the wrong thing in bringing him into my hall but I reassured him.

'My name is Hywel ap Cadell, the nephew of King Anarawd,' the messenger said in Ænglisc, giving me a brief nod of his head which I supposed was meant to be a bow.

'You are welcome, Hywel, come sit. Can I offer you some refreshment? Mead or ale and some bread and cheese perhaps?'

'That's kind of you,' he said smiling. 'Some ale would be welcome.'

I asked after Anarawd and we made inconsequential small talk for some time until I started to wonder if he was ever going to get around to the purpose of his visit. Rinan joined us, presumably having been told that there was an important Welsh visitor in the hall. I introduced him and then decided it was time to grasp the nettle.

'You didn't come here to discuss the harvest and the weather, Hywel. What can I do for you?'

'You will know that somehow that devil Hæsten and several hundred of his Danish pagans managed to evade your escort and invaded Wealas.'

His tone indicated that, if not actually complicit in allowing the Vikings to escape and ravage Gwynedd and Powys, I wouldn't have been altogether upset about it.

'Yes, Hæsten broke his oath to me and the Mercians escorting them out of our lands weren't sufficient to prevent them leaving.'

'It might have been prevented if Lord Æðelred hadn't given them scores of horses,' he said with some asperity.

For a moment he glared at me, then his face softened and he smiled again.

'Forgive me, lord. I know it wasn't your fault but the Vikings have done untold damage to our lands, pillaging our villages, looting our monasteries and taking our people as slaves.'

'I assume that you haven't been able to bring Hæsten to battle?'

'No, he always seems to elude us when we have gathered enough men to offer battle. That's where we're hoping that you can help us.'

'King Anarawd is proposing an alliance against the Vikings?' I asked, not daring to hope it was true.

'Yes, Hæsten appears to be heading back this way. My uncles warriors are hot on his heels but, even encumbered by hundreds of slaves, livestock and several carts full of plunder, we are unable to block his path and force him to face us.'

'Where is he now?'

'When I left the king, the Danes had crossed back from Ynys Môn to the mainland and they appear to be heading along the north coast.'

'Did they attack Aberffraw?'

'No, they avoided it, unfortunately. Had they done so the defenders could have held out until our main army caught up with them.'

Aberffraw on Ynys Môn was where Anarawd had his main hall and from where he ruled his kingdom.

'Where do you think they are now?'

'Probably seeking a ford over the River Conwy. My uncle should be about two days march behind them by now.'

'I take it that Anarawd wants me to act as a blocking force to delay Hæsten until he can catch up?'

'That is his hope, yes.'

'How many men has Hæsten got?'

'About seven or eight hundred in all. He's suffered some casualties but not enough,' he said bitterly. 'However, they are split into groups. There is a rear guard which we think numbers between two and three hundred and our scouts say that there are at least two hundred more escorting the slaves, livestock and carts. That leaves perhaps three hundred in the vanguard, who are the best part of a day's march ahead of the rest.'

I nodded. I could probably muster a similar number fairly quickly and I thanked God that Lady Æthelflæd hadn't yet left with her fifty men. A week later and she would have gone south.

'The best place to hold them is probably when they try to cross the Dēvā,' Rinan said, 'but the problem is knowing where. There are several fords they might use.'

'We need to put out scouts to watch them all and hold our forces back somewhere where they can move into position quickly enough to hold the ford, once we know where they are,' I told him.

'Thank you, lord,' Hywel said with a grin. 'I'll leave now and sail back along the coast to brief my uncle.'

'Not so fast, Hywel. There's a price for my help.'

His face fell.

'We'll free the people the Vikings have enslaved and you can have half the livestock but I want the other half. I also want half the silver, although you can have back anything obviously plundered from a church.'

Hywel looked dubious.

'If your king doesn't agree then I won't block Hæsten's path out of Wealas and you'll lose your people, all the livestock as well as the silver.'

'I think he'll agree in that case, lord, though I doubt he'll be happy.'

'Surely he didn't expect us to ally ourselves with him for no reward?'

'No, I suppose not.'

He turned to go.

'Oh, there is one other condition for my help.'

'What's that, lord,' Hywel said warily.

'I want him to agree to a treaty that will keep the peace between us. If I catch any Welsh raiders I'll return them to you but I want you to deal with them severely as a lesson to others; and I want your uncle to do the same to any of my people he catches raiding in Gwynedd. I don't want them killed out of hand as that will just cause bad blood between us. If I deal with them that won't occur.'

'It makes sense to me but I can't speak for my king, of course.'

'Put it to him and then come and find me at Tatenhale. Rinan will explain where it is.'

Tatenhale was a small settlement some eight miles south east of Cæstir and four miles from the valley of the Dēvā. From there I should be able to reach any of three fords in less than half a day. I just prayed that my scouts would be able to tell me which ford the enemy vanguard were making for in time.

✝✝✝

Hywel arrived just as the last of my men reached the muster point. Thankfully Anarawd had agreed to my conditions and had even said that he welcomed the proposal for a treaty between us.

All told I had around two hundred and fifty men, mostly experienced warriors. About half were mine or Æthelflæd's and the rest were Norsemen. Unfortunately Æthelflæd had insisted on accompanying her men and Cuthfleda had come with her. I had tried to persuade them to return to the safety of Cæstir but it was like hitting your head against a stone wall.

Abbot Æscwin and his few monks had insisted on joining us as well.

'I suppose I should be grateful that my wife and Æbbe haven't joined the rest of the family,' I muttered sarcastically to Ywer.

He smiled and pointed out that his brother and the monks would be useful.

'Men always fight better if they think God is with them,' he pointed out, 'and they can help Uhtric and Leofwine with the injured.'

I grunted in reply and went off to find Rinan. Now that I didn't have to fret about everyone arriving in time I could concentrate on thinking about strategy. A quarter of an hour later I rode off towards the river with my captain, Ywer and three men as escort. The three possible crossing points were similar. A low ridge sat above the ford in each case and there were small copses dotted here and there which could be useful. The ford in the middle was the one below Fearndune. Wolnoth had all but completed his fortress – essentially a hall, huts and outbuildings surrounded by a palisade.

I'd left five elderly warriors with him to defend it just in case it was attacked by Vikings foraging away from their main body. However, I rather hoped that's where their main body would try and cross as the stronghold would provide us with a redoubt in the middle of our shield wall. It would make it much more difficult for the enemy to break our line.

I rode back to camp satisfied that I now had a sound battle plan for whichever of the crossing points the Vikings chose.

187

An hour before dusk the next day two scouts rode in to the encampment at a canter. One was Skarde, Eirik's brother, and the other Oscgar, a Mercian who I'd rescued from the Danes many years before. Both had been sent out with Lyndon and three other warriors to find the Viking vanguard. By the animated look on Skarde's face I guessed that they had found them. In contrast Oscgar's face betrayed no excitement but then he was much older and rarely betrayed his emotions.

'The vanguard have camped alongside a stream not five miles away from the Dēvā,' Skarde blurted out as soon as they'd dismounted.

Oscgar gave the boy an annoyed look and cleared his throat.

'Greetings, lord. Lyndon sent us back to report that the Danes appear to be heading for the ford at Fearndune. Judging by their progress today, he estimates that they will reach the river around midday tomorrow.'

'Thank you' I said with a grin. 'Both of you,' I added seeing Skarde's crestfallen face. 'Go and get something to eat and drink. We march at dawn tomorrow.'

CHAPTER TWELVE

Early July 894

As much as I would have loved to take my place in the middle of the shield wall, I needed to be able to see what was happening. I therefore sat on horse to the rear of the right wing where my own men were stationed together with Æthelflæd's Mercians. I had managed to persuade her to remain in the fortress together with Cuthfleda, Uhtric and Leofwine. Æscwin and the monks would join them once they had celebrated mass amongst my warband and the Mercians.

I had stationed fifteen of my men on top of the palisade as well. Each one was an excellent bowman and their main task was to whittle down the Vikings' numbers. Of course, they were also there to hold the fort should the enemy try to capture it.

Another thirty of my warriors who were adept with the bow were deployed eighty yards back from the ford in order to wreak havoc as the Vikings tried to cross the river. That left the shield wall on the right flank with less than a ninety men but the archers had orders to withdraw and join their comrades well before they were overwhelmed.

Eirik and the Norsemen were stationed on the ridge to the left of the fort. I was more worried about their ability to hold the ground than I was about my flank. It wasn't because I doubted their fighting prowess but, whereas the extreme right of my line was anchored against a small wood, there was open ground to Eirik's left. That left him vulnerable to an outflanking manoeuvre. I had therefore kept ten of my men mounted as a reserve.

We had reached Fearndune two hours before noon and waited under the hot sun for the enemy to appear. After mass had ended boys dispensed water to the warriors who took their ease, chatting quietly amongst themselves. It was a good sign. It didn't matter how experienced a warrior was, everyone but an idiot felt fear before a battle. Waiting silently only encouraged that fear to grow. Talking to one another encouraged morale and kept one's anxiety at bay.

The sun had just passed its zenith when four of my scouts came splashing across the ford. They were led by Hrodulf, another Mercian who, like Oscgar, I'd saved from the Danes twenty years ago. He and his men had been sent to keep an eye on the Vikings and make sure that they didn't head for one of the other fords at the last minute.

'They are less than half an hour behind us, lord,' Hrodulf shouted to me across the heads of the lounging warriors.

The latter got to their feet and stood with shields resting on the ground watching the far ridge for the first signs of the enemy. In complete contrast to a few minutes ago the tension was palpable. Then the enemy horde appeared, first in dribs and drabs – mainly men mounted on shaggy Welsh mountain ponies – then more and more Vikings on foot crested the skyline and made their way down to the far river bank.

When they got there they halted and a heated debate started with much gesticulation. The banner carried by one of those in the group of horsemen was of a black raven on a triangular white background – the device used by Hæsten himself – and for a moment I thought that the Viking leader was present with the vanguard but the one who appeared to be in command was much younger and had a shock of red hair. It had to be Irwyn, Hæsten's sixteen year old son.

The estimate of two to three hundred in the vanguard seemed somewhat inaccurate from what I could see. My guess would be more like three hundred and fifty of the pagans. However, my greatest concern was that the enemy would decide not to cross here but would turn south and seek another ford. It would then be a race to see who got there first; one we could lose. Furthermore, we would lose two advantages: the enemy had been marching all morning under a hot sun whereas we had enjoyed a few hours relaxation and had slaked our thirst. Furthermore, having the fort in our centre gave us a strong defensive position.

Seeing Irwyn in charge was encouraging. I knew he was hot tempered and impetuous. I was confident that he would want to attack us without delay – and so it proved. Evidently he'd overridden the concerns of those around him who were older and wiser and, without even forming them up, he dismounted and led his men into the river.

They splashed through the river in a disorganised mass. So quickly had the attack occurred that my archers were almost caught unawares. They hastily nocked arrows to their bowstrings and a second or two later a score of Vikings were killed or wounded before they'd even reached mid-stream.

The enemy held their shields by their side or still had them on their backs, so intent were they in making their way through the thigh deep water as quickly as they could. Some realised how vulnerable they were and lifted their shields to protect themselves but most hadn't done so when the next volley hit them. Over a score more fell into the water, which had now taken on a pinkish hue in places.

Losing so many men before they had crossed the river didn't seem to deter the rest. If anything it merely maddened them. By now Irwyn and about fifty of his men had reached the bank and started to run towards the archers.

I'd put Ywer in charge and I willed him to give the order to turn and run but his archers nocked another arrow and let fly. This time the Danes had the sense to use their shields to protect their bodies. Nevertheless a few arrows found the gaps between the top of the shield and the brim of the helmet or the legs below the lower rim. One of those struck in the lower thigh was Irwyn and he stumbled before one of his men caught him and kept him upright.

Furiously Hæsten's son yanked out the arrow, which caused the flow of blood to increase dramatically. Nevertheless, he

191

gritted his teeth and limped on. I might hate the Vikings but I had to admire his courage.

At last Ywer gave the order and the archers ran back up the slope at a jog. The last volley had given them breathing space and they were able to take their place in the shield wall, passing bows and quivers back through the ranks to the boys who waited to take them. Others handed them their shields and they drew their swords just in time before the first of the enemy reached them.

I believed that no more than a hundred Danes had reached my right flank but it was a different story on the left. At least half of those who had crossed the river had angled towards our Norse allies. Perhaps ten or fifteen had fallen to the archers on top of the palisade but even so the enemy still outnumbered the Norsemen. After a while whoever was in command of the Vikings on that flank decided to withdraw and the next time they attacked he'd elongated their line so that it overlapped the Norse shield wall.

The extreme left of our line had no option but to fall back and turn through ninety degrees to avoid being outflanked. It was the moment I'd been waiting for. I led my horsemen behind the fort and along the back of the Norse line until we rode clear of it. I wheeled right so that we were behind the Vikings who were forcing the Norse line back. Then we charged, levelling our spears as we rode.

We struck the rear of the Danes, spearing them in the back. Surprise was complete. Some turned to face this new threat whilst others carried on to press back the Norse line. We withdrew and then charged again. Some of my horsemen still had their spears but most of us had lost ours and used swords or axes to hack down at the Danes. When my horsemen withdrew a second time we left carnage and chaos in our wake.

The Norse, heartened by our success, now attacked the Danish shield wall with renewed vigour and the latter broke. As the Danes streamed back down the slope we pursued them, hacking down several of their number. When we drew off to the side to avoid the main body of the retreating enemy, I did a quick head count. We hadn't lost a single man, although a few had flesh wounds.

Seeing what had happened to the other flank, the Vikings fighting my warband and the Mercians also withdrew. As I made my way back up the slope I saw Irwyn being supported by two of his men as they slowly followed the others back to the river. It would have been sensible to let them go as there were still Danes all over the slope but it was too good an opportunity to miss.

Calling to my horsemen, I dug my heels in and galloped across the slope towards Irwyn. By the time the Vikings had realised what I was doing and turned back to help their leader it was too late. We had surrounded him and his two companions. All three tried to fight us off but it was all over in a few seconds. The two companions were cut down and Irwyn was disarmed and taken prisoner.

✝✝✝

What remained of the Viking vanguard milled about on the far bank after Irwyn was carried into the fort to be treated for his wound. I watched from the top of the palisade with Wolnoth as their remaining jarls argued amongst themselves and then someone rode off on one of the ponies to the west.

'I don't like the look of that,' Wolnoth mattered. 'He's going for reinforcements.'

'Well hopefully Anarawd's men are keeping them too busy to help,' Rinan replied with a grim smile.

Both sides settled down to wait. The boys went amongst our men with water and bread and the enemy sat down to eat what they had with them. Evidently they didn't have much in the way of water with them as most made their way to the river to drink. That gave me an idea and I sent for Ywer.

Five minutes later forty archers together with a guard of twenty spearmen ran down the slope and stopped fifty paces from the water's edge. They strung their bows and picked men on the far bank as individual targets. Almost immediately those drinking or filling water skins withdrew to a safe distance. Having stopped the enemy from getting fresh water Ywer waited to see what they would do next.

Ten minutes later over a hundred Danes entered the water and waded across the ford. Whoever had decided that was a good idea soon had cause to regret it as my archers peppered the slow moving column. The enemy suffered around thirty casualties before they gave up and retreated once more.

Ywer and his men returned to the top of the ridge in high spirits but they didn't have long to celebrate before I saw something that made my blood run cold. The Viking main body came into sight driving hundreds, if not thousands, of cattle and sheep before them. It was impossible to see how many warriors came with them because of the dust cloud but I knew from previous reports that they numbered at least two hundred.

They halted on the far bank and, as the dust began to settle, I could see a column of captives and wagons come over the far rise and halt part way down the slope. It was difficult to make out detail at that distance; besides my eyesight wasn't what it once was, so I asked one of the younger warriors standing nearby to tell me what he could see.

'There seem to be hundreds of captives, mainly women and children, and over a score of wagons, lord,' he replied nervously.

'How many warriors guard them?'

'Warriors? I don't think...' His voice trailed off. 'They haven't left warriors to look after them and the livestock, lord; just boys.'

I groaned inwardly. I was hoping that they would have left warriors to guard their thralls and plunder and so reduce their numbers. As a rough estimate we faced over four hundred warriors. Even given our strong position, withstanding an attack by so many was a daunting prospect.

Whoever was in charge was no fool. As I watched, the Vikings surrounded the vast herd of cattle and drove them towards the ford. The water was too deep for the sheep to wade across and so they were left on the slope with the wagons and the captives.

There was no point in sending the archers forward to try and halt the cattle. They would just waste their arrows to no purpose and could well be trampled to death. For the same reason, forming a shield wall wasn't an option. Instead I ordered all the archers to defend the walls of the fort and told the rest to form up behind the rear wall of the fort.

The stampeding cattle split in two when they reached the fort, rather like sea parted by a ship's prow. When they'd passed the fort they kept going. At least, I thought inconsequentially, we'll be able to round them up afterwards if we win this battle.

By the time the last of the herd had passed us and our army had moved back to the top of the ridge, hundreds of Vikings were making their way across the ford and some had even reached dry land on our side. This wasn't the time for me to sit on my horse and direct the battle. The arrival of new blood and the use of the cattle had demoralised our warriors and it was time to lead by example.

I thrust my way through the men busy forming a shield wall five deep to get to the front. Everyone hurriedly moved out of the way when they realised who was trying to get past them; all, that is, except one of the Mercians. He glared at me as I thrust him out of the way and, when he saw who it was, the glare changed to a look of hatred. It slightly unnerved me at the time but I didn't have time to think about it, although I do remember thinking that he reminded me of someone.

I forgot the strange incident almost immediately; I had more important things to worry about. Once I'd reached the front rank and had taken my place between Ywer and Rinan I could see what was happening. The cattle had churned up the slope and there were cowpats everywhere. This meant the Vikings had to watch their footing and several fell over in the slippery conditions.

This robbed their charge of much of its momentum. During their slog up the slope the archers on the ramparts in the centre kept up a steady fire along most of the enemy's front ranks. Once again many made the mistake of not holding their shield in front of them, which hampered movement, and scores became victims to our arrows. However, the loss of these men didn't weaken their advance sufficiently and their numbers were enough to force us back a step or two when the two armies crashed into one another.

As ever, I concentrated on the Viking facing Ywer, who was on my left. My shield protected me from the man immediately to my front but the man facing my son was unprotected, his shield being on his left arm. I thrust my sword into the Viking's neck and he fell. Rinan did the same to the man immediately facing me. It was something we constantly practiced until it became second nature and the same was happening all along the line.

The more experienced Vikings fought in the same way, of course, but the young, hot blooded ones forgot and tried to kill the man to their front. In the first ten minutes of the attack Danes lost many more than we did.

I didn't know it at the time but the Viking leader had ordered all the Norsemen who had joined Hæsten to concentrate their strength against the middle of Eirik's line. There the fighting between one group of Norsemen and the other was more intense than anywhere else and many fell on both sides.

Whilst the front ranks of the two shield walls struggled against each other the archers in the fort kept up a withering fire against the Vikings in the rear of their line. Eventually the losses here discouraged the rest of the rear ranks and they turned and fled.

The job of those in the second and subsequent ranks was to push their shields against the man in front and so prevent the enemy from forcing the line back. Of course, those in the second row could also use spears against their opponents and they also had to be ready to step in to replace those killed or badly wounded in the front rank.

Once the pressure keeping their line firm had slackened with the flight of the rear couple of ranks, we began to gain ground, pushing the Vikings back down the slope. The footing became treacherous as we advanced; apart from uneven ground caused by the passage of the cattle, it was slick with blood and littered with the dead and the dying.

I had just stabbed my sword into the thigh of the Dane trying to hack at Ywer with an axe when I felt my feet slip from beneath me. The only thing that stopped me falling was the two men either side of me and the man behind. I fell back against his shield and managed to save myself from falling. However, I was unable to defend myself for a moment and my current adversary took advantage. Rinan was just a split second too late in skewering the man with his seax and in that moment the Dane managed to bring his axe down on my shoulder.

It wasn't a strong blow, thankfully, and the chainmail held but the blow broke my clavicle. I was out of the fight and in great pain. I was dimly aware of rough hands hauling me to the rear and I nearly passed out. I gritted my teeth and managed to hold on. Once behind the rearmost rank I was helped towards the fort. One of those who supported me was Dunbeorn but, although I could only see the side of his face, I was sure the other was the Mercian who'd glowered at me as I made my way forward before the battle.

Once they'd helped me into the fort Dunbeorn sat me against the bottom of the palisade and went off to find either Uhtric or Leofwine to come and set the bone. As soon as he'd disappeared the Mercian knelt beside me and spoke softly so that no one else could hear.

'You don't recognise me do you?'

I was in considerable pain and the question didn't strike me as odd at the time; indeed I wasn't really paying all that much attention.

'I thought I'd killed you at Fearnhamme but I evidently didn't hit your head hard enough. Well, I'll make certain this time.'

So saying he pulled his seax from its sheath.

'Wait!' At least tell me why on earth you want to kill me.'

He paused, glowering at me, then he spat in my face.

'You pushed my father over the side of the ship and left him to drown and then you killed my brother.'

I knew who he was then, he was Edda's younger son, the brother of Sexmund.

'Both your father and Sexmund tried to procure my death by using assassins, and I didn't kill Sexmund. One of my men did when your brother tried to kill me at a feast.'

He ignored my protest and continued, spittle flying from his lips in his rage.

'I was driven out of Wessex and forced to fight for the wretched Mercians in order to survive. My one hope was that one day I would meet you and wreak my revenge on you. Now it seems my wish has been granted.'

With that he thrust his seax towards my throat. My left shoulder might have been incapacitated but there was nothing wrong with my right arm. I scooped up a handful of dust from the ground and threw it in the man's face. It blinded him and some must have gone into his nose and mouth because he began to cough and splutter. Although it caused me immense pain as the two broken ends of my clavicle ground together, I swung my right fist at my would-be killer's jaw and had the satisfaction of landing a solid blow.

His head jerked back and he staggered backwards looking dazed. He wiped the dust from his eyes and swore at me before lunging for my throat once more. Suddenly he arched his back before the point could pierce my skin and he fell beside me. At first I couldn't believe what had happened and then I saw Æthelflæd standing looking down at his body, a seax in her hand.

'I never did quite trust him; it was lucky for you that I saw what was going on,' she said, throwing the bloody sword onto the ground. 'He told me he was the younger son of a Saxon ealdorman when he asked to join my warband.'

'That much was true, lady. He was Edda's second son.'

'That explains a lot. Oh, forgive me, Lord Jørren, you must be in considerable pain. I'll get someone to fetch a physician.'

'Thank you,' I said, 'my servant has already gone in search of one.'

I paused, looking at the blood which had seeped out the wound in the back of my would-be assassin's neck.

'Where did you learn to use a seax? Few women would know how to kill someone as expertly as that.'

'Don't tell my husband but Cuthfleda and I sneak away to practice with a warrior I trust implicitly whenever we can.'

At that moment Leofwine arrived. He gave Æthelflæd and the dead body a curious look but said nothing. Æthelflæd nodded to him and swiftly disappeared.

Ten minutes later Leofwine had strapped me up and Dunbeorn helped me climb up to the parapet. Every step was agony but I had to see what was going on.

To my intense relief I saw that the Vikings had broken off their attack and had retreated to the bottom of the slope. The slope was strewn with the dead and the dying but I was relieved to see that the great majority were Vikings. We had also lost men, as the bodies and the seriously wounded who were being carried to the rear testified, but their losses were far greater than ours. It was then that Ywer came to see how I was and to give me the bad news that we were nearly out of arrows.

Worse news was to follow. I had anticipated the arrival of the rest of Hæsten's men, hotly pursued by Anarawd's Welsh army.

199

Then the enemy would be trapped between us. However, just as the Vikings were forming up for a fresh attack one of the men I'd left to guard Cæstir rode into the fort with news that I didn't want to hear.

Hæsten was with the rear-guard and, once he'd been told about the ongoing battle at Fearndune, he'd headed for Cæstir instead, knowing that there wouldn't be enough men left to oppose him. He'd crossed the bridge, rode past the town, and headed for the border with Northumbria. Anarawd had been in hot pursuit of him and the Welsh had kept on after the Vikings. There would be no reinforcements for the Vikings already here but we had depended on the Welsh army. Now it seemed that we were on our own.

✝✝✝

Looking down at the battlefield I estimated that the Vikings had lost around two hundred men dead or too badly injured to fight, but that still left them with more men than we had. Ten men of my own warband were casualties and both the Mercians and the Norsemen had many more losses. My greatest sadness was that Cináed was amongst the dead. He had been one of my oldest companions. Of my original warband in the far off days of the Great Heathen Army only Wolnoth and Willum were left.

I struggled to shake off the depression which threatened to unman me. The pain in my shoulder didn't help. However, I had to get a grip of myself; I still had a battle to fight.

After milling about for a while the enemy formed up again ready for another charge. Wearily we lined up ready to repulse them once more. This time we couldn't count on much support from the archers. They were down to less than ten arrows each, so I pulled half of them out of the fort to bolster our shield wall. The remainder shared out the arrows that were left.

The enemy must have been even more tired than we were and it showed as they laboriously climbed the slope towards us. A volley of arrows rained down on them but the Danes had learned to hold their shields above their heads and few did any damage.

I turned to Wolnoth, who commanded the fort, and was about to say something when he yelled for his men to conserve the arrows they had left until the enemy had engaged our line. Then they could hit their rear ranks as the Danes pushed their shields against the man in front.

Tired men all along the line fought against each other. More men fell and then disaster struck. I heard a wail of despair from my left. Eirik had been badly wounded and was being carried to the rear. I was tempted to rush out and see how badly injured he was but my place was where I could see what was going on.

One of the other Norse jarls took charge but the loss of Eirik had disheartened the rest and gradually our left flank gave ground. I told Wolnoth to concentrate what arrows he had left on the Vikings pushing our Norse allies back. It helped, and the Norsemen stopped giving ground. Thankfully, the south palisade of the fort still anchored their right flank but their left was in danger of being outflanked.

I no longer had any horsemen to help them. They had long since joined the shield wall. However I did still have a total of twenty five men in the fort. The archers had all but run out of arrows and so I led them out of the east gate and along behind the Norsemen.

The Danes hadn't seen us and so, when we launched ourselves into their right flank from the side, they were taken completely unawares. Their flank crumbled and fled back down the slope leaving a score of dead and wounded behind them; not that I could claim any credit, I was merely a spectator from the rear.

Our combined strength was now more than that of our remaining adversaries and they were being attacked on two sides.

Minutes later they too joined the headlong flight back down the slope.

I seized the opportunity and, leaving Wolnoth to watch for any attempt by the routed Vikings to rally, I sought out the jarl who had taken command when Eirik had fallen.

'If we attack the remaining Danes in the rear we can still win this battle.'

He nodded in understanding and moments later he led his men around the front of the fort and fell upon the Danish rear. They were now trapped and what had been a fairly evenly matched struggle now became a slaughter. Now the enemy had only one thing on their minds – fighting their way clear and escaping.

The rout was complete and those who were still alive fled back to the river and kept going across the ford. Those already there joined them and the remnants of the Vikings ran towards the wagons full of plunder and the Welsh captives.

'Ywer,' I shouted, 'pursue them and seize the wagons. Make sure the Welsh thrall are safe as well.'

He nodded and immediately sent the Norsemen and Mercians after the retreating Danes. A few minutes later he rode out of the fort with fifty horsemen – all that remained of my warband – and soon overtook those on foot. Some of the Danes had stopped at the wagons to take whatever they could carry with them. It was a mistake which they paid for with their lives.

I watched until Ywer and my men had disappeared over the far ridge in pursuit of the remaining enemy and then sat down on the ground feeling incredibly weary. We'd won but it had been a very close run thing.

CHAPTER THIRTEEN

Autumn 894 / Spring 895

It was over three months before Eirik fully recovered. He was luckier than Irwyn. Despite the best efforts of Uhtric and Leofwine, the Dane's wound festered and his blood became poisoned. He died three weeks after the battle.

After a miserably wet September the weather had at last changed and warm sunshine bathed the land. Getting the crops in had been a struggle and we would have to be careful to use our food supplies sparingly over the winter but otherwise everything in the world seemed to be well.

Hilda and I smiled at each other as we waited in Cæstir's timber church for Æbbe's arrival. Eirik paced to and fro nervously whilst Ywer did his best to calm his nerves. My elder son stood in front of the simple wooden table that served as an altar resplendent in his abbot's robes.

Æbbe had insisted on tending to Eirik personally during his long recovery and it came as a surprise to nobody when they became betrothed. Whatever worries Hilda and I had about our daughter becoming a Norse wife had long since vanished. Eirik had been baptised a Christian a few days ago and several of his people had joined him in embracing Christianity. The majority of his followers still clung to their pagan beliefs but, contrary to my expectations, they seemed to have had no problem with their jarl changing allegiance to what they called the Nailed God.

My shoulder had taken six weeks to mend and it still ached slightly in wet weather but otherwise I was as fit as anyone else who had just celebrated their forty third birthday.

We'd heard that Hæsten had made it back to Ēast Seaxna Rīce and had constructed a new fortress on the banks of the River Lygan. I'd been confident that his army had been so weakened by the battle at Fearndune that he no longer posed much of a threat to Wessex or Mercia. I was wrong. Cuthfleda had come north for her sister's wedding and brought the latest tidings with her. Most of those who'd survived Fearndune had eventually made their way to the encampment on the River Lygen.

Even so that would have brought his numbers, with those who had escorted the families, to something between eight and nine hundred warriors. Unfortunately, it seemed that he had collected more recruits during his journey through southern Northumbria, the Danelaw and East Anglia. Furthermore, a fleet of longships had crossed from Frankia bringing another three hundred Danes and Norsemen to serve under his banner. The latest estimates put his current strength at just under fifteen hundred fighting men.

Much to our surprise and delight Ywer's twin sister Kjestin arrived two days before the wedding together with her husband Odda, eldest son of Ealdorman Eadred of Dyfneintscīr. As Kjestin had given birth just a few months previously I wasn't sure that they'd come. I'd have dearly loved to have seen my first grandchild but I fully understood why they had left him at home with his wet nurse.

One of the other guests attending my daughter's wedding was Hywel ap Cadell, King Anarawd's nephew. He was there to represent the King of Gwynedd who had confirmed our alliance shortly after our defeat of the Vikings. He had had the grace to apologise for leaving us to face the great majority of the enemy and he had expressed his gratitude for the release of the Welsh captives.

Anarawd hadn't been so magnanimous when it came to division of the livestock and the plunder, both of which I had taken back to Cæstir. As we had captured it without his assistance I told him that our original arrangement was no longer valid and the split should be reviewed. After a lot of haggling he had agreed to divide the livestock down the middle and to let me keep all the gold and silver except for what had evidently been looted from churches and monasteries.

That gave me enough cattle and sheep to stock every occupied vill and farmstead in Cæstirscīr and it replenished my coffers. I was as wealthy now as I had ever been, even after distributing half of it to every warrior who had survived and to every widow of those who had perished.

With the offer of livestock to every new settler I could attract, the population of my shire had grown over the past summer, although we could do with a lot more slaves to help work the land. As I stood awaiting the arrival of my daughter and her attendants I felt more confident about the future than I had for a long time.

I glanced over at Eirik. He was dressed in even finer raiment than usual. His trousers were dyed a rich red and were tucked into soft brown leather boots that came up to just below the knee. The latter must have cost a fortune all on their own. His tunic was made of bright blue wool through which silver wire had been threaded and his sword belt was studded with semi-precious stones. In the tradition of all Norse and Danish warriors, he wore several gold and silver rings on his bare arms.

I must have looked like a poor relative in comparison. My trousers of dark green were tied up to the knee with yellow ribbons and I wore my comfortable everyday shoes. On top of my plain linen under-tunic I wore a dark blue knee length tunic whose sole decoration was red woollen embroidery at the neck and ends of the sleeves. My sword belt was of plain black leather. However, I did wear my gold seal ring on my right hand and a chain of gold around my neck, symbolising my rank as an ealdorman.

A hush descended on the assembled family and guests as Æbbe entered followed by Cuthfleda as her principle attendant and several young girls - the daughters of local jarls and thegns.

Æbbe looked every inch a nobleman's daughter. Her under-tunic of embroidered white linen reached the ground. Over this she wore a fine woollen surcoat dyed a deep blue. It was ornately embroidered at both neck and hem and the ends of her three-quarter length sleeves were trimmed with fur. A red leather purse hung from a belt of the same colour which was decorated with gold studs.

As an unmarried girl she had worn her fair hair plaited. Now it was hidden under a loose white linen veil which was held in place by a plain silver circlet. I had always thought of her as my little girl but I realised with a start that she had grown into a very pretty young woman.

The ceremony itself was unremarkable except for one thing. Most marriages amongst the nobility are arranged by the parents and are either political or intended to gain land. This was neither; Eirik and Æbbe were in love and it showed throughout the ceremony. Even Skarde stopped scowling at his half-brother.

I was disappointed that Æðelred and Æthelflæd hadn't been able to come to the wedding. I knew it was a hundred and thirty miles from Glowecestre but, if Odda and Kjesten could come all the way from Escanceaster, I had hoped that they might attend; especially as it would be an opportunity for them to see what progress had been made with the defences of the most northerly part of Anglian Mercia.

It was only later that I heard that they had been summoned to Wintanceaster along with Edward. King Ælfred was gravely ill.

✝✝✝

Winter came early that year. In contrast to the mild weather of early October, the rest of the autumn was cold and miserable. Mornings were characterised by freezing fog which barely dispersed at all some days and chilly grey afternoons when it did. I don't remember seeing the sun at all until mid-December.

Although the weather over the period leading up to Christmas was generally fine, the sunny periods did little to warm the ground or even chase away the damp which still clung to everything. My shoulder ached in these conditions but I decided that I should visit as many settlements as possible to make sure that they were as well prepared for a harsh winter as possible.

I sent Eirik and Ywer out to visit the more far flung places whilst I concentrated on the nearby settlements. My last call was on Wolnoth at Fearndune. The last traces of the battle had long since been removed and any damage repaired. However, my old friend was not in such good shape.

He had collapsed two days previously and had taken to his bed. I found him surrounded by his wife, two sons and the one remaining unmarried daughter. We had known each other for nearly thirty years. He was an orphan who'd trained as a scout in Northumbria and had joined my warband after the capture of Eforwic by the Great Heathen Army. At the time he'd been fourteen, a year younger than me.

He'd soon proved himself to be a good tracker, hunter and pathfinder but he seemed to prefer his own company to that of others. Slowly that had changed over the years but he was always a man of few words; however, those words were always worth listening to.

I rode away from Fearndune sad at heart, knowing that I wouldn't see my old friend again in this life. His eldest son was now twenty and a credit to his parents. He would succeed Wolnoth as thegn and I had every confidence in him but that was small comfort to me. One's early forties was no great age to die but very few of my friends and companions had lived so long.

Two days later the wind changed direction and an icy blast from the north turned the damp that coated everything to ice. The clouds turned a much darker shade of grey and I felt snow in the air. I decided that there was just one last chance to go hunting and increase our supply of smoked meat before it was too late.

I decided to take Ywer, Eafer, Eomær, Arne and Skarde with me.

'Why Skarde?' Hilda asked me when I told her. 'The rest are close companions but he's just a petulant boy.'

'Precisely because he feels out of place here. He's the only Norse boy training to be a scout and his resentment at being here depresses everyone he comes in contact with. You know how fractious people can get when confined indoors in winter; I don't want him to get into a fight with serious consequences.'

'So you're hoping that by selecting him to go hunting with you, you'll establish a bond with him?' she asked sarcastically. 'It's more likely that the other boys will be jealous and the gulf between them will widen.'

I suppose she might have had a point but it was too late now. The invitation had been issued.

Even wearing my warm wolfskin cloak I felt cold as we rode out of Cæstir and headed towards the forest that lay five miles or so to the east. Behind the riders two huntsmen ran with a pair of boarhounds each followed by two slaves leading packhorses on which to carry back any kills we made. I sent Arne ahead with Skarde. Their job was to find the trail of any of the boars who lived in the forest; the dogs would then lead us to the animals – at least, that was my hope. Arne knew that he was also to look out for any sign of humans. Since the defeat of the Vikings, my shire had been relatively peaceful but that didn't mean that there weren't roving packs of Danes or Norsemen around who were bent on raiding.

We carried boar spears but we also wore byrnies and were armed with swords and seaxes. My hearth warriors also had bows and a quiver of arrows hanging from their saddle horns. Arrows wouldn't stop a charging boar; the bows were there in case we ran into trouble.

The spears we carried were specifically designed for hunting boar. They were shorter and heavier than a war spear and had a crosspiece on the spear socket behind the blade which acted as a barrier to prevent the spear from penetrating too deeply into the boar. If that happened it was liable to get stuck or break. Furthermore, it was designed to stop a furious boar, even a badly injured one, from working its way up the shaft of the spear to attack the hunter.

The icy wind chilled us to the bone and we were glad when we reached the relative shelter of the forest. For the first two hours Arne and Skarde failed to find anything and I thought that we might be getting frozen for no purpose. It was Skarde who spotted the faint traces of a boar's spoor.

It wasn't much – merely the broken end of a fern – so it showed how much the boy had already learned about tracking. He knew it marked the passing of a boar because of a couple of hairs attached to it. There's no mistaking the coarse bristles of a boar for those of any other animal. A little further on there was a patch of ground in the lee of a large oak tree that wasn't frozen like the surrounding area.

'What do you make of the tracks?' I asked Skarde.

He knelt down and studied the faint marks for some time before replying.

'There are three animals: a large sow and two of her young, probably squeakers about to become juveniles.'

Squeaker was the term for a piglet up to ten months old; those between ten months to a year were called juveniles.

'Why a sow and not a male boar?' I asked him.

'Because males are solitary animals except in the breeding season.'

'Very good, Skarde. Now which way are they headed?'

He studied the marks again.

'That way,' he said, pointing in the direction we were going.

I was impressed. Not many boys of his age could have discerned that from the faint marks in the earth.

It was time to let the hounds follow the trail. Given the temperature, the boars' odour would be faint, especially if the boars had passed here some time ago, but they quickly picked up the scent. Hopefully that meant that we weren't too far behind our prey.

It took us half an hour to run the boars to ground. Some hunters would have used the hounds to attack the animals first, to wound and weaken them, but I had more respect for my dogs than that. Inevitably some would end up injured, or even dead, and all because the hunters wanted to make their task safer and easier. It wasn't my way of doing things; it was our job to make the kills.

'Skarde stay back. Your job is done. Eafer, you take the squeaker on the right and Arne you take the one on the left. Ywer and I will tackle the sow. Eomær, stay ready to step in and help whoever needs it.'

We handed the reins of our horses to Skarde and advanced cautiously towards the three boars. The sow was enormous. She stood at nearly forty inches at the shoulder and must have weighed well over two hundred pounds. In contrast the two squeakers were less than half her size. They had lost the stripes that characterised piglets and I guessed that they were both females. They tended to stay with their mothers later than male squeakers. I estimated that the two youngsters were around eight months old, having been born in the early spring.

Boars are dangerous animals at the best of times; sows protecting their young are ferocious and quite fearless. Suddenly she charged towards me. Boars can't run that fast but they have tremendous momentum. I braced myself and held my spear ready to pierce her mouth. The quickest way to kill a boar was to penetrate its brain. Ywer stood to one side ready to aim his spear just behind the foreleg in the hope of piercing her heart.

The sow was cleverer that I'd expected. She moved to the side slightly just as I was about to strike and, instead of entering her mouth, my spear grazed the side of her face and penetrated her shoulder. Meanwhile Ywer had stabbed her side but the point hit a rib and was defected along her flank, giving her a shallow cut.

I was forced back by the ferocity of the sow's attack. Thankfully the spear point was lodged deep in her shoulder. Had she been able to shake it free she would have killed me, and probably my son as well. I held onto the shaft of my spear as the sow struggled to reach me but it was hard work and a couple of times she nearly wrenched it from my hands. Ywer had stabbed her again and, although he managed to thrust the point between her ribs this time, he didn't hit a vital organ.

I was tiring and the sow showed no sign of weakening. The next moment I was conscious of a horse riding past me. The rider stabbed down at the sow's back as he rode past and suddenly the fight went out of the animal. Her spine was broken and she was unable to use her back legs.

Ywer stabbed her once more as she lay helpless and this time he found her heart. I stood there exhausted and shaking with relief. I looked around seeking the identity of the horseman who had saved us and saw Skarde's grinning face looking down at me. Ywer came and embraced me. I think we both felt that our time had come. I thumped his back before letting go and holding my hand out to Skarde.

'I owe you my life, Skarde. Name your reward.'

I had expected him to ask for a silver arm ring or perhaps a purse of coins but he surprised me by asking to join my gesith. He was barely fourteen and, although legally an adult, no one had joined my hearth warriors at such a young age. However, he had proved himself a good tracker and he didn't lack courage.

'Very well. But first you must complete your training as a scout and prove to me that you have mastered the bow. All my hearth warriors are expert archers.'

'It will give me something to do during the winter,' he replied in near perfect Ænglisc, a broad grin lighting up his face.

I was puzzled as to why it had been Skarde who had come to our rescue and not Eomær but it transpired that Arne was also in danger. His squeaker had managed to evade his spear and had

211

gored him, not badly but Eomær had to step in and kill the squeaker before it did any more damage to Arne. Thankfully Eafer had managed to make a clean kill.

Eomær stitched the gash in Arne's side whilst the slaves gutted and loaded the boars onto the pack horses. Once back at my hall they would be skinned, butchered and put in the smokehouse.

We set off back to Cæstir in a jubilant mood but it didn't last long. The long threatened snow started to fall before we'd gone a mile. By the time we'd reached my hall it was snowing so heavily I could hardly see ten yards in front of me. It was going to be a long, hard winter.

✝✝✝

Thankfully spring came early. By early March the snow had all but gone but it left behind a morass of mud that made all but the old Roman roads impassable. Gradually the ground dried out and towards the end of the month a messenger arrived from Æðelred asking me to meet him at Glowecestre. A day later a pedlar arrived which caused Hilda and the other women considerable excitement. His cart included bolts of cloth, embroidery thread and other necessities for making new clothes. Of more interest to me and the other men was the news that he brought.

Ælfred was said to have made a full recovery, which came as a great relief. Hæsten had left his winter quarters at Meresai and had moved towards Lundenburg with his host – men, women and children. He was said to have halted at a place the pedlar called Herutford.

It was not somewhere I'd heard of but it meant the ford of the hart. The pedlar said that it was on the River Lygan some thirty miles due north of Lundenburg. As such it was in the Danelaw but in an area with no central ruler. As it was so close to an important port and trading centre the local Danes had come to an accommodation with the Mercians and lived in harmony with them. No doubt they were as unhappy with the arrival of the Viking horde as Æðelred must be.

I left Eirik and Ywer in joint charge of the shire and set off on the road south with my gesith. Following the losses we'd suffered at Fearndune it numbered a mere eighteen warriors, including the youngest member – Skarde. He had done what he'd promised and over the winter he had honed his skills as a tracker as well as becoming reasonably proficient with the bow. He still needed to build up the muscles in his arms and shoulders but he could hold his own with the majority of my bowmen.

I was afraid that he would be ostracised by his fellow hearth warriors, not because he was Norse – there were Danes, Norsemen, Saxons, Mercians, Northumbrians and Jutes in my gesith – but because of his youth. Most had to wait until they were eighteen or older before they joined. However, I needn't have worried. The courage he had shown during the boar hunt made him something of a hero.

The journey was uneventful and even the weather was pleasant. I had scarcely had time to wash the dust off and change my clothes before Æðelred sent for me. When I was shown into his presence I found him seated behind a table in a small chamber off the main hall. Æthelflæd sat beside him and I saw Cuthfleda in a corner with my great-nephew, the four year old Æthelstan. To my astonishment he was reading from a Latin Bible. He needed help from my daughter with quite a few of the words but he was remarkably proficient for a boy his age. Even novice monks couldn't read a word of Ænglisc until they were much older than he was.

I tore my attention away from them and concentrated on what Æðelred was saying.

'Ælfred has asked us to remove the Vikings from the vicinity of Lundenburg. Although it is within the Danelaw he doesn't trust Hæsten and thinks he could use it as a base to raid along the valley of the River Temes or even attack Lundenburg itself.'

'I see, and he expects Mercia to do this alone, lord?'

'No, he will support us with his army but it is a long way from Wessex and so Mercia has to be seen as the protagonist.'

'Even so, won't that compromise the tacit understanding we have reached with the Danes in the other half of Mercia?'

'It might, but I have been in touch with the local jarls and they would welcome our intervention. Hæsten expects them to feed his horde and he is actively recruiting amongst their young men.'

'How many men is Ælfred expecting us to contribute?'

'He has asked for a thousand. He is providing fifteen hundred from Cent and the eastern shires.'

My heart sank. That meant Edward and Oswine would be with his army. I suppose I should have expected it.

'How many men can you bring with you from Cæstirscīr?'

'When is he planning to move against Hæsten?'

'In May.'

'The fyrd will be busy preparing for harvesting; in any case I can't take too many fighting men away from the shire in case of attack.'

'Can you provide a hundred seasoned warriors?'

'Yes, just about. I have to leave some to garrison Cæstir and to patrol our borders.'

'That will have to do then.'

We spent the next hour or so discussing tactics before I was allowed to retire.

That evening Cuthfleda came to see me.

214

'Æthelflæd is worried about Æthelstan,' she told me. 'Edward is looking for a new bride and she has heard rumours that he wants to send his son to Cantwareburh as a novice.'

'What? He's only four! He's far too young.'

'I hear that Edward is considering Ælfflæd, the daughter of Ealdorman Æthelhelm of Wiltshire but Æthelhelm wants to be certain that it will be his grandson who becomes heir to the throne and not Æthelstan.'

'Surely Ælfflæd is far too young for marriage. What is she? Nine?'

'Ten, but we are only talking about betrothal at this stage, or so I've heard.'

'Why? Why Ælfflæd?'

'Because Edward is worried about a challenge for the throne from his cousin Æðelwold. Edward now controls the eastern shires but he wants a strong ally in western Wessex.'

It made sense. Æðelwold was the son of an elder brother who was the king before Ælfred. Æðelwold, or his brother, would normally have been strong contenders for the throne when their father died but they were too young at the time. The elder brother wasn't interested in becoming king after Ælfred but Æðelwold had made no secret of his desire for the crown. He wasn't an ealdorman but he had inherited many of his father's vills and consequentially he was both rich and powerful.

What depressed me most was that Ælfred was only two years older than me and already his son was making plans for when his father died. It was true that Ælfred had a weak constitution and had to be very careful about what he ate, whereas I still felt reasonably healthy, even if my joints and wounds ached at times. All the same it made me feel as if my days were numbered.

'What does Æthelflæd plan to do about her nephew?'

'If Edward sends for him she wants to send him to you in Cæstir and for you to train him to be a warrior.'

215

That was all very well but Edward already loathed me; if I thwarted him over his plans for his son it would only make relations between us ten times worse. However, I'd liked what little I'd seen of Æthelstan. He wasn't the bastard he was portrayed to be and I felt that robbing him of his inheritance was morally wrong. Edward might pretend that his son was illegitimate but I knew that he had married my niece and I had the proof. At that moment I decided that, come what may, when the time came I'd champion Æthelstan's cause.

CHAPTER FOURTEEN

Summer 895

It was early June by the time we reached Ælfred's encampment to the south of the Viking fort. The journey down Casingc Stræt had been uneventful; not that I had anticipated any trouble with such a large body of warriors. My warriors were all mounted but less than half of the rest of my little army had horses and so we travelled in three groups.

I led with my gesith followed by the wagons carrying everything we'd need for the camp, the servants and the Norse warriors on foot. The rear guard, consisting of Ywer and the rest of the mounted warriors, brought up the rear. We made slow progress, covering about fifteen miles each day, but I was in no rush to get there. In truth, I wasn't looking forward to encountering Edward again.

When we arrived we were shown to a site beside the rest of the Mercian contingent and, leaving Rinan to set up camp, Ywer and I went to find Æðelred. Unsurprisingly both Æthelflæd and my eldest daughter were present together with three other ealdormen.

'Ah, Jørren, excellent,' Æðelred said, full of bonhomie. 'You know everyone I think? Good. Ælfred has summoned a war council; come, walk beside me and tell me the latest news from Cæstirscīr.'

I nodded a greeting to the other occupants and then we made our way through the mud that had already been churned up by hundreds of feet towards the large pavilion at the centre of the camp. I told Æðelred the news from the north, such as it was, and then fell back to speak to my fellow ealdormen. I thought that I had noticed a few dark looks when Æðelred had selected me to walk with him and I was anxious lest they felt any animosity towards me. However, they included me in their group readily enough and seemed relaxed in my company; perhaps I was imagining things. One of them was in the middle of a bawdy tale about one of his priests when we arrived at the king's pavilion.

We were the last to arrive so we four ealdormen stood at the back whilst Æðelred made his way to the front to sit beside Ælfred, Edward and Archbishop Plegmund on a raised platform. Ywer had stayed behind with his sister and the Lady Æthelflæd. Her husband might regard her as his counsellor but the nobles of Wessex would have been scandalised had she attended the war council.

I studied Edward closely. He was now twenty and had filled out since I'd last seen him. He'd also grown a beard, not a long one such as the Vikings favoured, but one closely trimmed to the face. It made him look older.

His father looked more haggard than hitherto, no doubt a consequence of his recent ill health. In truth, he looked more like a man ten years older than his real age. However, his eyes still sparkled and, as we were to discover, his mind was as keen as ever.

'More Vikings are arriving by longship every week. We need to prevent any more joining Hæsten,' the king began after the usual prayers. 'They have stripped the surrounding area of food and so they are using their ships to raid and forage along the Temes estuary. If we can close the river to them we can starve them out without another pitched battle.'

Ælfred looked around the tent, his piercing eyes looking into those of every man there. Seemingly satisfied, he continued.

'To that end I intend to build a bridge across the river with a fort at each end. That will prevent the longships already upstream from raiding and others from joining. They are unlikely to sally forth to attack the forts because they would then be caught between the fortifications and our army.'

I had to admit that it was a clever plan. I would have probably used a chain boom to close the river but I could see why a bridge

218

was better. That way our forces could move from bank to bank as required.

The following day work started on clearing the site and the Mercians were given the task of defending the men – mainly slaves – brought in to do the construction work. They were forced to work from dawn to dusk – some sixteen hours with only a short break for bread and water at midday. By the end of the second day the ground was cleared and work on the bridge piers had started.

I was idly watching progress on the third day when Arne came to find me.

'Lord, there are two longships coming downriver,' he said breathlessly.

We had been caught off guard. We had men guarding all the approaches on land but neither Æðelred nor I had anticipated a foray by ship. I doubted that Hæsten was yet aware of the bridge being built several miles from his fort. It was pure mischance that his men had stumbled upon the construction work.

By the time I had gathered my archers to pepper the crews from the bank, the Vikings had backed up their ships and were busy turning them around. It wasn't an easy task in the confines of the river and one of them ran aground whilst attempting to do so. My archers ignored the hapless crew for now and concentrated on the longship now rowing furiously back upriver. Perhaps a quarter of their rowers were killed or wounded but they had made it around the bend by the time that enough of my men had mounted their horses and given chase.

Meanwhile, someone had gathered enough Mercians together to attack the grounded longship. I left Ywer to lead the horsemen who had set off in pursuit of the second longship and turned my attention to the stranded one. Its crew had made it onto the bank and had formed a shield wall. They were heavily outnumbered but they seemed determined to put up a fight. I called on the Mercians who were about to attack them to stop. Some of them were my men but many were from other shires and didn't know me.

Nevertheless, they hesitated. A few hotheads relished a fight with the hated Vikings but most were sensible enough to wait for orders. Just at that moment Æðelred arrived with two other ealdormen.

'Why did you stop my men attacking the heathen scum,' he asked angrily.

'Because there is no point in wasting lives, lord. I want to give the enemy a chance to surrender,' I replied calmly.

'What will you do with them if they do?'

'Offer them land in Cæstirscīr if they will swear to convert to Christianity and give me their oaths.'

'You'd trust them?' he asked, astounded by my reply.

'We need more settlers, and ones who can fight, if we are to defend the shire against the Northumbrians and against the Norsemen of Cumbria.'

He nodded thoughtfully.

'Very well, you can try. What will you do if they refuse?'

'I don't think they will. That's a Norse longship; its crew came here in search of plunder but I think they also came in search of a place to settle.'

Over the last few months I had improved my Norse; it wasn't too dissimilar to Danish and so it wasn't that difficult to master. Strictly speaking what we called Norse was more properly known as West Norse whilst Danish was derived from East Norse. The main differences were ones of pronunciation and grammar, rather than vocabulary. I therefore decided to speak to the crew who were eyeing us warily, weapons at the ready.

'Who's your jarl?' I called to them.

'Who wants to know?'

The speaker was a large man with iron grey hair and a long beard. Strangely the beard was more of a mixture of colours – grey in the main but interspersed with streaks of red and in one place a solid band of pure white. I guessed that the latter had grown over an old wound.

'I'm Jørren, Hertogi of Mercia.'

Hertogi meant commander and was the nearest word they had for the Ænglisc term hereræswa.

'I've heard of you, Jørren. It's said that you are an honourable man. What is it you want before we kill you and the effete Mercians with you?'

It was brave talk for someone whose men were outnumbered by at least ten to one but typical of the boastful Norse.

'You still haven't told me your name.'

'I'm called Bjørn Frami.'

Frami was a nickname which meant many things; amongst them ability, courage, fame, success and lucky.

'Well Bjørn, it seems that your luck has run out today. We don't even need to risk any of our lives to eliminate you. Keep a tight grip on your weapons as we send you all to Valhalla.'

I nodded at Rinan and forty archers stepped in front of the ring of steel which surrounded the Viking crew on three sides. Each man had an arrow nocked and now they raised their bows threateningly.

'There is an alternative, of course.'

The Vikings, who had been on the point of charging, intent on taking at least some of us with them, hesitated as Bjørn held up his hand.

'What alternative? If you're offering us thraldom, forget it.'

It was only at that point that I saw that there were women and children on the longship. They had evidently been crouching down below the gunwale but now their curiosity had got the better of them.

'You're not only risking the lives of your men but those of your women and children as well.'

Bjørn glanced behind him and yelled at those still on the beached longship to get their heads down.

'What good will that do? When you are all dead we can simply kill your families or sell them into slavery, as it pleases us.'

'You mentioned an alternative,' he said after a long pause.

'Yes, jarl. Are these men sworn to you or to Hæsten.'

'I'm no jarl,' he replied scornfully. 'These men have chosen me as their hersir; they are their own men.'

'Do you mean that you aren't sworn to serve Hæsten?'

'We left Orkneyjar because Jarl Hallad Rognvaldsson failed to protect us from the Danes who've taken our lands. We hate Danes but we heard that Hæsten was promising warriors who joined him land and riches. However, when we got here we found that he can't even provide for the followers he already has; so we decided to leave and seek our fortune elsewhere.'

I thought that Guthorm Sigurdsson was Jarl of Orkneyjar but presumably he'd died or been killed and this man Hallad had taken his place. By the sound of it the Danes were giving him as much trouble as they were giving us.

'If I offered you land and livestock in return for your oaths, would you serve me?'

'You're not a Norseman, not even a bloody Dane. How do I know we can trust you?'

'Why would I lie? What purpose would it serve? I need settlers because my land is underpopulated and I need warriors to help me defend it.'

'He speaks true, Bjørn Frami, I'm Eirik Fairhair, Jarl of Myrteland. I've given my oath to Lord Jørren, as have all the Norse jarls in Cæstirscīr. The land has good soil for farming, rich pastures and plenty of wood, unlike Norþweg or Orkneyjar.'

Bjørn turned to the warriors around him and there was a brief discussion before he replied.

'Given the choice between death or a promising future we've decided to choose the latter,' he said with a smile.

'There is one further condition,' Eirik added. 'Many of us are Christians now and you and your family will be expected to set an example to the rest, be baptised and follow the faith of the Nailed God.'

At this Bjørn's grin became even wider.

'You assumed that we are pagans, Lord Jørren, when you mentioned Valhalla. Like many in our part of Orkneyjar, we are already Christians.'

So saying, he pulled a silver crucifix from under his byrnie.

☩☩☩

I was feeling elated at the addition of thirty experienced warriors to my warband, not to mention more settlers for my land. However, my joy was short lived. The next day I received dire news.

The second longship had reached Hæsten's camp and that night the two dozen or so longships moored there had come downstream. Forced to flee before they were trapped upriver by Ælfred's bridge, they had decided to make a run for it now. I knew that my old friend Cei, the Sæ Hereræswa of Wessex, waited in the Temes estuary. He was there to stop any more seaborne Vikings from joining Hæsten so he wasn't expecting the sudden appearance of the enemy fleet from the River Lygan.

I was told that most of the Vikings managed to slip past Cei's ships in the darkness but his own ship encountered two of the enemy. Cei's longship was larger than the two snekkjur who attacked it but his crew was outnumbered. By all accounts his men fought bravely and killed so many of the Vikings that they broke off the fight and fled out to sea.

The rest of the Wessex fleet gave chase to the enemy until dawn. By then they were mere specks on the horizon visible only from the tops of our masts. However, they were heading east,

223

towards Frisia and not along the coast of Cent. That was good news but it came at a great cost. Cei, my companion when I'd left home in search of my brother three decades before, had been killed in the fighting.

I was saddened beyond measure. Jerrick, Cei's former deputy and commander of the fleet in the western half of Wessex, had been ill for a few months and had been replaced by a man I didn't know. By the sound of it Jerrick wasn't likely to recover. Now that Cei was dead practically all my old comrades were gone. Doubtless Ælfred would appoint some toady of Edward's as Cei's replacement and my last link with the fleet I'd been responsible for creating would be gone.

Ywer found me sitting slumped in a chair in my tent with an empty flagon of mead in my hand. I was so despondent after learning about Cei's death that I did something I'd never done before – I'd got blind drunk on my own.

'Father, wake up. What's the matter with you? Ælfred is asking for you.'

I opened my somewhat bleary eyes and peered myopically at my son. All I could see was a blurred image and my head felt as if someone was battering it with several hammers. I closed my eyes again.

'Go away,' I muttered, 'leave me in peace.'

'The king wants to see you. Wake up. God, you're drunk,' he said in disgust.

'Fine one to talk,' I mumbled. 'You get drunk all the time.'

'Yes, with friends, never on my own like this. What's got into you?'

'Cei's dead.'

Ywer hadn't been born when Cei had been one of my closest companions. He knew him, of course, but he and I had gone our separate ways by then. He had remained with the fleet when I'd ceased to be the sǣ hereræswa and we hadn't seen much of each

224

other after that. That somehow made his loss all the more poignant.

Then something struck me like a hammer blow. Even in my befuddled state I remembered that Cei had a family. They lived in the fortress at Dofras on the south coast of Cent. Cei owned no land and relied on his stipend from the king and on his share of the loot from Vikings and other pirates for income. All that would now cease.

That thought sobered me up more than the bucket of water that Ywer through over me. I spluttered with anger but it had done the trick. Instead of yelling at him I felt disgusted with myself, especially when I realised that I'd vomited all over my fine clothes in my drunken stupor.

My thoughts returned to Cei's family as I staggered to my feet. The least I could do was to offer them a vill. I tried to work out how old his eldest son was. I thought that he was probably fifteen; just old enough to become a thegn.

In response to Ywer's shout Dunbeorn appeared from wherever he'd been hiding and fetched me some clean clothes. The thought that he'd been so scared of me when I was in my cups that he had left me unattended did as much to sober me up as anything. By the time that I entered the king's tent I was almost myself again.

'Ah! There you are. What kept you so long?' Ælfred asked peevishly.

There were six other people in the tent. Edward and my stepson, Oswine, glowered at me whilst Æðelred, Æthelflæd and Bishop Asser merely looked annoyed that I had kept them waiting. I didn't recognise the sixth person but he was dressed like a Dane.

Ælfred didn't wait for an answer before introducing the stranger as Gunbiørgh, the nephew of King Eohric of East Anglia.

'Tell Lord Jørren what you told me,' the king said.

'King Eohric is weary of acting as host to the Viking horde. He's expected to feed them and put up with their marauding and pillaging. Furthermore, many of his young warriors deserted him to join Hæsten. He asks for your help to exterminate them once and for all.'

'Will your uncle face them in battle then?'

The young man shook his head.

'No, Hæsten is something of a legend to us. His exploits in the Mediterranean with Björn Ironside, the son of Ragnar Lodbrok, earned him a reputation which he enhanced considerably during his time in Frankia. Although we want rid of him, he is a hero, almost a legend, and few Danes would be willing to fight him.'

'I don't understand, cyning,' I said turning to Ælfred. 'If the East Anglians won't aid us what is Gunbiørgh doing here?'

'The longships moored in the River Lygan weren't the only ones to escape our clutches. Somehow Hæsten managed to spirit his whole army away last night, including the women and children.'

Ælfred gave Edward a disparaging look and his son lowered his eyes to the ground. I thought it probable that my nemesis had been in charge of the sector through which the Vikings had escaped; a suspicion I later found to be correct.

'However, thanks to Gunbiørgh, we know where they're headed. Eohric's fleet is at Mældun on the estuary of the River Blæcmere.'

I knew that Mældun was the principle settlement in Ēast Seaxna Rīce and one of the two places that Eohric had a hall. What I didn't know was how large his fleet was and so I asked.

'There's a mixture of longships and knarrs,' Gunbiørgh replied. 'I'm not sure of the exact number, especially as some will be away trading at this time of year, but enough to transport Hæsten and his Vikings wherever they want to go.'

I did a swift calculation in my head. We estimated that Hæsten had over fifteen hundred warriors before the longships had gone. Their departure had probably left twelve hundred men behind and there might be as many as five hundred women and children. There would also have been a number of thralls but they would have been killed or abandoned. He would need forty to fifty ships to move that many and I doubted that Eohric had anything like that number moored along the Blæcmere.

'What's your best estimate as to the number of ships at Mældun?' I asked the young Dane.

He shrugged. 'Fifteen to twenty?' he hazarded.

'In other words enough for eight hundred people at most. He needs more ships. My guess is that he's going to try and capture our ships in the Temes estuary. Without Cei, they are leaderless and vulnerable.'

'There are other men more worthy of command than that ex-slave was,' Edward scoffed.

I bit back an angry retort but I didn't have to say anything. Ælfred said what I was thinking.

'You forget yourself, Edward,' he said angrily. 'Cei served me faithfully for years, keeping the seas around the coasts of your kingdom virtually free of raiders and he gave his life in defence of Wessex.

'Lord Jørren is correct, however,' he continued in a calmer voice. 'We need an experienced sea commander to prevent the Danes from capturing our ships.'

His eyes swivelled towards me and I knew what was coming.

'Lord Æðelred, there is one man equal to the task of leading my navy against the Vikings and that is my former sæ hereræswa, Lord Jørren. If you and he are willing, he should take command as soon as possible.'

The look on Edward's face was priceless. He would now hate me more than ever but I didn't care. The thought of returning to the sea to fight the Danes filled me with delight.

'How can he take command of your ships, father? Even he can't walk on water,' Edward said contemptuously.

'Don't blaspheme, Edward!' Ælfred rebuked his son whilst Bishop Asser glared at the young man. 'However, you do have a point.'

'It's not a problem, cyning. I captured a longship yesterday. I'll go and find the fleet without delay.'

I saw Æðelred's eyes widen in surprise; he was about to say something when Æthelflæd put her hand on his arm. I immediately realised that I had offended him by taking his agreement for granted.

'That is, with Lord Æðelred's permission, of course.'

He nodded, somewhat mollified, and I left to find Bjørn Frami.

CHAPTER FIFTEEN

Summer 895

It felt good to be back at sea again. Bjørn had lost several of his crew before I'd persuaded him to surrender so I chose ten of my gesith to accompany me as well as Skarde who joined the ship's boys. I wondered whether he'd resent such a junior position having been in training as a scout and a warrior but he'd served as a ship's boy on Eirik's ships and he seemed pleased to be back with other Norse boys.

Æðelred questioned the wisdom of trusting my life to a ship's crew who'd been the enemy until recently but I had confidence that, having given me his oath, Bjørn wouldn't betray me. Besides, a third of the crew were my most trusted warriors including Acwel, Arne, Eafer, and Eomær.

I'd left Ywer in command of the rest of my men. I'd noticed a flicker of irritation cross Eirik's face when I'd put my son in charge. I suppose he was entitled to feel that I should have chosen him; after all he was my shire reeve. However, Ywer would be ealdorman after me and my men – although they had got used to serving with Eirik and his Norsemen – would respond better to Ywer. They had set off in pursuit of Hæsten but I doubted whether they would catch up with more than a few stragglers before the Vikings reached Mældun.

Then a thought struck me. It would take Hæsten time to find and engage our fleet; time in which those left ashore would be vulnerable to Ælfred's army. It didn't make sense for him to leave them waiting for his return with more ships at Mældun. They would make for somewhere safer and closer to the Temes estuary. The most likely place was Beamfleote where Hæsten had overwintered before.

However, if the Viking host divided en route to Mældun, Ælfred's scouts would easily spot it and would follow both trails. It was far more likely that half the Vikings had never have set out for Mældun but had headed directly to Beamfleote.

I was now impatient to find our fleet and go and see if my assumption was correct. If so, we could ambush Hæsten and hopefully defeat him once and for all.

'You were right, lord.' Eomær said when he returned to where we were hidden in the reed beds near Beamfleote.

It had taken me all day to find the Wessex fleet. Instead of the thirty or so ships I'd been expecting, there were only a dozen. The rest had either lost too many men to be effective and had headed back to Dofras or hadn't yet returned from chasing the Viking fleet heading for Frisia.

However, seven of them were the larger skeids – the proper name for what the Vikings called drekkar but with a cross mounted in the prow instead of a dragon's or serpent's head – with a crew of between seventy and eighty. The other five were the smaller snekkjur manned by thirty to forty. With Bjørn's ship, I now had seven hundred men and forty ship's boys.

Beamfleote lay near the end of an inlet off the Temes called the Beamfleote Hýþ. I'd dropped Eomær, Arne and Eafer ashore that morning so that they could check if my assumption about the whereabouts of the families was correct. If it wasn't, I had badly miscalculated. I was therefore vastly relieved when my scouts confirmed the presence of Vikings in the fort.

'Could you get any idea of numbers?' I asked.

'Several hundred but mainly women and children. The warriors we saw were either old men or beardless boys.'

That made sense. Hæsten would have wanted his best men to crew the ships at Mældun. I was now in a quandary. Did I wait for Hæsten and engage him on the estuary or did I capture the fort and imprison the occupants? I didn't know how many warships, as opposed to merchant knarrs, the Vikings would have but they would outnumber us in terms of warriors.

Furthermore, most of the men who crewed the Wessex ships were members of the sæfyrd, freemen who were fishermen, farmers or artisans and who manned Wessex's longships when required. They could fight but they weren't experienced warriors like Hæsten's men; far from it. In the limited time available for training, they spent most of their time practising rowing together and seamanship, not fighting on board ship.

I spent a sleepless night weighing up the options. I knew that I didn't have long before the Viking fleet from Mældun arrived. I couldn't expect any help from the rest of our army either. Even if I somehow managed to get a message to Ælfred, it would take him the best part of two days to reach Beamfleote overland.

As dawn broke I made up my mind. If I managed to capture the fort and their families, the Vikings would undoubtedly try and free them. If I could hold out until the main army got here, we would have the Vikings in a trap.

Once I'd made my decision the next problem was taking the fort.

†††

There was no point in secrecy. The Vikings weren't going anywhere and I wanted them to be fearful. I sent the smallest longship in the fleet off to Mældun to find the king and let him know about Beamfleote and my conclusion about Hæsten's intentions. I impressed on its captain that he had to stay well out to sea to avoid the Vikings and make landfall only when he was sure that he'd passed them. His crew had a hard task ahead of them. They would have to forego the sail and row. Then, with a boy up the mast, they should be able to spot the sails of Hæsten's fleet without being seen themselves.

We surrounded the fort on three sides just before dawn the next day and waited until the alarm was sounded. The palisade was in good order but the gates had been removed, perhaps by the local thegn, to avoid the place being used again by the Vikings. If so, it was flawed logic. They would be easy enough to replace and, as I stood outside the fort, I could see that a start had been made to do just that. Trees had already been felled in preparation and a sawpit had been constructed to turn the trunks into planks. A day later and new gates would have been in place.

It would have been easy enough to charge in through the open gateway. I now had four hundred men with me and, although over half were men of the sæfyrd, they would be more than a match for those who were gazing at us from the parapet. There were about two hundred of them, either greybeards or else boys who were still training to be warriors.

A red-haired woman appeared on top of the palisade and scowled down at us. I had only seen her once before but I recognised Hæsten's wife.

'What do want here? Have you come to kill defenceless women and children?' she sneered.

I took off my helmet.

'You know me: Jørren of Cæstirscīr. I don't kill defenceless women and children if I can avoid doing so. Surrender to me and no blood need be spilt today.'

'I heard you allowed Jøns to die in agony. I would no more trust you than lie down with a wolf.'

I had to think who she meant for a moment and then I realised that Jøns was Irwyn's name before he was baptised. No doubt her younger son had also forsaken his Christian name of Godric and had reverted to Guðmarr.

'We did everything we could to save Irwyn but his wounds became infected. There was nothing we could do for him. Believe me, I would rather have had a live hostage than a corpse. You can take some comfort that he was given a proper Christian burial, not left in the open for the beasts to feed on.'

'A pox on your Christian burial. Now he's food for the worms and his hugr is going to Folkvangr instead of Valhalla. He should have been allowed to die with a sword in his hand and been cremated.'

I had learnt enough about their pagan beliefs to know that the hugr or soul was thought to leave the body after the remains were fully destroyed through decay or burning. Only then could the hugr start its journey to the realm of the dead. Although Vikings could be buried, cremation was the quicker way to the hugr's final destination.

'He was baptised a Christian and died a Christian death. Let that be an end of the matter,' I called up to her. 'Forget the past; I'm more concerned about the present. Surrender to me and your lives will be spared. Refuse and we'll storm the fort and many will die.'

'Do your worst, skitt.'

I smiled grimly. If she thought being called a turd would upset me, she was wrong. I'd been called far worse things in my life.

I signalled to Arne who blew on his horn and we advanced in line towards the gates. It was tempting to rush forward en masse but I suspected that the Danes had warriors waiting just inside the gateway as well as a few archers up on the parapet.

233

I saw the bowmen suddenly appear and I gave the order to raise our shields. The half a dozen arrows did no damage and then warriors appeared to block the entrance. They were all old men but they stood ten deep. Because the gateway was only fifteen feet wide our superior numbers would avail us little. So I held my hand up and we halted.

'Archers to the fore,' I called and fifty of my men - both those of my gesith and men from the longships – handed their shields, axes and spears to the ship's boys behind the rest and grabbed bows and quivers.

To shoot directly at the row of warriors blocking the gate would be a waste of time and arrows. Instead they took aim at those on the parapet and over the heads of the first few rows of the shield wall. Several bodies fell onto the ground in front of the palisade and more toppled off the walkway into the fort. Even more encouragingly, howls of dismay and the screams of the wounded came from those in the rear ranks of the enemy shield wall.

One or two Danish bowmen unwisely poked their heads above the parapet. Before they could loose an arrow they vanished again as my men fired first. After that there were no more arrows from the top of the palisade.

After a final volley into the enemy's rear ranks, we advanced again and clashed with the Viking shield wall. Now it became a matter of shoving and heaving to force the line back and thrusting at exposed eyes, legs and feet. Although those in the Danish front row were experienced, they were old and slow. They also tired quickly and they lost men twice as fast as we did.

It seemed like forever but it was probably less than quarter of an hour before we pushed them back out of the gateway and into the fort. Now we could bring our greater numbers to bear and it wasn't long before they were outflanked and they broke.

After that it was a matter of hunting them down through the fort. There were few huts, mainly lines of tents, and so there were few places for them to hide. At one point I saw the vivid red hair belonging to Hæsten's wife amongst a group of Danes who had been surrounded by my men. Then I had to concentrate on a boy of no more than ten years old who was trying to hamstring me with a dagger. I stomped hard on his forearm and I felt the bone snap. He howled in pain and I let him be. I should really have put my blade through his neck but he was out of the fight and would recover to become a slave, provided someone else didn't kill him. I looked for the red-haired woman again but she'd disappeared.

It took two hours before the fort was captured and the last of the enemy were rounded up. We had lost a score dead and twice that number wounded; most of whom should recover in time. Against that, over a hundred of the old men and boy warriors had been killed and about eighty had wounds which would heal. There were also some casualties amongst the women and young children. There had been the odd case of rape and I'd killed two of the sæfyrd who I had caught humping a young girl. However, there were some three hundred and fifty captives taken alive.

One of the dead was Hæsten's wife. I was told that she had gone down fighting and had killed two men before succumbing. I had half expected her surviving son to be with her but there was no sign of him and I assumed that he must have gone with his father.

One of my remaining concerns as ealdorman was the lack of bondsmen and women to help work the land and care for the livestock in my shire. It wasn't altruistic. I needed slaves to work the land in the vills I owned; furthermore, the more prosperous my shire was, the more everyone paid in taxes. To achieve that the thegns and freemen needed the cheap labour that slaves provided. These Danes might be the solution to the problem, provided that Ælfred, Edward and Æðelred didn't see them as the spoils of war whose sale could help defray the cost of the campaign.

235

I quickly came to the conclusion that I should dispatch them to Cæstirscīr before Ælfred and the rest arrived. The problem was one of transportation. What I needed was knarrs, not longships. The former were ideal for carrying cargo, horses or people whereas a longship couldn't carry many more than its crew. There was a possible solution but it involved a great deal of risk.

Now I prayed for Hæsten to arrive before the combined armies of Wessex and Mercia.

†††

'The lookout said to tell you that there are ships coming up the inlet, lord,' Skarde told me breathlessly.

He and the other ship's boys were taking it in turns to stay with the sentry on the palisade whose job it was to watch the inlet, ready to act as messengers.

'Did he say how many and what type?'

'No, lord, sorry, but I could see at least four knarrs coming up the creek; I could just about make out many more ships in the estuary but I'm not sure how many.'

I thumped him on the shoulder in my excitement, which caused the boy to jerk away and look at me as if I'd gone mad. I'd been fairly confident that Hæsten wouldn't see the need to bring all his stolen ships up the creek to fetch the families and their protectors. After all, he was expecting to pick them up in the knarrs and then continue on his way, a task which shouldn't take more than an hour or two.

It was time I was elsewhere. Leaving Acwel in charge of the fort and the prisoners, I made my way as quickly as I could to where my fleet was moored in the reed beds. I'd chosen a location just over half a mile from the junction with the Temes estuary. It would take a little while to get underway and so I'd sent Arne on ahead in the hope that, being younger and fitter than me, my fleet would be ready to sail as soon as I got there.

I arrived sweating and panting to see that the crews were nearly all aboard and a few of the masts were being stepped.

'Don't bother with masts,' I yelled. 'The wind's coming from the south. Get the oars out.'

I sent the smallest of my longships to block the entrance to Beamfleote Hýþ to stop the knarrs escaping before clambering aboard Bjørn's ship. We rowed slowly to the edge of the reed bed as I impatiently peered ahead from the bows. It was impossible to achieve any speed as the reeds would have snagged the oars, destroying the rower's rhythm and leading to chaos. Once we were in open water it was a different matter and the ships surged ahead.

As we had planned, we divided into two groups; one to cut off retreat downriver and the other to prevent the enemy escaping upstream towards Lundenburg. We had caught Hæsten's fleet off guard. He had eight longships – five of them the larger drekar with seventy to eighty men aboard and three the smaller snekkjur with around thirty crew. In addition there were two more knarrs, both crammed with warriors. I did a swift calculation and concluded that the enemy numbered around eight hundred. They had slightly more warriors than I did but, as two hundred were aboard the knarrs, which lay upwind of the longships, I could forget about them for now.

The Vikings panicked. Some started to row towards us whilst three others made off towards the far shore. I spotted Hæsten's raven banner flying from the masthead of one of the ships heading towards the coast of Cent and gave chase with one of the other skieds and a snekkja, leaving the rest of my group to cut off escape upriver.

I glanced to my left and saw the other half of the fleet making for the open sea. Then disaster struck. The captains of what had been Cei's fleet should have known the Temes estuary like the back of their hands but perhaps a recent storm had altered the sea bed. Whatever the reason, the leading skeid suddenly came to a grinding halt. They must have run into a mud bank just under the surface.

I dreaded to think what had happened on board. The rowers would have been catapulted forward, smashing chests and bones against their oars. Doubtless the sudden impact would have sprung the planks of the hull, letting in water. Even if the captain managed to plug the hull and get her off as the tide rose, one of my largest ships was out of the fight.

Moreover, the other ships in the group had backed water frantically to avoid the same fate. They succeeded but they would have to proceed cautiously, taking soundings to get around the mud bank and that would allow the enemy time to escape.

Those Viking ships heading upriver came about when they saw what had happened and they too now headed for the Norþ-sǽ. I now had a difficult choice. I could come about myself and try and head the escaping longships off or I could continue to chase Hæsten.

Whatever I decided now, my strategy had turned out to be a fiasco and I could imagine the look of glee on Edward's face when I reported my failure to Ælfred and Æðelred. There was only one way I could mitigate my humiliation and that was to capture or kill Hæsten. We therefore pressed on with our pursuit.

The three Viking ships were more than halfway to the far coastline when they tacked and raised their sails. The wind from the south now carried them along at a spanking pace parallel to the shore. My rowers were tiring and, with the mast in its cradle on the desk, we were unable to raise our own sails. I saw my one hope of salvaging my reputation disappearing in the wake of the enemy ships.

We heaved to so that we could step the mast and raise our own sails, not an easy task as we wallowed in the swell, but by then the three enemy vessels were level with the island of Sceapig, the location of Hæsten's first surrender two and a half years previously. I cursed him to hell and back, the man had the luck of the devil.

Then something happened to change the situation completely.

✝✝✝

Many Danish ships, including the ones Hæsten had taken, used red and white striped sails whereas Wessex used undyed wool to weave theirs; resulting in a dirty white appearance. They differed in this respect from those of Mercia who tended to dye theirs brown. The six ships which I now saw heading along the estuary towards me all displayed off white sails. I concluded that they were part of the missing fleet which had been following the Viking longships which had escaped from the encampment on the River Lygen.

Their arrival was certainly timely. However, instead of heading for Hæsten's three ships near the coast of Cent they made for the rest of the fleet near the northern shore. It was where the other seven Viking ships were and whoever was in command of the new arrivals naturally saw them as the priority.

Their longships were now spread out with the cumbersome knarrs trailing in the rear. It wouldn't be long before our leading ships caught the knarrs up. I turned my attention to Hæsten's three ships. Although they weren't drawing away from my group, we weren't gaining on them either. Night wasn't that far away and I knew that we'd lose them in the dark.

I had a difficult decision to make. Ælfred would expect me to stay on the heels of Hæsten. However, my priority was to ship the hundreds of slaves I needed to farm my shire to Cæstir before anyone else could lay claim to them. To do that I needed to return to Beamfleote and take charge there.

Bjørn could see the indecision on my face. He too had a vested interest in seeing his share of the slaves safely delivered to the lands I'd promised him.

'Send our other two ships to shadow those three,' he urged me, pointing to the longships a mile ahead of us, 'whilst we return to the Beamfleote Hýþ and get the captives loaded onto the knarrs.'

Neither of us doubted that Acwel and the men I'd left with him in the fort had secured the four knarrs by now. There would have only been a few sailors on board as each would have needed all the available space for the Viking families. Typically each merchant ship carried a crew of between six and ten, depending on size, and so they wouldn't have been able to put up much of a fight.

Bjørn's intervention helped me make my mind up and, ordering the two ships accompanying us to continue after the three Danish ships, I gave the order and Bjørn's longship went about. Two minutes later we were heading north-west, back to where we'd come from.

✝✝✝

In the end the sea battle had been a partial success. We had captured three of the Viking longships and one of the knarrs. Thanks to our tactic of standing off and peppering the enemy with arrows before boarding, our losses had been lighter than theirs. By the time that they had surrendered less than a hundred remained alive. Of those, a score were too badly injured to survive.

Unfortunately, two of the longships and the other knarr had succeeded in escaping during the fighting and were now disappearing towards the north-eastern point of Cent in the wake of Hæsten's other three ships. That meant that something like four hundred Vikings had survived to pillage the south coast of Wessex. I doubted that Ælfred would be pleased and Edward would seek to discredit me. Even Æðelred would be disappointed in the outcome.

Taking the captives for myself would hardly improve matters but I was determined. I left Acwel and a dozen men at the fort with those too badly injured to sail with us. I took Leofwine and his assistants to tend to the more lightly wounded. Acwel remonstrated with me as many of the wounded in the fort would die without proper attention but Uhtric was with Ywer and the rest of my men and they should arrive the next day. There were also a number of monks who were skilled healers with the army.

Two of our longships had been damaged in the battle with the Viking ships and so I left those behind and distributed their crews amongst the rest to replace the dead and wounded. We now had a total of seventeen longships in addition to the knarrs. My plan was to take the fastest skeids with me to chase Hæsten and leave the rest to escort the knarrs.

However, the captains of Ælfred's ships refused to obey me. They were happy enough to chase the remainder of the Viking ships but not to escort my slaves back to Cæstir, a place that most hadn't even heard of. I couldn't blame them but it meant I had to compromise. Bjørn's longship would have to escort the knarrs on its own whilst the rest of us hunted Hæsten down.

We loaded the captives onto the five knarrs with enough men to guard them and then the fleet set sail once more. I had left the bulk of my warriors on Bjørn's ship but I took Arne, Eafer, Eomær and Dunbeorn with me when I transferred to the largest of the Wessex skeids, which was captained by a man called Edgar. He told me that he had served with me before when I'd been Ælfred's sæ hereræswa. I didn't remember him but, as he'd been one young man amongst many in those days, it wasn't surprising.

241

Taking nearly a score of ships to deal with six of the enemy seemed a bit excessive and it meant leaving the coast of eastern Wessex undefended. However, there were still a few Saxon longships making their way back from Frisia and I was conscious of the fact that Hæsten had allies in Dyflin. If he arrived there before we caught him we could end up facing a lot more than half a dozen ships.

On the fourth day we were hailed by a fishing boat coming out of the natural harbour that led to Cicæstre. According to the fishermen, the Danes had landed and attempted to pillage the settlement the previous day. Ealdorman Cyngils and many of his warriors were with Ælfred and Edward but the shire reeve had mustered what remained of the fyrd and had opposed the Danes' landing. After losing a score of men they had beaten a hasty retreat and headed back out to sea.

It was excellent news. It meant that Hæstan's lead on us had been reduced by at least half a day. We sailed on in high spirits but the excellent weather conditions hitherto were about to change. As night fell we anchored in the narrow stretch of water between Whitlond and the south coast of Hamtunscīr. Just after sunrise we headed out of the sheltered channel and back into the open sea.

The wind had continued to blow from the south all week. Some days it was a stiff breeze, on others it was no more than a gentle zephyr and we had to row to make progress. This morning the clouds above us were no longer white and fluffy in a blue sky but had become overcast. Within the hour it had changed to a forbidding dark grey. The wind had picked up quite considerably and the ships' boys had difficulty in reefing the sail. Much as I wanted to chase after my quarry, I decided that the prudent course of action was to seek shelter and so we made for the coast. Luck was with us and I offered up a prayer of thanks as the entrance to Poole Hæfen appeared out of the gloom.

The storm lasted for two days. Whilst we were riding it out at anchor in the shelter of the natural harbour I found myself hoping that Hæsten had been caught out in it. If so, his ships would surely have been wrecked on the rocky coast.

However, I wasn't that lucky. On the second afternoon a fishing boat rowed out to us with a message. Vikings had landed at Sonwic further along the coast and were raiding inland. I tried to recall what I knew of Sonwic from the time I'd been in the area two decades previously when we had Guðrum's fleet bottled up in Poole Hæfen. I seemed to remember that it didn't have a harbour as such but that there was a long strand of golden sand where the fishermen drew up their boats. If Hæsten had beached his ships there and pulled them well up onto the sand they would have been safe from the storm.

We had a chance to trap him against the shore but the wind was still too strong to row into the teeth of it and out through the narrow entrance to Poole Hæfen. I waited impatiently for conditions to improve and spent a sleepless night with the wind still howling through the rigging from the south and rain beating down on us.

Just after dawn things improved. The rain died away, the wind moderated and then backed to the east. I waited irritably whilst the large stones that acted as anchors were laboriously hauled aboard and the ship's boys hoisted the sail. Under power from both oars and mainsails we raced out into the open sea. There was still a heavy swell which threw the ships around not dissimilar to a cork bobbing about and spray repeatedly drenched us. However, I was scarcely conscious of it as I stood in the prow eagerly searching the expanse of water ahead as the coastline curved to the south away from Poole Hæfen.

The spray made it difficult for me to see more than a few hundred yards ahead of us but the boy up the mast on lookout duty had no such problem.

'Ships ahead,' he suddenly called down in a piping treble voice. 'They're just backing off the beach.'

'How far away,' I yelled up.

'Perhaps two miles?'

I swore. They would have seen us and be making off as fast as they could go. The coast ran due south for a mile or so before turning westwards and they would be around the point and running before the wind long before we could catch them. I told Edgar to change course to head directly for the point. At least we would have reduced the distance between us by the time that the Vikings could turn.

We continued to pursue the enemy throughout that day but they remained a mile and half ahead of us and there seemed to be nothing we could do to reduce the distance. The wind was strong enough to blow us along at near our maximum speed through the water and so rowing merely served to exhaust the oarsmen without appreciably aiding our progress.

As dusk fell the wind shifted to the north-east. At least our motion through the water was now a little more comfortable but I fretted that we would lose the enemy during the hours of darkness. I spent another sleepless night and by dawn I was feeling jaded and exhausted. It was as I had feared; there were no craft in sight expect for own ships. Hæsten had given us the slip.

CHAPTER SIXTEEN

Autumn 895 to February 896

I had little alternative but to continue to sail westwards, hoping that Hæsten was doing the same. The other options were that he'd doubled back, which I thought extremely unlikely, or that he'd turned south and headed for Frankia. If that proved to be the case, he was unlikely to return across the Sūð-sæ at a later date. However, I still thought that he might head for Dyflin to recruit more men.

It wasn't until we were off the southern point of the Kernow peninsula – the south-western tip of the island of Britannia – that we finally caught sight of the Viking fleet. The wind had dropped the previous day and we had to resort to rowing. The knarr carrying a hundred of Hæsten's warriors had been becalmed and the other ships had to resort to towing her. The added drag of the merchant ship had evidently exhausted the rowers in the longships and when we caught sight of them they had stopped for a rest.

Furled mainsails were stowed on a cradle amidships and so we were far less visible than we would have been when sailing. Consequently, we had closed the gap to about two miles before we were spotted. The sight of an ever increasing number of ships closing on the Vikings evidently panicked them and they cast off the knarr in order to make good their own escape.

Becalmed, the knarr looked like easy prey but it still had a hundred armed Vikings aboard. I therefore left four ships to deal with her and carried on past her in pursuit of the rest of the enemy ships.

Their rowers might have been tired but the sight of us bearing down on them evidently gave them a new burst of energy and the gap closed only marginally over the next few hours. By that time our own oarsmen were close to collapse.

One or two had simply given up and I had them removed and replaced them with archers and the two eldest ship's boys. Then another buckled under and I took his place. It was a long time since I'd plied an oar and I was far from a young man. I felt every sinew in my arms, back and legs straining as I powered the heavy blade through the water. After a quarter of an hour I felt as if I'd torn every muscle I had but I was determined not to give up. Then I felt the blessed touch of a breath of wind coming from the west. Ten minutes later we had shipped the oars and hoisted the sail.

I was ready to lie down and rest but I saw Skarde smirking at my obvious distress as he sheeted home the ropes that controlled the angle of the sail. I was damned if I was prepared to let the little sod see how tired I was. I straightened my back and glared at him. He looked away hastily and I turned my attention to the Vikings ahead of us.

By dusk we were some twenty miles further along the north coast of Kernow. Normally we would have sought a cove or sheltered bay where we could spend the night. This coast was notorious for its rocky shoreline and with the wind pushing us to leeward sailing at night was especially dangerous. Nevertheless, the Vikings showed no sign of seeking an anchorage and so we pressed on. They had turned slightly so that they were heading more out to sea and we followed suit. Now my worry was that we would lose touch with the other ships in the fleet during the night.

We solved that problem by taking in sail slightly and displaying a torch from the stern. Fire is always dangerous aboard ship so I assigned two men to keep watch on the torch in shifts throughout the night. The rest of our ships soon did the same and so I went to find a spot to catch some sleep confident that I had done all I could to keep us together and on the tail of the enemy.

'Wake up, lord. It's sunrise, although you wouldn't have guessed.'

I opened my eyes groggily to see Dunbeorn's face above me. I looked up at the sky but all I could see was an expanse of white. I touched my face and my hand came away wet. The wind had died again during the hours of darkness and a sea fret had descended. I stood up and looked about me but all I could see was a blanket of fog.

The silence was eerie, broken only by the creak of oars against rowlocks and the lap of the sea against the bows. My heart sank into my boots. Not only had we lost touch with both the enemy and the rest of my fleet but we had no idea where we were or what dangers surrounded us.

Edgar had taken the precaution of putting a leadsman in the bows. I watched as he cast his weighted line ahead of the ship, pulled it in and called out the depth according to the markings on his line. It was some relief when he called 'no bottom'. The line was six fathoms long and so the depth of water here was over ten times our draught.

I vaguely heard the same phrase seconds later like an echo and I looked about me bewildered.

'It means that there's another ship within fifty yards of us at a guess,' Edgar said softly.

'Probably ours then?' I whispered back.

'Unless we've overtaken one of the Viking longships in the night.'

'In which direction is it, do you think?'

It was a stupid question and I regretted asking it as soon as the words were out of my mouth. Fog is disorientating and no one has any idea where a sound comes from.

'Forget I asked,' I added hurriedly.

He grinned and pointed aft. For a moment I thought that he knew the direction from the sound but then I saw the bows of another longship looming out of the fog. To my intense relief it bore a cross on the prow. It was one of ours.

'Bear away,' Edgar called out sharply as their bows threatened to crash into our stern post.

I saw the startled face of their leadsman before he called back for the steersman to put his steering oar over to starboard.

'Ship oars,' Edgar called just in time as their bows came abreast of the rearmost rowers.

A split second later the same order was given by a disembodied voice in the mist. The two ships glided past each other until the stern of the other ship came alongside ours.

'Any idea where the rest are,' I called across.

'There's two more just astern of us,' their captain called back, but I've no idea where the rest are.'

'I suggest we heave to until this clears,' I called across.

'Yes, lord. I'll pass it on to the other two.'

It took three hours before the fog started to clear. A gentle breeze sprang up tearing the white blanket into wisps of mist, then the wind strengthened and suddenly visibility improved. I was relieved to see another twelve longships dotted around the sea behind us but there was no sign of the other three. Nor was there any sign of the enemy fleet.

We hoisted the sail and I spread our ships out in a line to cover as much water as possible whilst still keeping in sight of at least two other ships: one to larboard and one to starboard. However, there was still no sign of Hæsten's ships.

I had assumed that he was heading for Dyflin and therefore making for the Íralandes Sæ to the north Kernow. We were perhaps thirty miles to the west of the border between Kernow and Dyfneintscīr when the longship on our starboard side lowered and raised their sail. It was the universal signal to indicate that he had a message for me.

'This better be important,' I muttered to Edgar as we repeated the signal to the ships to larboard.

248

'What's the message,' I hollered as soon as we were within range.

'No idea, lord. The message seems to have been passed along the line to us.'

Fearful of losing the rest, I got Edgar to raise and lower the sail twice, meaning follow me, and headed to the north-east to intercept the ship nearest the coast.

We had been in the middle of the line with each ship three miles apart. That meant that the innermost ship was within sight of land. I didn't have to ask why he wanted to speak to me. There ahead of him was the Viking fleet in the channel between the south coast of Wealas and the north coast of Somersaete. I'd been wrong about Dyflin. Hæsten was heading for the mouth of the River Sæfern; he intended to raid southern Mercia whilst Æðelred and his army were still in the east.

✝✝✝

'I'm sorry, lord,' Edgar said firmly. This river mouth is the boundary between Wessex and Mercia and we cannot sail any further.'

We had reached a point where the estuary narrowed and became the River Sæfern. The boundary was clearly demarcated by the mouth of a tributary to our left which ran into the Sæfern. I ground my teeth in frustration as I watched Hæsten's ships sailing on up the main river towards Glowecestre.

There was nothing to be done about it. The chase was over as far as the Wessex fleet was concerned. Hæsten and his remaining men were now Mercia's problem.

'Well, I'm not returning with you,' I said firmly. 'My duty is to continue to pursue the Vikings so that I can report where they've gone.'

'Do you want me to put you ashore, lord?' Edgar asked, trying to hide a grin.

He knew very well that my few companions and I would be stranded afoot with no means of following the enemy longships if he did so.

'No, we'll wait here until the other four longships catch us up. Hopefully they will bring the captured knarr with them.'

'You intend to go after six Viking longships in a knarr manned by just the five of you?' Edgar asked incredulously.

'No, we'll pick up more men at Glowecestre,' I replied brusquely.

He still looked dubious. No doubt he thought I was mad to chase a fleet of longships in a knarr.

'At least we're not likely to lose them along the Sæfern,' I added dryly.

It was mid-afternoon before the ship's boy up the mast yelled down that several sails were in sight.

'How many?' Edgar shouted back.

'Four.'

My heart sank. Did that mean that they hadn't managed to capture the knarr, or had they lost one of the longships in doing so?

'No, wait; there's another sail well behind the others.'

I breathed a sigh of relief.

An hour later I took possession of the knarr and, with forty three Danes tied up in the cargo space, we hoisted the sail and headed up the River Sæfern to Glowecestre.

The grizzled old warrior who'd been left in command of the garrison of boys, old men and the night watch was dubious about taking responsibility for the Danish captives until I pointed out that doubtless Lord Æðelred would reward him for giving him so many able-bodied slaves.

He confirmed that the passage of the Viking longships had been reported to him but he'd done nothing about it. The least he could have done was to send out riders to warn the settlements and farmsteads upstream. Now that they were in the confines of the river they would have to row and, as the Sæfern meandered, a rider alternating between trotting and cantering could easily outdistance the ships and warn those near the river. I was tempted to tell him that he was an idiot but there was no point. I just hoped that it wasn't too late.

I picked several local boys who could ride and dispatched them along the right bank to warn everyone as far north as Wirecestre. Once there it would become the responsibility of whoever the Ealdorman of Wirecestrescīr had left in charge to alert his own shire.

There was nothing further I could do until the next morning. There were rocks and shoals further along the river and I was certain that the Viking fleet would have moored up for the night. I chewed my lip as I went over my options in my mind. The priority was discovering their destination. Winter was only a couple of months away and I expected Hæsten to find somewhere defensible to overwinter and then spend the next few weeks foraging for supplies and seeking plunder and slaves to keep his men happy.

There was little point in following the enemy up the river in the knarr; that could be done on horseback. I chose Eafer and Eomær for the task. Once they had found out where Hæsten had halted they were to bring me the news at Cæstir. Meanwhile I would choose a few men and boys to help me sail the knarr home around the coast of Wealas.

I knew I was taking a risk but it was getting late in the year for pirates to be looking for prey in the Íralandes Sǣ. However, I

251

made sure that everyone on board could use a bow and took a few barrels of spare arrows with us just in case. If we encountered several longships we would be in trouble but I thought that bombarding a lone vessel with arrows would convince any attacker to try for easier game.

As it turned out it wasn't pirates we had to worry about, it was the weather.

†††

We had rounded the north-western tip of Wealas, near the island from where I'd rescued Ywer over a decade ago, and were heading towards the straits between Ynys Môn and the mainland. Half an hour later and we would have reached sheltered waters. As it was, Ynys Môn was still a dark shadow on the horizon when the wind veered to the south-west and gained in strength. The dark clouds overhead scudded across the sky and I knew that we were in for a storm.

The entrance to the straits lay between two peninsulas, the gap between them being no more than four hundred yards. We were approaching the channel on a broad reach with the wind on our starboard quarter. Knarrs make quite a lot of leeway as they are broad in the beam with only a stubby keel and we were being pushed towards the northernmost of the two peninsulas.

By now the pressure of the wind on the mainsail was threatening to tear the mast out of the ship and it was already reefed as much as possible. I had no option but to drop the sail. Arne and I leant on the steering oar with all our weight, trying to force the head around to starboard. Slowly the ship came around so that it was pointing towards the southern peninsula. However, the wind was now on our beam and we were still being forced sideways towards the south-western tip of the island.

Thankfully the shore at that point consisted of gently shelving golden sands. At the last moment, when being driven ashore was inevitable, I brought the bows around and headed for the beach.

'Grab something and brace yourselves,' I yelled above the noise of the howling wind.

Arne and I let go of the steering oar and quickly lashed ourselves to the sternpost. A few seconds later the keel grounded on the soft sand and the ship came to a sudden stop. I was thrown forward by the sudden loss of momentum and I felt a pain in my chest where the rope secured me. For a moment I thought that I might have broken a rib or two but I was just badly bruised. Arne was in the same state.

Most of the others were just badly bruised or had torn muscles but one of the boys I had recruited in Glowecestre had let go on impact and had been thrown against the mast, breaking his neck and killing him instantly.

I was amazed that the mast hadn't been torn loose but the rigging had flexed and held. The chests containing our possessions were in the hold and some had broken free of their fastenings. The coffer containing the hacksilver, arm rings and coins - my share of the plunder taken from the Danes during the campaign - had been smashed and the contents were strewn all over the hold.

There was nothing to be done until the storm abated. We ate some cheese washed down with ale from the one cask that hadn't been broken open and collected up the contents of the coffer. I put it all in a number of leather sacks for ease of carrying when we left the knarr. I had no expectation that we could re-float her. She had been driven too far up the beach for us to drag back into the water and the planks at the bows had sprung apart on impact.

We settled down to get what sleep we could and hoped that the storm had blown itself out by morning.

I stood up and stretched, trying to get the stiffness out of my muscles. The grey clouds and wind of the previous day had disappeared to be replaced by blue skies and a gentle breeze. The only reminders of the storm were the swell on the sea and the fact that we were stranded fifty yards up the beach.

I looked inland towards the top of the dunes to see a man and two dogs watching us. I could also see the odd sheep and came to the conclusion that he was a shepherd. He disappeared and I roused the others.

An hour later, burdened with what we could carry, we reached the top of the same dunes. All we could see was a flat pasture with a wood in the distance. The grassland was dotted with clumps of gorse and with sheep placidly grazing. I looked for the shepherd and his dogs but there was no sign of them. Presumably he had gone hotfoot to his settlement to tell them of our shipwreck. This was confirmed half an hour later when we saw some thirty men coming towards us led by the shepherd and his dogs.

We had a problem because none of us spoke their language and they didn't speak Ænglisc, Danish or Norse. However, they did manage to convey menace and their gestures made it clear that they meant to attack us. I didn't want to have to harm them but we were more than prepared to defend ourselves if necessary. We loosened our swords and seaxes in their scabbards before stringing our bows and nocking arrows to them.

That gave them pause for thought. We might only number eight but we would cause them serious harm if they attacked us.

'Anarawd ap Rhodri?' I asked.

They might not understand us and my pronunciation might be a little strange but they recognised the name without a doubt. Their whole attitude changed. No doubt they thought that we were Vikings come to raid them at first. However, Vikings were unlikely to ask for their king by name.

We accompanied them back to their settlement and a young man set off to the north on one of the few shaggy ponies the place boasted. We were given a basic meal of broth and a weak ale to drink and shown to a hut in which to rest. Three hours later the young man returned bringing several more riders with him. I recognised one of the newcomers with relief. It was Hywel ap Cadell, the king's nephew.

'You seem to have suffered something of a misfortune, Lord Jørren,' he said with a grin.

'I'm pleased to see you too, Hywel,' I said sardonically. 'Our ship was driven ashore in a storm but that's unimportant for now. I need to see your uncle urgently.'

'The king? What can be so important?'

'Hæsten is back,' I said succinctly.

The grin disappeared and he frowned.

'Where is he?'

'All in good time. Is Anarawd at Aberffraw?'

'He's away hunting. Come, you'd better talk to my cousin, Idwal.'

I had heard of a man called Idwal the Bald, Anarawd's eldest son. He was said to be against his father's alliance with Mercia. I groaned inwardly but I had little choice.

I was lent a mountain pony but the rest of my men had to walk. By the time we reached Aberffraw it was dusk. I was taken to see Idwal straight away but I had to leave my sword and seax at the door. The king's hall was similar to ours and to those of the Vikings but it was more crudely built of whole logs with the gaps filled with mud. There were no windows and the roof was made of turf. Consequently soil dropped down occasionally from the underneath of the turfs to land on the straw covered earthen floor or on the people gathered in the hall.

The interior smelt of smoke, unwashed bodies and wet straw. In that way it didn't differ from many of our halls except that the

255

stench was more intense and the windowless interior lent the pungent atmosphere a gloomy feel.

It took my eyes a while to adjust to the interior, lit only by the fire in the central hearth and two tall candles on the table at the far end. A balding young man I took to be Idwal sat on the smaller of two chairs between the candles. Around him stood four older men who I assumed were members of the king's council.

I waited whilst Hywel went and whispered in his cousin's ear. Idwal scowled at me and then beckoned me forward.

'Hywel says you have important information about the bastard Danes who raided our land last year,' he said in heavily accented Ænglisc.

'Yes, lord.'

He held up his hand.

'You will do me the courtesy of addressing me as tywysog,' he said angrily.

I knew that tywysog meant prince in his language but we weren't speaking Welsh.

'Certainly, tywysog, if you will do me the courtesy of calling me lord. I'm the Ealdorman of Cæstirscīr and the Hereræswa of Mercia.'

I saw his face turn red and he glared at me for my impertinence. He said something in Welsh which made his councillors laugh. I'd had enough and I turned on my heel to leave.

'Where are you going? I haven't dismissed you!' he shouted.

'I'll wait until your father returns. No doubt he'll show me more respect. I doubt if he'll be pleased with you after I've spoken to him, especially as I bring news about Hæsten.'

A look of concern passed over his face.

'I'm sorry if I have offended you, Lord Jørren, it wasn't my intention,' he said smoothly.

I hesitated.

'Perhaps some refreshments would be welcome,' I suggested. 'At least the people who found us had the good manners to feed us and give us some ale.'

His face grew red again and he barked out an order in Welsh. A minute or two later I and my men had been given a goblet of ale and some bread and cheese. There were no tables in the hall, which I found strange, so we had to eat and drink standing.

I told Idwal very briefly what had happened over the past summer, some of which he evidently knew from the impatient way he waved his hand, telling me to get on with it. I curbed my annoyance and came to the point.

'Hæsten has only a small number of men left now, perhaps as few as three hundred. We chased him all the way along the southern coast of Wessex until he entered the mouth of the River Sæfern. The Wessex fleet refused to leave their own waters but I followed him as far as Glowecestre. He continued up the Sæfern in his longships shadowed by some of my scouts. Meanwhile I was returning in a knarr we had captured from the Vikings to Cæstir, intending to raise a force of warriors to travel back down and attack Hæsten once I knew where he intended to overwinter.'

'But you don't know where he is now?' he said scornfully.

'No, but I expect my scouts to tell me as soon as I return home.'

'Very well.'

He held a whispered conversation with his advisers and then turned back to me with a smile.

'I'll help you on your way on one condition; you come back and tell my father where Hæsten is as soon as you find out.'

'I'll certainly let you know as soon as I find out, tywysog, but I'm no messenger.' I said curtly.

'But my father will want to meet you to decide what to do about Hæsten, lord,' he said in a more conciliatory tone. I nodded.

'Once I know where the Vikings are holed up I'll agree a place for us to meet; somewhere midway between Aberffraw and Cæstir so that no-one's dignity suffers.'

I saw a hint of wry amusement in Idwal's eyes before I gave him a curt bow and took my leave.

✝✝✝

We watched the Vikings' newly constructed fort at Brigge all winter but we didn't attack it. Brigge was as far as the Viking ships could go up the Sæfern and they must have hauled them over the shallower stretches to get as far as they did.

Hæsten had chosen a good site for his winter camp. It stood on the top of an almost vertical cliff high above the river. The other three sides were defended by a fifteen foot high palisade with a single gateway protected on both sides by a tower. We could have stormed it, of course, but neither Anarawd nor the Ealdorman of Shropscīr - in whose shire Brigge lay - nor I wanted to lose men when we could starve the Vikings out.

They had abandoned their longships below the cliff but evidently they had managed to gather enough provisions to see the winter out before they arrived and had carried them up to their fort. As time wore on I became convinced that they weren't running short of provisions. There were no cremations of the dead and the men on sentry duty showed no sign of growing thin through lack of food.

I decided that I was wasting my time at Brigge and returned to Cæstir in the middle of December. It wasn't an easy journey; snow lay thick on the ground and there was a chilly wind which permeated the thickest of cloaks. However, I was determined to return and mark Christ's birth with my family, not least because I now had another grandchild. Æbbe had given birth to a healthy boy and the newly converted Eirik had said that he would bring them both over to celebrate Christmas with us.

The celebration of Christ's birth came and went. It was a pleasant time and I wasn't particularly keen to return to Brigge. The weather had been milder in late December but at the beginning of January the snow came back and the roads became impassable, so it wasn't until the middle of February that I was able to return to the siege.

When I told Hilda that I had to leave again our period of happiness turned to acrimony. Hilda lost her temper with me and, when that didn't have any effect, she tried to wheedle me into staying. I was tempted to send Ywer in my place but I was the Hereræswa of Mercia and it was my responsibility.

Once more I left Hilda under something of a cloud. Our arguments made me increasingly weary, especially as I would have much rather stayed at home. I needed to restore prosperity to Cæstirscīr and make it strong enough to be able to withstand attacks by the Norse pagans from Cumbria, the Northumbrians and Viking raiders from Mann and Íralond. I wasn't even certain that the truce with Gwynedd would last, especially if anything happened to Anarawd and Idwal came to the throne.

I put these concerns behind me as the Viking stronghold came into sight. Nothing seemed to have changed very much. I was met by a grumpy thegn from Shropscīr who had drawn the short straw and had been detailed to maintain the siege over the Christmas and New Year period. I could understand his ill humour and that of his men because they should have been relieved six weeks ago. Instead they had to endure the snow and their supplies had almost run out.

We settled down to wait. A few days later a small contingent of Welshmen from Gwynedd arrived together with a thegn called Edgar representing the Ealdorman of Shropscīr. He had brought even fewer men than had the Welsh which displeased me. After all, the Vikings were camped in his shire, not mine.

259

I expected that the Vikings would either attempt to break through our lines or else negotiate. Knowing Hæsten, I expected the former; he only negotiated if there was no other option. I was therefore pleasantly surprised when the Vikings sent a messenger to request a meeting. However, I thought it rather strange that the request came from someone called Ulfbjørn Bearslayer and not from Hæsten.

I agreed to the meeting and, accompanied by the representative of the King of Gwynedd, Edgar and Rinan, I rode to within two hundred yards of the fort and dismounted. When the gates opened a young boy and three men rode out. All were swathed in furs against the cold but I recognised the boy when he dismounted. It was Hæsten's younger son, Godric – at least he had been called Godric when he was in my custody; I had forgotten what his pagan name was.

My curiosity was now piqued. Why would Hæsten send his thirteen year old son to negotiate on his behalf?

'You know who I am, Lord Jørren,' Godric began in a voice typical of a boy on the cusp of puberty. 'This is my father's deputy, Jarl Ulfbjørn Bearslayer.'

I nodded at the Dane who looked rather like a bear himself. The other two weren't introduced and I took it that they were bodyguards.

'My father died in his sleep two nights ago,' the boy said.

My heart pounded with excitement. Hæsten's reputation had been what drew men to his banner; despite the lack of success he'd enjoyed since landing in Cent over three years ago. With his demise I dared to hope that the invasion of our lands was over.

I could hardly sympathise with Godric on his loss; that would have been hypocritical of me. However, I was curious about the cause of his death and so I asked.

The boy was tried to hide his grief but a tear left a clear mark on the left hand side of his grubby face. Vikings took great pride in their appearance and the filthy appearance of Godric and his companions led me to believe that, however much food they still had in store, there was a shortage of water in the fort. Presumably they could melt snow but perhaps all the clean snow had already been used. Godric tried to answer me but the words wouldn't come, so Ulfbjørn replied instead.

'Hæsten was a larger than life character who we all thought was indestructible but old age catches up with us all. He would never say how old he was but he must have been well into his sixties. I suspect that this, coupled with the privations we've been forced to suffer ever since we came to this benighted island, finally laid him low. It was sudden though. On the night he died he was his usual self at first, laughing and drinking. Suddenly his face contorted and went grey. He complained of a pain in his chest and seemed to have difficulty in breathing. A few minutes later he died. It was all so quick.'

I said nothing for a moment. What was there to say? The old warrior hadn't died in battle with a sword in his hand so, in accordance with their pagan beliefs, he wouldn't go to Valhalla. That must have upset them. However, I needed to negotiate the Vikings' surrender and so I eventually broke the morbid silence.

'So who leads the Vikings in the fort now? You? Or Ulfbjørn?'

'If you mean who leads the warband, neither of us. We all agree that we don't want to go on fighting. I'm only here to negotiate arrangements for my father's funeral. Jarl Ulfbjørn and I will meet you again after that to discuss the future.'

'No, it doesn't work like that,' I told him firmly. 'You obviously want to give Hæsten a farewell appropriate to a Dane of his rank and standing. However, before I will agree to that I want to settle the terms of your surrender.'

'We'll fight on then,' Ulfbjørn said belligerently.

'Don't be a fool, man! To what purpose? If you want to die here we'll oblige you but I think you want to live and to make a future for yourselves.'

'You will spare our lives then?'

'Perhaps, if you can meet certain conditions. Foremost amongst them is a solemn oath to end your raids on our land for good.'

I sensed a certain amount of tension amongst my two companions and so I added 'of course, anything we agree will also have to be acceptable to King Anarawd and Lord Æðelred.'

I didn't think that would be problem. Everyone, including Ælfred, just wanted peace. Provided the price wasn't too high I was certain they would support whatever I proposed. Edward might argue against it, of course, just to be perverse, but he was presumably far away in Cent and by the time he heard what had been agreed it would be far too late to change anything.

'Can we continue this somewhere a little more sheltered,' Godric asked, a trifle plaintively.

I was glad he had suggested it. The bitingly cold wind high above the river was chilling me to the bone. There was a shepherd's hut not far from the fort and I had it cleaned out ready for our use the next day.

In the end I agreed to allow them to use the smallest of their longships to give Hæsten a Viking cremation provided they surrendered all but one of the other ships. That would be given to those who wished to return to Frankia. I intended to keep two of the larger skeids for myself to supplement Bjørn Frami's ship. They would form the nucleus of a fleet to patrol our shores. The other ships would be given to Æðelred as he would expect something out of the arrangement.

Some of the Vikings were Northumbrians or East Anglian Danes and they would be allowed to return home, but at a price. They would have to buy their freedom with silver arm rings or weapons and armour.

That left eighty men including young Godric and the elderly Ulfbjørn Bearslayer.

'If you are prepared to give me your oaths, I will give you land on condition that you fight for me whenever I need you to.'

I held up my hand before they could reply.

'There is another condition; you must be baptised and become Christians. This time, Godric, you must mean it.'

'To betray our gods is a serious matter, lord.' Ulfbjørn replied dubiously. 'We need to discuss this with our men.'

'Of course. Do that and meet us again tomorrow at noon.'

A few slipped away rather than become Christians but they were too few in number to bother me. Ulfbørn gave his oath to me along with seventy other Danes. Those who were married would be allowed to purchase the freedom of their families through additional taxation.

I intended to give them land on the borders of my shire where they would have to defend their vills and farmsteads against the Cumbrian Norse and their fellow Danes in Northumbria. Godric himself agreed to enter my service and train as a warrior.

✝✝✝

I watched as the Vikings carried the lifeless form of my enemy for the past three and a half years onto the ship and lay him down on a pile of brushwood before placing both his hands around his sword. As men pushed him out into the current using long poles other Vikings threw lit torches onto the brushwood. Soon it was burning merrily as the pitch covered logs caught fire. Hæsten's final resting place was the shallows in the middle of the river where the blazing longship went aground.

The water around it sizzled and steamed as the fire consumed both ship and corpse. The next morning all that was left was the blackened keel and the ribs of the hull. The Viking leader's ashes had been carried away by the current. His life, full of destruction and pillage, had at last come to an end. Godric told me later that he was sixty three – a great age for anyone, let alone a man who had lived by the sword.

The story of Jørren's family and the unification of Anglo-Saxon England, including the key roles played by Æthelflæd and her nephew Æthelstan, will continue in H A Culley's next series of novels –

The Birth of England

The first book

Ælfred's Daughter

is due out in spring 2021

HISTORICAL NOTE

Apart from Hæsten's route to Brignorth in the latter part of 895, the events portrayed in this novel are based on what is known about his invasion. He crossed to England from Boulogne in the autumn of 892 at the head of one of two great Viking armies. The account below is taken from various sources, which inevitably don't agree, but it seems to me to be the most likely sequence of events.

Hæsten appears to have been the same man as the Hæsten who was the co-leader with Bjørn Ironside, the Norse King of Sweden and one of the four sons of the notorious Ragnar Lodbrok, who raided the Mediterranean coast between 859 and 861.

As part of a Viking-Breton army he killed Robert the Strong, Duke of the Franks, at the Battle of Brissarthe in 866. He went on to sack Bourges, Orléans and Angers before the Franks became too powerful and he was forced to retreat to an area north of the River Seine.

A large Viking army led by Rollo, founder of the Dukedom of Normandy, and Hæsten sailed up the River Seine and lay siege to Paris. However, Count Odo, son of Robert the Strong, successfully defended the city and later became King of the Franks. Odo began a campaign to drive the Vikings out of Frankia and it was at this point that Hæsten decided to invade England in search of plunder.

Hæsten would have been well into his fifties or even sixties at the time that this novel begins. As life expectancy at the time was around forty he would have been an old man by the time he landed in Kent. Of course, it's possible that there were two quite different Hæstens but the ease with which he seemed to attract new recruits would seem to indicate that he had quite a reputation.

His was the smaller of two invading armies who landed from a fleet of some eighty longships near Milton Regis in Kent, just south of the Isle of Sheppey in the Thames Estuary.

Another two hundred and fifty longships under an unnamed leader crossed the English Channel from the estuary of the River Somme and rowed up the River Rother to seize the settlement of Appledore. They appear to have spent the winter at or near where they landed.

In the spring of 893 King Alfred (or more correctly Ælfred) positioned the West Saxon army between the two groups of Vikings to keep them from uniting. Hæsten apparently then agreed terms, including allowing his two sons to be baptised, and left Kent for Essex. The larger army attempted to unite with Hæsten after raiding Hampshire and Berkshire in the late spring of 893 but was defeated at Farnham by an army under the Ætheling Edward, Alfred's eldest son. The survivors eventually reached Hæsten's army at Mersea Island, after a combined West Saxon and Mercian army failed to dislodge them from their fortress at Thorney.

Hæsten, now leading the combined Viking armies, withdrew to a fortified camp at Benfleet, Essex and used this camp as a base to raid the nearby Danish jarldoms in eastern Mercia. However, while the bulk of his men were out raiding, those left to guard the fort at Benfleet were defeated by the fyrd of eastern Wessex. They captured not only the fort but also Hæsten's ships, the treasure the Vikings had plundered as well as their women and children. This included Hæsten's own wife and sons.

Hæsten constructed a new stronghold at Shoeburyness at the mouth of the Thames Estuary where he attracted reinforcements from the Danes and Norsemen who had settled in East Anglia and southern Northumbria over the past two decades. Shortly afterwards, according to the Anglo-Saxon Chronicle, Hæsten held talks with Alfred, possibly to discuss terms for the release of his family. The outcome seems one sided. His two sons, who had been held hostage since he'd agreed to leave Kent, were released.

What Hæsten had conceded in return isn't recorded. All the Anglo-Saxon Chronicle says on the subject is that Alfred and his son-in-law, Aethelred (or Æðelred) of Mercia, had stood as sponsors (i.e godfathers) to Hæsten's sons at their baptism in early 893.

If Alfred's strategy was to broker a lasting peace then it was a failure. Not long after this Hæsten set out on a path of pillaging and destruction all along the Thames valley and then along the River Severn. Hæsten was pursued all the way by Alfred's son, Edward, and Aethelred. The combined Mercian and West Saxon army were reinforced by a contingent of warriors from the Welsh kingdoms at some point. The reason the Welsh came to assist their old enemies, the Anglo-Saxons, remains a matter for speculation.

Eventually the Viking army was trapped at Buttington on the River Severn (location not certain so I have chosen the peninsula of Sudbury, near Chepstow, in my version). At the resulting battle a few weeks later they fought their way out, losing many men in the process, and returned to their fortress at Shoeburyness.

Meanwhile Alfred had been forced to muster an army drawn from the western shires of Wessex to deal with threats to both the north and south coasts of Devon. According to Max Adams in his book *Ælfred's Britain* (2017) Northumbrians from Cumbria on the west coast had invaded northern Devon whilst Danes from East Anglia had landed to besiege Exeter. As both invading forces withdrew before Alfred could bring them to battle, it seems likely that they were taking advantage of the situation in the east of the country but Alfred's prompt action to confront them made them think again.

Hæsten's men, bottled up in the fort at Shoeburyness, were reduced by hunger to eating their horses. Eventually they broke out of their fortress to mount a desperate assault on the combined Saxon/Mercian army but they were routed after a hard fought battle. Many thousand Vikings were slain, according to the records, and the remainder fled leaving Edward and Aethelred in possession of the battlefield.

The surviving Vikings left East Anglia in the late summer of 893 and eventually arrived at the ruined Roman fortress of Chester. Presumably, lacking ships, they must have marched from the east coast all the way across the country to the west coast. It seems that Hæsten's plan was to rebuild the fortifications and use Chester as a base for raiding northern Mercia. However, the Mercians quickly laid siege to the fortress and attempted to starve the Danes into surrender.

The besieged Vikings broke out of Chester and marched south to devastate most of Wales, staying there until the summer of 894. Afterwards they returned via southern Northumbria, the part of the Danelaw called the Five Boroughs and East Anglia to their fort at Mersea Island in Essex.

In the autumn of 894, the army towed their ships into the Thames Estuary and up the River Lea to a new fort, although the records don't say where these ships came from. One presumes that they were somehow captured; there wasn't time to build a significant number of new ones.

In the summer of 895 Alfred arrived with the army of Wessex and blocked the River Lea downstream from Hæsten's stronghold by starting the construction of a fort either side of the river connected by a bridge. Before the work was completed the Vikings abandoned their camp and made another great march across the breadth of England to a site on the Severn where

Bridgnorth now stands, being harassed all the way by the Saxons and Mercians.

My tale diverges from the accepted history at this point. Because a trek back across England to Brignorth, harassed all the way, would make for tedious reading I have chosen to allow Hæsten to escape from the River Lea by sea.

According to John Lowerson's book, *a Short History of Sussex* (1980) there was a battle at Chichester on the south coast of Sussex in 895 where the local fyrd defeated a large force of Danes, killing hundreds. This raid may have been unconnected to Hæsten's invasion but I have chosen to include it.

Hæsten stayed near Bridgnorth until the spring of 896 when the Viking army finally dispersed into East Anglia, Northumbria and - according to the Anglo-Saxon Chronicle - those who were penniless found themselves ships and went south across the sea to the Seine. At some point around this time Hæsten disappears from recorded history.

Ælfred died on 26th October 899 and was succeeded by Edward. He was opposed by his cousin Æðelwold who was supported by the Danes of Northumbria and East Anglia but that's a tale for the next series of books.

Printed in Great Britain
by Amazon

10962270R00159